RUN

LISA BRANDENBURG

PAGE PUBLISHING, INC.
New York, NY

First originally published by Page Publishing, Inc. 2018

ISBN 978-1-64138-392-9 (Paperback)
ISBN 978-1-64138-393-6 (Digital)

Printed in the United States of America

Dedication

I thank God for all His signs that pointed me in the right direction. I thank my husband Joe for being the right direction and I thank an old childhood friend for giving me direction. When I saw all the amazing things he and his wife were doing, I told him I felt like I've done nothing with my life. He simply replied, "It's never too late to make a difference." He was right.

John Verdi, immeasurable thanks to you and Ayana for planting literal and figurative seeds at the Verdi EcoSchool in Florida. The roots have spread further than you know.

Prologue

I'm about ten seconds from walking down the aisle, and for the first time, I'm scared. An overwhelming sense of clarity has just surfaced. Standing in this church, it's like God has sent me a personal message and the message is *run!*

Chapter 1

Richard and I met out of pure frustration. I was so over the whole dating scene and wanted nothing to do with men. And there was my married sister and her friend trying to live vicariously through me. A good equation this does not make.

I can't even remember why I invited them over. In the years that have passed, it all became a blur. Perhaps (and this really might not be stretching the truth) they actually came over uninvited to slip away from the monotony that had become their lives. I'm not sure what was so thrilling about my life, but every now and then, they would show up at my door.

What I can recall is for about the hundredth time in my life, I successfully avoided divulging my innermost private secrets with my sister. Yeah, can you believe that? I spent most of my life avoiding sisterly chats with my sister. You really can't blame me though. She uses everything I say against me. But I digress...

So there I was, dodging questions about my virginity when suddenly her friend blurts out, "I have someone for you."

Trust me when I tell you I was not excited about the prospect of training some guy to dodge questions on his end as easily as I do.

"No. Absolutely not, I'm not interested," I protested. Then came the "Are you a lesbian?" questions (thank God I loved dodgeball as a kid). Like a stealth ninja, I made my escape.

When I was safely back in the confines of my bedroom, I began thinking how great it was not to be fighting all the time with my significant other the way my sister did or to not have a man get me pregnant and run out on me the way her friend did. I get to pick the movies to watch, the dinner to eat, and most importantly, I don't have to worry about sports. Yeah, life was good! And then I thought, *Who wants to go to the movies by themselves, loser?*

Sheepishly, I walked out of my room and back to my imminent death. As I passed by the phone, I knew I was crazy. "Okay, I'll call the guy," I started explaining to them. "No. Better yet, you have him call me."

"So you're not a lesbian after all?" There it was. The trap was in motion, and there was nothing I could do to stop it.

Chapter 2

I went to work the next day wondering if this guy even existed. After all, it could have been one elaborate plot by two bored moms to poke fun at the single girl with no love life. I figured if I told myself he didn't exist, then I didn't have to be let down if he didn't want to meet me.

Yet two days later there he was, a voice on my answering machine. "Hi, Lani, this is Richard..." I think I almost fainted. I had been without a man for so long I forgot how nerve-wracking the whole ordeal could be. My face was turning red, my palms were sweaty. He liked me; he wanted to meet me. I couldn't believe how desirable I was. (Uh, wait, reality check. He didn't like me. He was just desperate enough to give me a shot and that was good enough for me). My hands were shaking so much that I had to play the message twice to write the number down.

With trembling hands, I picked up the receiver (yes, these were the days before cell phones). I clicked the ominous On button. I pressed the number 1 and my heart started palpitating. I clicked the Off button.

"You can do this" was how the pep talk with the little voice in my head started. "You have spoken to men plenty of times. Pretend you don't care if he likes you or not." Then I started practicing my opening line, "Hi! Is Richard there?" "Hello... may I speak to Richard please?" "Hello, is this Richard?"

There was just way too much pressure. And then, as if God was throwing me a Hail Mary, the phone rang. It scared the crap out of me at first, but then I was relieved. I wasn't going to have to dial his number.

Clearing my throat and mustering the most pleasant telephone operator voice, I picked up. "Hello?" (I even surprised myself with how amazing I sounded).

"Ha ha ha...you thought I was him, didn't you?" my sister taunted. "Where did you pick up that accent?"

"Shut up. What do you want?" I asked.

"Did he call?" She just had to know.

"Yes, as a matter of fact, he did," I told her.

"AND?"

"And nothing. I haven't called him back," I responded.

"What do you mean you haven't called him back? You have a live one on the hook and you're waiting?" she scolded.

In reality, I wanted to tell her I was nervous; that I didn't think I was good enough, that I wasn't sure he would like me. I needed her reassurance in such a desperate way but instead, "I like to make men sweat it out," came out of my mouth.

"Well, the way things are going for you, I wouldn't wait too long, spinster." And with a chuckle, she hung up.

So there I was again, alone with the phone and knees that were ready to buckle. Being a spinster was not something I aspired to be, so I clicked that ominous On button again. The dial tone was ten times louder than I recalled moments earlier, so I didn't hesitate to hit the *1* this time. I stared at the second number on the Post-it note for so long, that an annoying beeping sound came out of the receiver, and I got so nervous I dropped the paper.

I clicked that wonderful Off button, and like magic, my knees were working and my heart was beating at the right pace. There was just one problem. When I looked down to get the paper, I couldn't find it. Turning to the left and then the right did no good. Feeling like I was doing the "hokeypokey," I turned all around and still couldn't find it.

Defeated, I took it as a sign that Richard was not in fact "Mr. Right" and headed to my room. As I glanced in my mirror, I noticed a bright yellow paper sticking on my shirt right under my boob. Apparently, cars aren't the only thing with blind spots.

With a quiet trepidation, I headed back toward the phone. After going through the whole rigmarole all over again, I made it through the second, third, fourth, and eventually all numbers.

A man answered, "Hello?"

"Um...hi...um...Richard please?" It barely came out of my mouth and who the hell says, "so and so please" when they aren't at work? I obviously needed to practice that opening line more than I had.

"Yeah, hi, this is Richard. Is this Lani?"

"Yes, yes it is. Wow...you remembered my name?" I was so impressed.

"Well," he advised, "I have it written next to the phone."

I guess I had to take what I could get, "Oh, that's smart."

Anyway, the conversation was pleasant enough. At least I think it was. Heck, all I could hear in my head was a little voice saying, "Don't say anything dumb." I think he mentioned a desk job and living at home with his mom, but honestly, who could hear over the drone of "there's a real man on the phone with you" that was pounding in my head. He just might have been telling me he's a successful lawyer who lives in a penthouse in Manhattan. At least that was what I was hoping he said!

We didn't speak for too long. He was apologetic in saying he had to rush off so his mom could make a call, but we did manage to make arrangements to meet on Saturday.

Immediately after hanging up, I went to my closet to figure out what on earth I was going to wear. Shoving hanger after hanger over (and cursing myself for not color-coding the shirts when I made a mental note months ago to do so), I determined I had nothing exciting to wear. Before the panic set in, I reminded myself it was only Wednesday, so I had two and a half days to get myself in order.

Chapter 3

At work the next day, I snuck out for a "longer than usual" lunch to slip into the different stores around my building. Truth be told, I didn't even know half of the places existed since I'm usually catatonic on my way to work and "head down in a hurry" on my way out of work. But lo and behold...they were there.

You would think the tall, thin, impeccably dressed, perfectly manicured blonde would have been a clue that I didn't belong in the first shop...ahem, excuse me..."boutique" I stepped into. The second clue would be the way her nose twitched and her lips tightened at the sight of me. Not gonna lie...I thought it was dust.

My final clue was when she asked me who I was shopping for. It wasn't a "Hi, welcome, how can I help you today?" inquiry, it was an all-out, "there's no possible way I would allow our clothes to touch your dreadful skin" attack.

"And who do you know that belongs in our couture?" she began. "They must have exquisite taste if you chose our store for the gift."

"The gift?" I asked, "I'm sorry, I don't understand, what gift?"

"Well, dear, seeing as your current, let's call it 'wardrobe,' does not exactly, let's say, 'blend' with our fashion-forward trends, my assumption can only be that you are shopping for a present," she finished.

"Um...no...actually, I was here for myself."

"Oh...well...I apologize for the misunderstanding," she backpedaled.

"You know what?" I asked her. I followed it with, "I've decided that the thousand dollar shopping spree I was about to go on won't happen here," and I stormed out. I have no idea where that came from, heck, I was lucky if I had $75 to spare, but seeing the expression on her face when I made that comment (at the very moment where a person who looked like a manager came out from the back) was priceless.

I was feeling very "Pretty Woman-ish" in the next store and was extra confident I could find something more appropriate for my tastes. How did I know this? Easy...the store had Sale signs on some racks. That was definitely more my speed.

I went to the first sale rack and spun it around until I found my size. Then I sorted through the vibrant colors noticing something very disappointing; these clothes were out of season. Yes, the color on that sweater was just my style, but it was not sweater season. And I would even consider that cute gray dress if it wasn't made of wool. *UGH. How could I show up in a turtleneck when the weather was high sixties?* I thought.

Feeling my wallet tremble in my pocketbook, I walked over to the "what's new" section. There was a shirt I was instantly attracted to. It was mainly purple with flowy three-quarter sleeves, and it looked like it would accentuate my boobs without showing off my muffin-top. It had some paisley patterns, which was perfect for hiding unwanted bumps.

After finding my size, I pulled it off the rack, walked over to the mirror, and held it up to myself, nearly poking my face with the hanger. I pushed down the shirt with the palm of my other hand and did a little sashay with my right hip then reversed my hands and flounced to my left. Honestly, I have no idea why women do this move when you consider that in real life, no one walks or poses this way.

In any event, that runway show in front of the mirror (especially with the black pants I was wearing) proved that this was the shirt for me. Looking at the price tag though, reminded me that I am neither a high-paid runway model nor a high-priced Julia Roberts prostitute.

"$59 for a shirt," I said to no one in particular but secretly hoped someone would overhear and agree that the pricing in the store was egregiously wrong. How could I buy a super cute wool dress for $7.99 but have to spend sixty bucks for something that will be $9.99 in a matter of months? It was completely unfair, so in a huff, I shoved the shirt back on the rack not caring if it got wrinkled. I was of the opinion that someone who could spend that much on a shirt probably sent it out to the drycleaner for a pressing first.

That gray dress was willing me to pick it up, so I obliged. This go around, I didn't waste any time in front of the mirror; I went straight to the dressing room. Imagine my surprise though when the dressing area was one cavernous room with hooks and mirrors adorning the walls. I had no idea these places even existed.

Normally, I'm quite shy about these things, but seeing as no other woman was there and my already long lunch was getting longer by the second, I threw caution to the wind and took my shirt off. I then proceeded to put the dress on and although it gave me a really hard time (especially over my boobs, which up until today I didn't think were that big), I finally got it on.

Unfortunately, it looked terrible, and I attributed it to those black pants causing the muffin top. So I kicked off my sneakers (which I wear whenever I walk outside because navigating all the holes our sidewalks and streets have in any sort of heel is a suicide mission), pulled my pants off, and was still disgusted by what I saw because the white socks I was wearing threw the whole outfit off.

Bending down, I ripped the socks off (making a mental note that I really needed to change the polish on my toes) and stood up and not even that helped. Turning around to see what my back looked like, I did the awkward "twist your head as far behind your right shoulder as you can" motion all the while praying my bra wasn't so tight that I had sections of fat pop-ping out. But naturally, there were plenty of fat sections, so I adjusted the bra straps trying to displace said "fat sections" to no avail. My bra was not going to be Spanx for my boobs. This was not the dress for me.

Realizing I was away from my desk for almost two hours, I quickly pulled the dress over my head. At least I tried to. My boobs, which were never big in the past when I wanted them to be, were now a complete and utter hindrance to my life.

I took a deep breath and tried again. The dress went up a little higher than before but nowhere close to getting off. Another deep breath and one more try—complete failure. Panic started creeping in as I looked around for a pair of scissors, which at this point was my only option.

Not seeing any, I tried again, and this time, my arms got stuck over my head and I imagined what the snob in the other store would think about me. She thought I was a mess before, thank God she wasn't there as I shimmied and wiggled and twisted trying to get that darn thing off.

A little relief came when I got the dress back down, but the relief quickly turned to horrific shame when at some point during my transgression another shopper came in and was staring at me. I hadn't heard her over the beating of my heart, and I certainly didn't see her behind the curtain that my arms and dress created around my head. What must she be thinking? And oh God, what underwear was I wearing?

"Looks like you could use some help," she implied.

Knowing there was no way on earth I was getting this off solo, I graciously accepted, and in a matter of moments, it popped off my head, and I wondered if that's how a baby felt when they were born.

Getting dressed quickly, I thanked the woman over and over and begged her to never tell anyone about this encounter. She said she wouldn't, but I can't blame her if she did. There was a "discard" rack just outside the dressing room for the clothes you weren't taking and there was no doubt in my mind that hideous, once cute, gray dress was a "discard."

As it swung back and forth on the rack, I caught a glimpse of the tag. In my haste to get away from the pricey items, I didn't check the size. It was two sizes smaller than I usually wear. Loser.

A two-hour lunch with nothing but shame to show for it was definitely not worth it. I didn't even have time to pick up something to eat, and there was no way I could go out again. As I sat listening to the sound of my stomach reminding me I forgot about it, I assured myself that missing a meal was exactly what I needed to do so I was never in that predicament again.

Chapter 4

In a rare occurrence, I dropped by my sister's house after work unannounced. When we were teens the one thing that truly brought us together was our clothes. We seemed to get along really good as long as one of us needed to borrow some of it.

"Oh, hi, Aunt Lani," my niece said with a warm hug. I hadn't realized it at the time, but I really needed that hug. I held her a little tighter (and longer) than usual, and it was she who finally broke away.

"So...whatcha doing here?" she asked.

"I came to see your mom. Is she around?"

"Sure, she's in the back cleaning my room."

Hmmm..."Wait, why is she cleaning *your* room?" I questioned. "Isn't that your job?"

My niece was quick to inform me that if her mom wanted a clean room, it was her prerogative. She was not going to interfere with her mother's happiness.

Honestly, I should have corrected her, but I wasn't in the mood to get into a philosophical debate with a kid. I was sure given my current downtrodden state, there was no way I would win.

With an "I hope you change your mind one day," I headed down the hall to find my sister. Just as my niece promised, she was fiddling with some dollhouse as I approached. She jumped out of her skin when she turned around, and I noticed she was holding a feather duster.

"Who the heck uses feather dusters?" I asked. "I thought they were only for French maid outfits," I remarked.

"Who the heck sneaks up on someone in their own home?" she retorted.

"Good point." If only she realized what a true "sneak up" felt like—arms in the air, full body exposure. I shuddered just recalling it.

"Hey, you got anything I can wear on Saturday night?" I asked.

"Why...what's Saturday night...Oh my God, you are going out with that guy, aren't you?" she figured out.

"Yes, I—"

"Where are you going? What is he like? Did he see a picture of you yet? No, he couldn't have," she rambled.

"Wait, what do you mean he 'couldn't have'?" I asked.

"Oh, don't be so sensitive. I'm just teasing you. What's he like?" she pried.

"I don't know," I said honestly. "He seems normal. We didn't really get to talk much. His mother interrupted."

"Wait, what?" She pounced on that comment with a reckless abandon. "Don't tell me he lives with his mother," she said.

"Okay, I won't."

"Oh God," she sighed.

I told her not to worry about that and asked if we could get to the business at hand. She went into her closet and started tossing item after item (most of which I tossed to a "discard" pile).

When I was satisfied that I had enough to put some sort of outfit together (although I really wish they made Garanimals for adults), I headed for the door. At that point, my sister invited me to stay for dinner. As I'm not much of a cook myself, I gladly accepted a home-cooked meal.

Whatever was cooking smelled fantastic, and knowing my sister, there was probably some pasta involved. Sure enough, when she put the food on the table, the most delicious-looking baked ziti stared me right in the eye daring me to dive in.

I took a nice, heaping spoonful and was about to go for a second when I remembered the fat sections bulging from my bra. The salad would have to do for my second helping. We all made some polite chitchat; my brother-in-law talking about the promotion he got and my niece jumping in with "and now he'll have an office and can hang all my drawings up."

I'm not sure, but I thought I caught a glimpse of...what was it?...sadness perhaps...at least that's what I thought I saw from my sister. I made a mental note to ask her about it later.

My niece started rambling on about this boy in school who she thought liked her, but she wasn't sure because he didn't actually say anything, but she could tell that he was being extra nice to her and he even gave her the ball at gym today and no one ever gives up the ball especially when it was dodgeball because everyone loves to throw balls at other kids because you can't get in trouble for it...

I hated to admit it, but I was tuning out rather quickly. She might have mentioned something about a dance and "Chrissy likes him" and something about Spanish class, and I just couldn't tune in until she stopped and it was really quiet and I managed to nod my head to make her think I was listening, and unfortunately at that point, I was because after a moment of silence, she blurted out, "Aunt Lani, how come no boys like you?"

My brother-in-law spit his drink all over the table, and my sister chastised her daughter for asking such a terrible question; my niece thought it was a completely rational question to ask and continued with, "But, Mom, it's true. You even said that the other day," to which my sister had to do damage control and pretend she was talking about something completely different when I knew all along my niece had it right.

I assured them it was no big deal as I simultaneously lost my appetite and just played with my food. I was completely grateful when her phone rang and used that as an excuse to head out. My last image was my brother-in-law sopping up his drink from the table and my sister holding the phone to one ear while trying to gesture to my niece to apologize as I left.

There was a faint voice from behind me that could have been a "sorry," but I can't be sure. I called out and thanked her for dinner and the clothes as I shut the door. At that point, I knew children were not on my bucket list; they were way too honest for my liking.

Chapter 5

By the time I got home, I was exhausted but knew time was ticking away, so not trying on the clothes wasn't an option. All I really had to do was try shirts since my black pants were already on. After my ordeal with the tight gray dress, I decided to go for the biggest-looking shirt.

It was a boxy-looking shirt; the kind that looks like an unflattering square. Seeing as the lilac coloring was pretty and we all know that nothing looks as good on a hanger, I chose to give it a shot. Boy oh boy, that was a mistake for sure.

The good news was it slid right on me. The bad news was I looked like some sort of feminine Sponge Bob Square Shirt. Not even pressing down with my hands or sashaying could help this pathetic shirt. No wonder I never saw my sister in it.

The next shirt was promising. It was a green and black striped number with a plunging neckline that I thought might accentuate my "after today's debacle I guess they are big" boobs. It had two strings that tied in the back. The shirt went easily over my head and stretched comfortably over said boobs. I pulled it down and quickly tied the strings in the back secretly wondering if they were going to be irritating on my back when I sat in a chair. No sooner did I stop tying that I realized the strings were the least of my problem.

My breasts looked amazing. Seriously. They were more awesome than I could have dreamed, but my stomach...what was up with that? Somehow my stomach was protruding out more than I had ever seen it before. I knew I could stand to lose a little weight, but not to the extent that I looked...pregnant? *I totally look pregnant*, I thought.

Shuddering at the thought, I whipped that shirt right off and looked at the tag to figure out the size and everything was suddenly clear. It was a maternity shirt. Who knew that a maternity shirt could work so well that it made the complete opposite of a pregnant woman look like she was with child?

After a few more shirts, none of which I was completely happy with, I settled on an orange button-down. I could create my own "plunging neckline" and orange went surprisingly well with my coloring. I didn't love it, and for a split second I thought about going back to the maternity shirt because it accentuated my top half so beautifully, but decided it was best that he didn't think I was knocked up.

I threw my dirty clothes in the laundry making a mental note that I had to make sure those black pants were washed by Saturday and got on my pj's. The ones I chose were less frumpy than usual. Apparently, plunging necklines that showed off my unknown voluptuous cleavage got me feeling a little sexy. Hmm...*sexy*, a word I didn't usually use to describe myself but for the first time in a really long time, I did in fact...feel sexy.

These were red, and although they weren't a sexy (or even cute) pattern, the way the shirt draped over my breasts excited me. It clung enough to show off my curves which were just enough to hold the fabric off my stomach so I looked thin. I did a little happy dance in the mirror as I told myself I could pull this date thing off.

I went to bed with a smile on my face and slept more soundly than I had in days. I'm not even sure I had any dreams because I slept straight through the night. When I woke up the next morning, I practically pranced out of bed. It was Friday, my favorite day of the week. Fridays were my favorite because I was able to work (which I actually enjoyed) and relish in the fact that I could relax for two days.

Quite frankly, I was surprised I *was* relaxed considering the big day ahead of me. The work day flew by though, and when five o'clock rolled around, I grabbed my things and headed off imagining the possibilities. Maybe Richard was the one.

Chapter 6

When I opened my front door, I heard my answering machine, which I quickly went over and checked. "Hi, Lani, it's Richard..." My heart sank. He was going to cancel on me. "Just wanted to say I am looking forward to tomorrow." Whoopee! I jumped up and down three times just hearing that. I didn't erase the message. I listened to it a half a dozen times (or more) and got more and more excited with each playback.

This was real. It was happening. I had a date, and he was looking forward to me...*me*! I giggled and thought about calling my sister to tell her. Being part superstitious, I aired on the side of caution and didn't. Who knew what negative jinxing I would stir up by doing so.

In a very rare splurge, recalling how God awful my toes were, I went for a pedicure. Don't get me wrong...I do like being girly at times. I have even gotten my nails professionally done before. My sister insisted on matching nails for all her bridesmaids some years ago and I had to admit, it was nice to be pampered.

Having said that, there were two things I didn't enjoy. One, the price; and two, I couldn't figure out what the woman working on me was saying. But seeing as I didn't have to shell out $60 for an outfit, I had the first objection covered. I'd just have to work very hard at communication.

With an excitement I hadn't felt in a long time, I headed out to the nail salon. Forgetting that most other women pamper themselves regularly, I was completely surprised when the place was full on a Friday night...duh.

"What you need?" came out of a woman hidden behind some sort of surgical mask.

"A pedicure please."

"Okay...you pick out your color. Give us one minute, okay?" she asked while vehemently nodding her head yes so I had no choice but to agree.

Walking over to the wall of colors, I was overwhelmed by the selection. This was not how I remembered my sister's soiree. Then again, we were all matching so the selection wasn't mine.

I tried to look at the nails on the women already being taken care of. The one with red had long and curled over nails. I imagined what it must be like trying to blow her nose or worse yet, how did she wipe herself after a bowel movement? Ick. I was nauseous just thinking about it and decided that red was not my color.

The next woman had a brownish gold and I couldn't tell if I liked it or hated it. I tried to casually look at her face, but her back was toward me. Luckily there was a mirror in front of her, so I maneuvered myself so I could see her reflection. Right at the moment I realized she was considerably older than me and that "brownish gold" was an "old lady" color, I slightly lost my balance and knocked a ceramic, Asian-looking cat off the edge of the counter. Thank God it didn't break, but the woman gave me a dirty look from behind the surgical mask anyway.

I finally gave up the stalking and settled on a light pink because it is pretty neutral (a.k.a. boring). Thrilled that step one was done, I took a seat in the small, magazine-filled, kind of dirty leather couch area to wait "one minute." Mentally, I noted it had already been at least five.

When fifteen minutes had passed and no one seemed to be moving to the drying phase, I asked if it would be much longer. The "doctor," as I imagined she must be given the surgical mask, said, "Just one more minute, you be patient, it all good," and started nodding her head again. Since I had nowhere else to be, I figured I could be patient.

Another ten minutes had gone by when it looked like someone was being moved to the dryer. It was a slow process though. She had to carefully twist and slide out of her chair and allow the pedicurist to help her with her pocketbook. Then, she shimmied in what looked like paper flip-flops to the dryer while her hands (which had also been polished) were spread out all "jazz hands" like. I swear it had to be another five minutes before the woman was safely seated at the drying station and spraying some sort of hairspray on her feet.

Meanwhile, the pedicurist was scrubbing her work area down and prepping it for me. When it was finally ready (almost forty minutes from when I was told it would only be "one min-ute") I made my way over to the chair, kicked off my shoes, got on the chair, and the woman began rolling up my pants.

You could say I was slightly mortified when she made a comment about how much hair I had on them. She really said, "You got lot of hair. You need waxing." I brushed her off by saying I'm going to shave later. She shook her head at me.

The pedicure was going well except I couldn't help but wonder what she thought of me as she was taking off the old polish that had been on for at least six months. I didn't even know how I still had any color on my toes, but there it was mocking me. Seeing how there wouldn't be a need for her ser-vices if not for people like me, I talked myself into thinking I was doing her a favor. Hey...whatever works.

Now, if there is one thing I can't stand, it's the sound of nails on a chalkboard. If there is one thing I can stand even less, it's the sound and feel of a nail file on my toes. And honestly, I knew my toes needed some managing, but not to the extent that she was taking a good two minutes on each toe. Perhaps it wasn't a whole two minutes, but it felt like forever and only by the grace of God did I not pull my foot out of her grasp and kick her.

When that ordeal was over, she moved on to some device that looked part coral, part stone, and she scrubbed the bottom of my foot with it. I didn't recall this part from the last pedicure, so I wasn't prepared for the painful ecstasy it brought. It felt really good in certain spots, but when it got to my arch, oh man. The sensation that went through my body was almost unbearable. There was this (I don't really know how to describe it) sensation that jolted through my foot, up my leg, and into my crotch (no...seriously). A warmness came over me in the final destination area but leading up to it was pure torture.

When my sister was pregnant, she taught me the breathing techniques she was learning and they certainly came in handy. Even still, I pulled my foot away once or twice, but to her credit, she was like a snapping turtle; the moment I pulled away, she lunged for my foot and continued her scrub. Knowing I had to go through the same motions on the other foot was terrifying to say the least. Fortunately when that part was over, we moved on to a much more relaxing phase...the massage.

Now had I remembered there was a leg massage involved I might have been keen enough to have shaved. Poor woman, no wonder she was trying to get me to wax. Que sera, sera.

She began on my left leg and it was heavenly. I closed my eyes and pretended I was on a tropical island being completely pampered on the beach. She must have rubbed that leg for a good five minutes before switching to my right one. I started understanding why the wait was so long until...wait...did she really spend all that time on my left leg and then gypped my right one? I distinctly remember her holding my left foot up and rubbing it at least ten times (I was counting) and then she went over each toe individually. There was a lot of time on my calf because that was when I was dreaming about what frozen beverages I'd be sipping on. She totally didn't do each toe individually and at most rubbed my right foot four times.

How is that fair? I was going to be lopsided. My paradise was just screwed up by someone who doesn't value the importance of consistency. It didn't matter how relaxed I was a mere three minutes ago, I was now completely agitated and gave her dirty looks through the final phase of polishing.

One thing I can give her credit for was the value of upsell. She mentioned at least two more times that I needed a wax... especially on my lip. I finally caved because nobody wants a woman with a mustache.

She helped me do that "shimmy out of the chair" move and got me on my feet. I wasn't really sure how to walk in those paper sandals though. Every time I lifted my foot, the toe part would flip under so my newly, revitalized toes and balls of my feet were touching the dirty floor. Admittedly, I'm not a germaphobe or clean freak by any means, but it would have been nice to have immaculate feet for at least an hour.

Deciding that dirty feet were better than tripping on my face, I grinned and bore it and made it to the small room where she asked me to lay down on bed/chair apparatus that looked like it was from a dentist office. She pulled a round light from above down toward my face, and I swore I was about to get my teeth clean. Maybe, just maybe given the surgical mask and this quasi exam room, this place moonlighted as a dental practice.

Instead of approaching me with a water pick, she had a tongue depressor with what looked like honey on it. She put it down above my lip, and it was unexpectedly warm and comforting, like a little massage for my mouth. Being it felt so relaxing, I began entertaining the thought of waxing my legs. That took a turn rather quickly. Following the honey massage, she approached me with a tissue of some sort and for an odd moment I felt like I was about to be chloroformed given the way she hovered over me with a devious look on her face.

Thankfully, she only put it on my lip and smoothed it down. Just as I was calculating in my head how much of a tip I needed to give her based on the awesome massages, she took a corner of the paper and said, "You ready?"

"Ready for what?" I asked.

"For pain."

"Pain? What pain?" I swear, I was completely clueless then...

RIP.

"Ooooooouch!" I screamed. "Oh my God! That was horrible."

"No, no, you fine," she assured me. "I do other side now."

"Wait, no...I can't," and as I tried to get up, she put her hand on my shoulder to push me down. At this point, I felt like she was going to have to use chloroform.

"You have half mustache. You need other half gone."

I couldn't argue; she was right. It's one thing to have some whiskers; I've seen women with them, but it's another to look like you took steps to remedy them but stopped halfway through. Help me Lord!

"Okay, okay...please be gentle."

She got more "honey" you know, the stuff that mere moments before was a gift of happiness but now was nothing more than torture cream. But I'll be damned, when she applied it, I momentarily forgot the pain and was transported to my happy place again. Once that paper went down, that bubble burst into a million pieces. She didn't even ask me if I was ready this time. She just ripped it and even continued to dab at my lip like she was trying to spot clean milk from it. It was horrible. I finally sat up and told her it was enough.

"No, no. You still have hair," she informed me.

"What?" Seriously, how much hair could I possibly have and geez...what if I said yes to the leg wax. I'd be there so long I'd miss the date.

"Okay, okay, no more wax." That's when she grabbed the tweezers (this woman was relentless). Thankfully she only had to grab three or four and then she applied some cream. When she was done, the devious smile was replaced with pride as she held a mirror up for me to see...

"What happened to my face?" I panicked. It was all red and blotchy.

"You no worry. It go away few hours," she informed and walked out of the room.

All I could do was shake my head and vow to never get my lip waxed again. I stood up, brushed my clothes down, smiled at my pretty toes, rolled my eyes at the dopey paper sandals, and looked in the mirror once again. What on earth was I supposed to do? Instinctively, I touched it and...wow...it was super smooth. It looked hideous, but man...it felt awesome. Feeling somewhat optimistic, I walked out of the room and right into a salon full of people staring at me.

Had the blotchiness been that bad that they saw it so quickly? That couldn't have been it. So, why on earth were they staring as I walked over to the register? It finally dawned on me when good-naturedly someone asked, "Are you okay?"

"Yes...why wouldn't I be?"

"Well, the screaming. We were nervous."

OMG! They heard me, they all heard me. "I'm fine...thank you."

I never paid for something so quickly in my life, and I knew the moment I stepped out the door I would never walk into that salon again.

Chapter 7

The first thing I did when I got in the car is pull down the visor. I had to see just how bad the damage was. I flipped open the mirror, and as the light came on, I adjusted the visor so I could see my red lip.

My fingers were once again drawn to the rash that had taken up residence under my nose. It's truly amazing how something so ugly could draw me in time and time again. I went from prodding with one finger to poking with two fingers to smoothing with three fingers. Eventually I stopped for fear I was going to make it worse. That's when I finally started the car and headed home.

Halfway there, a little voice in my head suggested I touch that wonderfully smooth lip again, and I succumbed to the pressure by rationalizing that instead of making it worse, I could actually be smoothing the bumps down.

When I got home, I went straight to the mirror to survey the damage. Needing to give credit where it is due, I silently acknowledge that the "doctor" was right. The bumps were already starting to go down. Additionally, I had to pay myself some credit because after all, I did contribute by smoothing the bumps down.

I slipped into that "sexy red number" from the night before and went through my refrigerator and cabinets before settling on cereal for dinner. Considering I didn't have anything else to eat, the choice wasn't difficult.

Given the lack of inventory, I pondered over why I wasn't skinny. Looking at the box of Cheerios (the store brand version because they were cheaper), I knew I was being "heart healthy," but why wasn't the weight pouring off?

Fake Cheerios were dinner for me at least four times a week. Why on earth weren't the pounds shedding? When I placed my bowl in the sink and instinctively walked over to the freezer to see what ice cream I had, the answer was clear. As quickly as I could, I slammed the freezer shut and went to the couch.

No sooner do I get into a comfortable spot when the phone rings. Odds are it wasn't Richard since he already left a message, so I was calm when I picked up the phone.

"So...are you nervous about tomorrow?" my sister asked.

"Well, no. At least I wasn't until you just called."

"Oh...sorry. My bad. Eh...it will be fine. If nothing else, you'll get a free meal out of it."

I told her, "That's very encouraging."

Usually when I make mental notes, they come back to me at the most inopportune times. Like the mental note to put my frozen leftovers into the fridge so they could thaw out for dinner. I remembered that one the minute I stepped on the train to work. Another winner was remembering my mom's birthday after I left her house. Yep. That one cost me some points in the will.

This time though...my mental state was spot on.

"So," I started, "I noticed you didn't seem too happy at the sound of Paul's promotion. What's that about? I'm sure you could use the extra money."

"I prefer the extra help at home," she confessed. "He's going to be working longer hours, and with all the after school activities, I'm constantly rushing to get from one place to another. I spend most of my time in the car, and by the time I get home, I'm wiped out and don't have the energy to clean. It's hard enough to get dinner ready."

"Gee, I'm sorry," I told her. "I didn't realize you were stressing. If it means anything, dinner the other night was delicious."

"Oh, thanks. It was actually leftovers from the freezer."

Seriously? My sister who runs around like a chicken without a head all day remembers to take stuff out of the freezer, but I can't. Loser.

We hung up, and I made a mental note to stop by her house more often and see if I could help with things.

After scanning through a hundred channels and realizing there was nothing to watch, I turned off the TV and went to bed. I had a difficult time falling asleep because I was sure I had forgotten something. Unfortunately, I just couldn't put my finger on it, so I assumed it must not have been that important.

Counting sheep never worked for me, but no matter how many times those sheep let me down, in these situations, I always gave them another chance. By the time I got to fifteen, my mind was wandering with thoughts of Richard, my sister, my blistered lip, my recent outings to buy an outfit...CRAP! My black pants. That's what I forgot. I sat straight up in bed and looked at the clock. It was 11:48 p.m. UGH! I didn't even realize I had been lying there so long.

There was no shot in hell that a laundromat was open, and even if there was one, I could only imagine the company I'd share at midnight on Friday (or is it technically Saturday?). The whole "one minute turned into forty minutes" experience at the nail salon completely threw me. No wonder my mental notes were off.

Seeing as there was nothing I could do about it, I lay back down and tried my darndest to fall asleep. No matter how much I concentrated on those sheep, nothing worked. I swear, if I could have just kept my mind focused enough on them so they would jump over the fence in a beautiful, consistent arc, other thoughts wouldn't have room to enter. But alas, the furthest I got was thirty-three and then it was total anarchy with the sheep. One was jumping over the fence and never landing, another was doing summersaults, one even donned a black ninja outfit and kicked his way over the fence. I mean...you can't make this stuff up.

And those damn sheep were as relentless as the "you need wax" lady. Once they started in with their shenanigans, they were committed. Trying to get them back into beautiful arcs was impossible. Just as I gave in to the "doctor" (and ended up looking like a kid with an unkempt fruit punch mustache), I gave in to the sheep and let them run rampant in the meadow of my mind. After a few minutes, I sat up again and found the TV remote.

When the TV came on, I felt like my memory must have been erased the way Will Smith's was in *Men in Black*. Seriously...the TV was definitely not as bright when I shut it off. Same thing happens to me when I turn on my car in the morning. I get blasted by how loud the music is. The night before...I'm straining to hear it. The next morning...I'm having a seizure while trying to turn the knob down. It doesn't seem right.

At that moment, had I been one single ounce of vampire, I would have been ash in an instant. I went under my covers and hid like a child who fears the shadows on their ceiling. I peeked my head out from the blanket ever so slowly to allow for proper eye adjusting. Had anyone been in the room, they would have sworn I was a creepy peeping Tom.

With fully adjusted eyes, I began to peruse the channels. For the most part, they were infomercials and admittedly I considered getting the George Foreman Grill. Seeing as I don't cook, it looked like an easy way to cook without cooking and removed the risk of lighting my aluminum siding on fire using a traditional BBQ.

I began wondering if the girls Richard dated were cooks. I definitely couldn't compete with them if they were. Well, perhaps if I had a Foreman I could. It cooked burgers, chicken, steaks, veggies, everything. It was an awesome machine, and I needed to decide if $59.85 plus ten dollars for shipping and handling would be a good investment in my love life (seemed a smarter use of my $60 than a shirt).

The next channel vied for my hard-earned dollars by show-casing some weight loss system that would naturally get me to my perfect weight. There was something undeniable about put-ting my dollars toward looking better as opposed to something that will have me eat more. Decisions, decisions...

Who knew how many obscure things were on late at night? I can't be 100 percent positive, but I am pretty sure I saw the guy from *The Dukes of Hazard* hosting a show and the red hair guy, Conan something. Truth be told, I was zoning out. Around 1:00 a.m., I finally turned off the TV and went to bed for good.

Chapter 8

I woke up around 8:30 a.m. with an urge for a nice, juicy burger. It was then that I knew the right investment for me was the George Foreman, to hell with the weight loss. Instead of the burger though, I settled for Cookie Crisp cereal. If fake Cheerios was a staple for dinner, Cookie Crisp was my go-to breakfast. I flipped through the TV to see if anything interesting caught my eye.

I must confess, I landed on cartoons and watched them while I ate. There was something liberating about Saturday morning cartoons and Cookie Crisp cereal. I enjoyed that breakfast without a care in the world. Richard was miles away from my mind although he was replaced by Justin, my first crush.

Justin was quiet but really cute! He had black hair that was a little longer than the other boys, and he was tall and tough-looking (well as tough-looking as you could be in third grade). He raised his hand to answer a question and was right every single time.

While most of the other boys giggled at me because I was heavy, Justin used to sit by me at lunch. He didn't say much but just the fact he was breathing the same air as me made my heart flutter.

The other boys were jealous of him, and I knew all the other girls liked him too but deep down inside I knew that Justin and I would get married someday...especially after "the incident."

It was a regular day like any other. Our teacher walked us to the cafeteria, and I sat down in my usual spot with a couple of my girlfriends. Justin sat down next to me, smiled, and opened his He-Man lunchbox as a couple of the other boys from class sat down across from us. When I opened my Smurfs lunchbox and took out my thermos, I got covered in fruit punch. Somehow the lid was not tightened properly and the whole drink spilled on my beautiful white shirt.

One of the boys jumped up, pointed at me, and started laughing saying, "Lani, got harpooned and now she's bleeding." At the time, I didn't even know what *harpooned* meant, but when my girlfriends looked at me, they really thought it was blood and started screaming and running from the table.

The other boys were hysterically laughing and pointing, and I started to tear up. Justin, who witnessed the whole thing, took the napkins from his lunchbox and started blotting my shirt. He told me it would be okay, and he gave me his drink.

"Don't worry about them," he said. "They're just dumb boys."

"I thought they were your friends."

"Nah, I don't need friends who treat people like that," and he went right back to his sandwich like nothing happened.

From that day forward the teasing stopped, and I started hearing the other girls say they had crushes on different boys. Justin, either intentionally or not, put everyone on notice that there was one girl for him. *Me!*

At the end of the school year, Justin's family moved, and I never saw him again. My heart was broken but there was nothing I could do except vow to never settle for anyone who wasn't as good to me as he was. Years later while catching up with old friends, I was told Justin had a special needs brother. It was then that I realized where his compassion came from, and I was beyond thankful for his brother.

Reality came back to focus when I was down to the last three cookies in my cereal bowl, and I played a little game with myself to see how long it would take me to get all three on the spoon. Surprisingly I did it in two tries, and I was grateful for the victory. At that point, I'd take any win I could get!

After rinsing out my bowl, I knew I had to get my butt in gear. I still needed to get to the laundromat, which would take at least two hours when you factor in travel. I also needed a minimum of one hour to get ready and another half hour to eat lunch, so I wouldn't be starving when it came time for dinner. The last thing I wanted was to act like a gavone when the food came out. I'm sure it wouldn't go over well with Richard if I dove into the bread basket like a cat on a laser light.

Honestly, hanging out at the laundromat was the last thing I wanted to do, so I went to my closet to see if there were any other pants that would work. That activity consumed at least half an hour before I realized it was fruitless. The laundromat was my only option.

Chapter 9

Since it made no sense to shower when I had to shower closer to date time, I threw my hair into a bun, tossed on some sweats, brushed my teeth, and headed out the door. I just about had the key in the car door when my "didn't you make a mental note about something you're forgetting" radar turned on.

Not learning my lesson from the night before, I figured if I didn't remember it, it must not be that important. I got in the car, turned it on, flipped it into reverse, and remembered what I forgot. I put the car back in park, turned it off, got out, headed upstairs, unlocked my door, and went in. I forgot my black pants. Loser.

The laundromat was super empty, which was awesome because I pulled right into a spot near the door. Normally, I have to lug a huge bag across the lot praying my arms don't give in and I drop my "grandma undies" for the world to see.

Instead, I walked right in and took the closest washing machine there was. There was no airing of my dirty laundry today.

I filled the washer with my black pants, a couple of shirts, pajamas, and some underwear. When I started seeing the water spray into the machine and drown my belongings, I thought about my "grandma undies" and realized I didn't have any "sexy" undergarments. What if (and this was a big "what if") we hit it off...I mean *really*...hit it off?

Ugh...only I could go from thinking "he's not going to like me at all" to "what panties will I be wearing when he undresses me" so quickly. I did a mental inventory of my choices. There was a pink one that might have a small hole, a blue one that was cute if it didn't curl down under my fat roll, that hideous one that couldn't decide if it was yellow or green (but man it's super comfy), that lacy one that wouldn't fit (even though a year ago I vowed to lose the weight so it would) and a couple of plain black ones as a last resort.

Deep down, I knew I should go with the hideous, comfortable one because I didn't want to come off as desperate by jumping into bed with him on the first night. Bad underwear was always a good deterrent for those things. If push came to shove, I could always make sure the lights were off.

My fantasy was quickly ended by a loud bang caused by the laundromat door flying open and hitting the wall behind it. A couple (who must have been in a hot and heavy lip-lock) came staggering in and had the guy not had her in a vice-like grip, there was no doubt that she would have been on the floor. The woman, whose sleeve was way farther down her shoulder than the designer intended, made eye contact with me, looked at her man, and started laughing. He took a step or two back, which finally helped her get upright, adjusted his pants at the waist, and then flattened his pants at the thighs with his hands. At that point, I was able to see just how much he "appreciated" his date.

The two looked around for a moment (most likely wondering how they ended up there) then kissed a little more. When they broke their embrace, she straightened out her neckline (to a more respectable "off-the-shoulder" look), twisted her skirt back into place and in the loudest, sloppiest way declared, "I'm gonna marry this guy someday." At that point, he got very nervous, held her at arms' distance, snapped into soberness, and clearly stated, "Hey, baby...this is great and all, but we only met a few hours ago. We got a good thing...let's not mess it up."

She looked at me for some sort of support, but really, I had nothing for her. Truly, I never had an encounter such as hers. I was never drunk to the point of being half-naked the next morning with some stranger fooling around in a shopping complex where I was so unaware of my surroundings that I busted through a laundromat door.

But she seemed so downtrodden I had to say something. "I wouldn't worry if I were you. If it's meant to be, it will be." She seemed satisfied, a look of relief came across his face, and he led her out the door by her hand and I couldn't help but notice how much he didn't "appreciate" her anymore.

He led her across the street to a car service dispatcher, and having nothing else to do, I watched to see if one or two would get in the car. In less than ten minutes, she was in a car riding solo, and he was smoking a cigarette walking down the street.

I decided it was probably best to not discuss marriage at all with Richard. It seems to have an extremely negative effect on men, and I didn't need any help in that department.

To pass the time, I replayed that scene over and over in my head. Each time I did, I thought of a different scenario that would have led them there. My favorite was the bar they were at was closing so they went to a park to continue their escapade. While getting "down and dirty," her skirt got...well...dirty, so they had the idea to go to the laundromat to clean them only they didn't have any money so they were going to secretly toss her skirt into someone else's load. Upon doing so, she'd take that skirt off and reveal...torn, grannie panties and the guy would run out of the place and she'd go chasing after him yelling, "I thought you loved me." Now that scenario would have made me feel much better about my collection of undergarments!

About twenty-five minutes later, I got to witness the complete opposite spectrum of love. A little old man with a cane held the door open gently while his wife with a walker entered the laundromat. He guided her to a seat and left. She smiled at me and I said, "Hello." Moments later, he came back carrying a small sack of laundry. His wife beamed as he walked in. Had I not been so caught up in the sweetness of it all, I would have been smart enough to jump up and grab the door.

"I'm sorry...I forgot my manners, I should have gotten the door for you."

"It's okay," he started. "As long as God gives me the strength, I'm happy to be independent."

"Yes, but still...," I insisted.

"Oh, don't you worry yourself, honey," his wife added, "Ed is as strong as an ox. I love watching him do the chores."

"Well, she ought to. She spent over fifty years doing them for me. Now it's time for her to relax and let me have my turn," he explained.

I spent the remainder of my laundry time observing the couple; the way he gingerly placed the items into the washer, how she lovingly gestured for him to sit down next to her when he placed the final item and pressed the Start button.

They talked about their grandchildren and how they still missed their son who died of cancer. On several occasions, he stroked her thinning white hair, and she laughed heartily at something he said. I was a fly on the wall, soaking in the beauty of their relationship, appreciating every bit of love they shared. It was a privilege to observe a love that lasted the test of time and I prayed they still made men the way they used to.

When the dryer beeped, I shook my head to get back into reality and grabbed my clothes. I realized I was slightly depressed about leaving my new role models. Before I walked out, I said, "You two are very inspiring. I have a date tonight, and I hope it turns into something, and we're still in love when we're—" And I stopped myself realizing I was about to offend them.

"Old?" she said. "It's okay, dear, we know we're old. I hope you find the happiness we have."

"Thank you."

"And look," Ed added, "don't let that boy have his way with you. I know about these young fellas, and they're only after one thing." I could feel my cheeks turn red.

"Ed...you know very well you were only after one thing too at that age. And you got it, might I remind you." She pecked him on the cheek, and they giggled like kids as I walked out the door.

Did true love still exist? I guess I'd find out soon enough.

Chapter 10

When I got home, I did something I rarely ever do; I put away my laundry right away. Normally I let it sit for a few days, and when it's down to just one or two items (from having sifted through them for clothes to wear), I'll put them away. But in this instance, I could not risk my pants wrinkling (which they very well could have in a couple of hours) and/or the thought of my intimate wear being out should the date go so well that Richard came home with me.

When my room was laundry free, I checked the fridge for lunch choices. There really wasn't much, but I was excited by a Tupperware container whose contents were a mystery. I fought a moment or two trying to figure if I had to press or pull to open it and was aghast when I got to the contents. It was left-over spaghetti and meatballs. It had been in there so long it was fuzzy and truth be told, I couldn't even remember when it was from.

While trying to stop myself from gagging, I quickly chucked the hairy worms and moldy rocks into the garbage and tossed the Tupperware in the sink. I turned the hot water on as high as it would go, praying I didn't damage that expensive piece of "unique food storage" (per the pushy Tupperware lady). After burning my hand in the midst of adding dish soap so it could soak, I decided today wasn't a "domestic lunch" day. I grabbed my keys and headed out the door again.

Wondering if I should stuff myself (so I would hardly eat on the date) or just grab something light (so I don't shock him on future dates), I drove aimlessly for five minutes. Looking for inspiration, I turned on the radio and got my answer. I had to hand it to McDonald's, their jingles were very catchy and alluring.

Rather than waste time going in, I used the drive-thru and was greeted with posters of the cool Happy Meal toys. All of a sudden, I made the grown up decision to buy a kid's meal because I wanted the Disney prize (if I saved it in its wrapper long enough it had to be worth something down the line).

"Welcome to McDonald's. Can I take your order please?" was statically asked through the box.

"Yes, thank you. I'd like the cheeseburger Happy Meal with a Sprite."

"Can you repeat that please?" she asked.

"Sure...can I have a cheeseburger Happy Meal—"

"Did you say cheeseburger?" she interrupted.

"Yes, the cheeseburger Hap—"

"Would you like fries with that?"

At this point, I'm getting frustrated. "Well, don't the Happy Meals come with them?"

"Oh," she said, "you want a Happy Meal?"

"Yes. With a Sprite please."

She wanted to know if it was for a boy or a girl. I told her it was for me.

"It's for you? Are you over twelve?"

"I'm in your drive thru," I explained.

"Yeah, but are you over the age of twelve."

I wasn't sure if this was a joke or not and quickly realized that "fast food" isn't really fast.

"Of course I am. How could I drive a car if I'm under twelve?"

"Well, I can't sell you the Happy Meal."

"Wait...what?" I asked her.

"Happy Meals are for kids." That's when the car behind me, or was it the one behind that one or it could have been behind that one as well, honked the horn.

"Listen, I don't have time for this, and you have a really long line. It's for my kid (I almost said in the backseat but realized she would notice their absence when I drove up to window) waiting for me at home."

"You already told me it was for you ma'am. I can't sell it to you."

With that, I peeled away from the static box and did something I hadn't ever done before. As I drove passed the window, I gave her the middle finger...and it felt good! Unfortunately, that error in judgment forbid me to go in the restaurant, demand to speak to a manager, and get the Happy Meal I wanted. In the long run, it was probably best that I didn't do that anyway. I can only imagine how foolish I'd look; a grown woman fighting for a kid's toy.

So, I did the next best thing. I went to BurgerPalace, ordered their kid's meal, and went home slightly depressed that I got a generic toy instead of Disney and soggy onion rings instead of deliciously, salty, shoestring French fries.

By the time I was done eating, I had a few hours left. I could not believe how fast the time was flying by. I wondered if Richard was as panicked as I was and if he had a hard time deciding what to wear. Men have it so much easier than women; they really do. Unless Richard had unexpectedly long hair, he wouldn't have to worry about it and if he worried about makeup, then I wasn't so sure he was the one for me. Most men have one pair of nice shoes and one pair of sneakers, so that's not a major issue. All they have to worry about are pants and a shirt. Life just didn't seem fair sometimes.

In a way, there was too much time for me to start getting ready (who wants to be all dressed up and worry about getting wrinkled while you sit on the couch watching the clock deciding what time would get you there early enough not to be late, but late enough not to seem desperate?) but not enough time for me to start any major tasks.

I paced my living room adjusting the few pictures I had and looked out the window a few times expecting "I don't know what." I felt heat welling up in my stomach, so I jumped up and down a bit, wiggling my arms to shake the nervousness out of me. Just when I recognized one of the issues was my house being too quiet, the phone rang and scared the bejeezus out of me!

Clearing my throat, I answered, "Hello?"

"Hi," my sister said. "Just wanted to wish you good luck tonight."

"Oh...really? That's nice of you."

"Yeah, I figured you could use a little. Let me know what happens."

As if, I thought but said, "Okay."

Deciding it was better to err on the side of caution by not waiting too long to get in the shower, I shimmied my way out of my comfy (but nowhere close to date appropriate) clothes and went to the bathroom. It was one of those times I willed a bowel movement. By going right then and there, I would accomplish two things. One, my pants would fit a tad better; and two, I ensured there wouldn't be any issues during the date.

The odd thing about bodily functions is that some people can control them. For instance, my brother-in-law is proud of the fact that he can "poop at will." If he's bored at work, he gets up from his desk and makes his way around the cubes talking to his team. If there are no issues and the chats go rather quickly, he'll just go into the bathroom and...well..."poop at will." Meanwhile, I could sit there for an hour praying to the "poop gods" and not so much as a goober leaves my body.

After sitting there for fifteen minutes and knowing full well I had an oval imprint on my butt, I threw in the towel, went through the proper motions, and made my way to the sink. A good hand washing was followed up with an even better tooth brushing before I made my way into the shower.

I'm not quite sure why I felt the water needed to be scalding hot, but there I was torturing my toes by sticking them in and hoping the pain would subside and miraculously my whole body would adjust. I let a good sixty to ninety seconds go by when finally I decided to adjust the water, and when it reached a temperature between "scalding hot" and "lukewarm," I proceeded to bathe.

Since I told the good doctor at the nail salon that I was going to shave my legs, I thought the honesty gods would get me if I decided to skip it. Shaving is a chore for me. To say I hate it is an understatement. A task that takes me thirty minutes to complete is sabotaged the moment I step out of the shower, get hit with a cool breeze, and get goose bumps. The stubble pops out like groundhogs looking for their shadows. Fortunately, you don't see the five o'clock shadow but rub my leg against the grain, and I'm ready to hide in a hole with the groundhogs for six weeks.

I did my best to avoid those pesky points by opening the shower curtain enough to let some of the steam out and cool air in. When it was finally time to turn off the water and pull back the curtain in its entirety, I was pleasantly surprised that my little trick worked. I didn't get caught in a draft, so my legs remained smooth.

Drying off was awesome. I loved how the towel glided up my leg and didn't get snagged. There was no white fuzzy residue, and I wished the "doctor" could see my legs at that very moment.

Instead, "at that very moment," the phone rang and instinctively, I ran to grab it. The second my big toe hit the tile, I got that chill I had so meticulously avoided and like rain sprinkling down on a thin iron roof, I could hear the *ping, ping, ping* of little hairs forcing their way from the follicles that were nobly trying to keep them at bay.

Figuring smooth legs was a battle I would never win, I relished in the fact I took one shower where I came out looking like a spokeswoman for Nair. My shining moment ended though when the phone rang again and reminded me why I sacrificed my smoothness.

"Hello?" I answered.

"Is Gina there?"

"Who?" I inquired.

"Gina? Is she there? It's Tom."

"Um...no. There's no Gina here."

Tom proceeded to ask me my name, and when I foolishly told him I didn't have time to talk because I just got out of the shower and was in a towel, he insisted that we meet.

"What about Gina?" I asked.

"Gina who? You sound better than her anyway."

"I'm sure my husband agrees. Goodbye," and with that, I hung up the phone. I'm not sure why I told him I had a husband. It could be because I wanted a way to get him off the phone without hurting his feelings, but a more probable reason was not wanting him to know I was alone. If he was a psycho, he could very well find out where I live just to get a glimpse of me in my towel. I said a small prayer for Gina and went back to the mission at hand.

First task was to get enough product in my hair so my curls looked fabulous. This is no easy feat. I had to put the mousse in first, then gel, then hairspray. The mousse and gel have to be applied in sections because if I missed even one, my whole hair would be thrown off. (Think of a bad apple in the bunch. It's very hard to concentrate on the beautiful, shiny, glowing apples when one has a big, brown, messy dent. You're wondering if that apple's disease is contagious and will spoil the lot even though you know that's completely impossible. It's the same with my curls.)

So, there I was, separating my hair and strategically applying the proper amounts of product to each section. By the time I made it to the hairspray, my arms were killing me from holding them up for so long. I had to admit though...my hair looked amazing!

My freshly washed, black pants went on without incident and my sister's shirt was fitting beautifully. When I gave myself the onceover in the mirror though, I had a dilemma. My outfit was perfect...for Halloween.

Looking at the clock, realizing there was literally no time to panic, I told myself I looked good and to get going with my makeup. Not being a "girly girl," I stuck to neutral colors because you couldn't screw up light brown as much as you could screw up purple. I was completely pleased with my look at that point when I realized I hadn't planned for shoes.

Sticking my head in the back of my closet to find the cute shoes I rarely wore was an issue. I didn't want to tussle my hair, but my arms were not long enough to get in the back. I decided to give my arm one last attempt at getting the shoes before pulling all the hangers off the rods to make room for my fab hair. The good news was I got the shoes, the bad news was I pulled a muscle doing it. And this wasn't just an annoying pull, this was a "you have lost total use of your arm and it is dangling on your side doing nothing" pull. Argh!

With the minutes ticking down, I worked with my left hand to get my shoes on and thank goodness, they went really well with the outfit. I started performing compressions on my right arm with my left hand willing it to operate. I tilted my neck as far left as I could, hoping the stretch would work all the way through to my fingertips. Eventually I worked it out to the point I felt confident I could leave the house.

Chapter 11

Since I have a habit of dating men who are less financially stable than me, I had to drive (so much for the penthouse I hoped he had). It took me a while to inspect my car and make sure there weren't any fast-food wrappers or dirty socks (don't ask) lying around, but when all was said and done, the car got an 80 on the "cleanliness" scale. That would have to do because a true detailed cleaning would lead to sweating, which would lead to hair frizzing, and after making it as far as I had, there was no way I wanted to screw up my fabulous curls before Richard got to see them. So...an 80 it would stay.

On the drive, I spent so much time replaying the chaos I just endured that I didn't even realize how quickly I reached my destination. I parked my car outside of his house and waited. The house was nice in a sort of "maybe we can use it as an exterior shot in a horror movie" way. You know those houses... they're tall and curved on the top. They have huge windows that no one would ever bother to clean, and when the lights are on, it looks like a pair of eyes peering out at you. Other than that, I imagined the house was charming inside.

When he stepped out of the door, my reaction was, "not bad, but what's with the nose?" I mean, he was tall, had an average body (not too flabby, not too muscle-y), he was dressed in a pair of cargo pants and a plaid button-down, but when I got to his face, that nose was...well...let's just say, "prominent feature." None of us are perfect though.

As he rounded the car, I started panicking. Was I supposed to get out and open his door for him? Do women do that? Should I have started the tradition? If I got out, would I greet him with a handshake? Is a handshake going to be awkward as we're both sitting in the car? Do you even shake hands on the first date? Why am I so lame?

Meanwhile (as I found out later in our relationship) while I was going through an emotional, internal frenzy, he was just thinking, "good cleavage." It must be nice to live as a guy, not caring about details, you know, living for the simple things like cleavage. Probably makes going to sleep so much easier. They don't have any mumbo jumbo floating around in their heads, just visions of boobs. On the plus side, I got the reaction I was hoping for, so I shouldn't complain too much!

Getting back to our first encounter...he suggested a dinner and movie when we spoke on the phone. I agreed but thought, *How cliché.* I was hoping we'd at least be able to spend the night talking until we could barely keep our eyes open. After all, getting to know each other is a lot easier when you aren't confined to looking forward in the dark for two hours.

I will admit though, the alluring thing about a movie theater is the popcorn. Not just because I love the taste of salty fake butter left on my tongue long after the popcorn has been swallowed, but oh...the anticipation of our fingers reaching for that one special kernel that we both creep upon at the same moment. Who doesn't love the thrill of a thick, slightly calloused finger gliding up the side of their hand moments before that finger meets their mouth? But I digress...

First, there was dinner. He began by ordering us the cold shellfish platter then went with the chef's recommendation: dry aged sirloin with shallot butter. The waiter advertised it was served with a cheddar and bacon baked potato and the most amazing creamed spinach your tongue will ever taste. As I was drooling over the prospect of sinking my teeth into a perfectly pan-seared steak and gorging myself on an overstuffed potato, that little voice in my head called me a "cow" and reminded me that men like their women in shape (and not a circle as I was surely heading if I went down the path of heart attack on a plate).

When the waiter turned to me, my mouth dried up. Seriously...it was as if my saliva was afraid I was going to gain weight by simply imagining the creamed spinach and all its calories sliding down my throat. "I'll have the spinach salad with the fat-free raspberry vinaigrette." It came out as a gravelly whisper, and as I said it, I immediately regretted my decision. I knew that food envy was only moments away.

When the waiter left us alone, we began our tango of conversation. First, he would take the lead and ask a question and I would answer in an alluring, seductive but to the point way. Then smoothly, I would turn the conversation around and lead him with a step or two of questions.

"What do you enjoy most when you are not working and why?" I'd inquire.

He'd respond curt and to the point with seductive eyes, "I like to find the right woman...because I enjoy a good partner." Then he'd throw it back to me..."And what about you?"

Caught up with the music I heard in my head (one, two, three, four. One, two, three, four. One, two, three, four), I actually responded in time, "I, like, to, work. I, love, to, dance. I, go, to, beach."

"I'm sorry...what? Are you okay?" he asked.

"Um...yes. Sorry, I was just thinking of something," I blurted. Apparently, he wasn't envisioning the two of us (me dressed in a tight red dress with a sweeping hemline that gives a tease of my legs in black fishnet stockings and he is hotter than hell wearing perfectly tailored clothing; black slacks, white button-down shirt, and black suit jacket that he abandons mere moments after the music starts so he can hold me and twirl me with a fierce recklessness that leaves me wanting more). No, more likely than not, he was focusing on not being bored.

Before I could embarrass myself further, the waiter came back with our appetizer. He delicately placed the seafood platter in the center of the table. My eyes immediately caught sight of the most succulent-looking shrimp. I worked my eyes clockwise and was greeted by a delicious-looking lobster tail cut in half; no doubt to avoid people looking like foolish messes trying to do it themselves. Another adjustment of my eyes...more of that mouthwatering shrimp and then ewww....oysters on the half shell.

I never had oysters before. As a matter of fact, I never even saw one up close. I wasn't sure if my eyes were deceiving me or if the rumors were true. Oysters looked like a woman's most intimate lady parts.

Richard encouraged me to "dive right in," so I took a shrimp to be polite. I don't know if I should have been secretly thrilled or not, but Richard went right for the oyster, and I was now educated why some people call a woman's vagina "fishy."

As he lifted the shell off the plate, there was a yellowish liquid that dripped off and hit the lobster (I made a mental note to not eat the lobster). He brought it up to his mouth and with a lick of his lips and a gleam in his eye, he sucked in the oyster like he owned it. I was almost slightly turned on given what the creature looked like when all of a sudden, after two chews, he opened his mouth really wide and stuck out his tongue as if he had to prove to me that he did it.

If that image wasn't bad enough, he finished his gesture with, "Okay, now you try." I tried to get out of it by saying I was so happy with my shrimp, but he wasn't having it. He told me he would "dress" it up for me, whatever that meant.

There I was at a crossroads. To not eat the oyster might make him put me on the "she's not adventurous" list but to eat the oyster might make me gag and, worse off, make me ask myself the "Are you a lesbian?" question.

Before I knew it, there he was, holding the oyster across the table for me to accept lovingly. While I was in my head trying to work out what to do, Richard had already "dressed" it with cocktail sauce, horseradish, and lemon.

"C'mon, Lani," he encouraged. "Don't be a chicken. Nobody likes a chicken." As if this decision wasn't humiliating enough, he started making chicken sounds. "Bock...bock, bock, bock....bock." At this point, the couple nearest to us started to look at me.

"Okay, okay, I'll do it," I said, and I took the shell. He advised I should just drink it down like I would NyQuil. What he didn't realize is I gag on NyQuil, so when I put it in my mouth and tried to swallow, I couldn't. So I had to start chewing and, ugh...that texture and oh God, the horseradish was starting to burn the roof of my mouth, and I couldn't figure out why there was secretion building up in my mouth. And that little voice in my head pushed me over the edge by saying, "I just figured it out...it looks and feels like snot."

My eyes were filled with water. I tried everything in my power to get that snot shot down, but it was never gonna happen. For a moment, it was as if time stood still; everyone was frozen, and I could discretely take my napkin (I didn't care that it was cloth) and remove the foreign object from my mouth.

But no, that didn't happen. Instead, Richard sucked down another one, I started coughing, and my oyster flew out of my mouth right onto...you guessed it...the succulent shrimp I was so looking forward to enjoying.

The waiter came rushing over and asked if everything was okay. With head down, cloth napkin over my mouth, and left hand over my eyes as if I could make myself invisible, I shook my head yes and prayed he go away.

But he didn't.

"Miss, are you okay? I have never seen anything like that before. Was the oyster not to your liking?" he questioned.

Trying to be polite, I looked up at him. That's when I noticed all the tables staring, and Richard trying to remove the evidence using his paper napkin from under his drink. Thank God he had the decency to ask the waiter if he could please give us a moment.

Without missing a beat, he said, "I guess the rest are mine." And although I'm sure Richard wasn't as thrilled with my gag reflexes as I was about him eagerly eating a fishy lady part, he didn't make me feel uncomfortable in the least.

By the time the waiter arrived with our main courses, my face was back to its normal color, and my eyes were no longer watering. I was happy I went with the salad because it was pretty hard to choke on.

The rest of the meal went without a hitch. He even let me try his delicious steak and get this...he fed it to me off his fork. Our conversation was a little less tense for me now (I mean after what just happened, there really wasn't anything left for me to do to embarrass myself). It was confirmed that he did live with his mom, but that was just a temporary situation. She wasn't in good health, so he felt it best to stay with her. Since he came and went as he pleased (and she didn't pay him much mind), he said it felt the same as living alone.

When dinner was finished and dessert was no more than a few crumbs and some remnants of ice cream in the form of soup on the plate near Richard, I started an internal discussion about how I should handle the bill. I totally didn't want to pay (what girl does?), but I didn't want him to think I was a money-grubber. I know it sounds like I'm a money-grubber because I didn't want to pay, but it's not like I ordered the most expensive thing on the menu and then didn't want to pay. That...would be a grubber in my opinion. No, this situation was entirely different. I simply wanted him to treat me like I was special.

The best that could happen was Richard putting his hand out when the bill came. Yes...that is always the best thing in these moments because if the waiter just happened to put it in the middle then there's that "reach toward the bill" and see if he stops you move that can be awkward. You have to be slow enough that he beats you to it, but fast enough that he doesn't think you are shying away from it.

Once it's in the man's hands, you have to do the right thing and ask if you could at least leave the tip. You pray he says, "no," but you prepare yourself for that, "Well, okay, if you insist" moment where you can't let the disappointment show on your face.

In the middle of pontificating in my head, Richard excused himself to go to the bathroom. At least that's what I think he said over the drone of my own inner voice. And this is where things really got awkward.

The darn waiter brought the bill when Richard was gone. I mean, who does that to a woman? Maybe he thought since I was so comfortable hacking up my dinner on him that we must have been a married couple so it didn't matter. But oh...it did. This was the first date, the "Is this guy a 'hand out for the bill' sort of guy" test and this dope just screwed up the whole thing.

What's worse is he hadn't bothered to clear the dessert plate that was closer to Richard so he put the bill down close to me. *Really?* Like a stealth cat, my eyes darted around the table trying to picture a way to rearrange the dinnerware, so I could "innocently" get the bill closer to the center. Because time was of the essence, I decided to just go in for the dessert plate, move that more toward the corner and slide the bill nearer to its rightful owner.

But as soon as I raised my hand to move, Richard was back. In a slick change of direction, I went for my water glass instead (thank God Richard didn't notice it was empty). It was a good thing it was empty too because had it not been when Richard announced, "Wow, you didn't have to pay, that was really sweet of you," I would have entertained that nosey couple next to us yet again by spraying the whole table like a sprinkler.

Seeing as it was so close to me, Richard naturally assumed I took care of it. "No problem" came out of my mouth, but "I'm going to kill that waiter," cheerfully played in my head.

It pained me to take out my wallet and credit card, but there was no turning back. If I thought the maneuver to intentionally not have to reach the bill was awkward, I could imagine just how bad the "Oh...me? No...I didn't pay" conversation would have been.

Out of pure revenge, I deducted a dollar from what I would have normally tipped. I would have liked to have left him a note as well telling him he needs to learn how to read situations better, but honestly, he was already going to be talking about the girl who choked on her oyster for the rest of his days as a waiter, I didn't have to call attention to myself any further.

Richard helped me with my jacket, and we headed out the restaurant and back toward my car. Another test I would have liked to see was if he'd open my car door for me. He didn't, but I spent the next five minutes trying to determine if that was because I was driving. I'm not sure if the dynamic changes when it's not the passenger door the girl gets in.

Anyway, when we got to the theater, it was a madhouse—wall-to-wall teens. I hadn't been to the movies on a Saturday night in I can't even remember, but I do remember there not being this many kids. And when did teens become so loud, or worse yet, when did I become so old that a Saturday night out was "too loud"?

We stood on line, and I prayed those kids were going to any other movie but ours. I was feeling optimistic because our movie was Rated R, and those kids were much too young for that. A sigh of relief came over me when I was close enough to the front to hear one of them ask for the PG-13 movie. Whew! Crisis averted.

Richard let me pick the movie. I thought that was very chivalrous of him. I chose the upbeat, light-hearted comedy about two people who accidentally meet and begin a courtship. The comedic part is how the man tries to navigate his way through dating a blind woman who is a klutz to boot.

Normally, this isn't the typical movie I'd like to see. No...I'm more of a shoot 'em up, chase them through the dark woods sort of girl, but I once dated a guy who had nightmares after watching *The Shining*, so I decided not to risk it.

When we were called up to place our ticket order, like the gentleman I want him to be, Richard puts his arm behind me to let me go first. Like the money-grubber I don't want him to be,

I'm concerned that he thinks he found a sugar mama and wants me to pay again. Thankfully, his wallet comes out this time, and I don't even hesitate in the least to keep my mouth shut!

He asked if I would like popcorn, but I am completely stuffed, so we made our way to the movie. Luckily, there weren't too many people in the theater so we chose seats dead center and a little back.

When we sat down, I suddenly realized that by rejecting his offer for popcorn, I lost the opportunity for test number three; what would he do if our fingers collided reaching for that one special kernel?

I'm not how sure how long I waited thinking of ways to change my mind and sheepishly (with the most seductive eyes I could muster up) ask if we could get popcorn. I was brought out of my haze by the giggles and whispers of people...teenage people. Apparently, they snuck in to watch the movie. Shortly after they found their seats (directly behind us and only two rows back), the lights went down and the previews began.

During the previews, my heart fluttered a bit when I realized I could conduct test four, just slightly altered. Since there was only one arm rest, I'd wait for him to put his arm up and then "mistakenly" put my arm on top of his. If I situated my arm the right way, my hand could land close to his. I mean, I knew it wasn't going to be the most comfortable position to lay my arm, but as a woman, we risk our comfort all the time for men. Just think about the shoes that are sold. Case closed!

As the previews were winding down, I felt something at the back of my head. I actually thought I had imagined it until I felt it again and then heard the giggles. I turned around and the teens were flinging popcorn at one another, and I got caught in the cross-hairs.

When Richard inquired what was happening, I explained and he stood up, turned around, and asked if there was going to be any more issues during the show. That seemed to scare them into better behavior just as the movie began.

The movie opened with the woman struggling to get out of her pajamas shortly after her alarm went off. She was standing in front of a mirror wrestling with her shirt twisting to the left and the right and eventually falling on her bed backward and her little Yorkie jumped on top of her. Had she not been blind, she probably would have seen that the buttons were tightened up to her neck (*Cute opening*, I thought. *But why does a blind person need a mirror in their bedroom?* I wondered).

Meanwhile, they cut to the man who is meticulously brushing his teeth in the mirror. He moves on to his hair gel and leaves the bathroom in nothing but a small towel (his body is so hot, that I'm almost blinded myself by his beauty). He opens his closet and everything is perfect.

A little later, he is driving down the street in his impeccably stellar convertible. It shines, it sparkles, and it hits a little dog that comes running across the street as a woman screams, "Fluffy." The dog goes flying through the air in slow motion while the man hops out of his convertible in real-time, slides over the hood of his car, and catches the dog as he's falling.

The man is perplexed that the woman is still screaming, "Fluffy," as he approaches her with the dog. When she bumps into a light post, he realizes she is blind. A crowd gathers around him taking pictures and asking for his autograph; the dog pees on his leg.

This is how their romance began, but I was already drifting out of their reality and into mine. Yes, I was patiently waiting for Richard to put his arm on the armrest, but he didn't. Then I started thinking he might go for the "yawn and put his arm around me" maneuver and that was fine too.

When the movie ended, I was disappointed. He hadn't tried to hold my hand, brush against my finger, or throw his arm around me in a yawn move. *But...*he never brought up the oysters, and that was fine by me. As he left my car saying he had a really great time, he didn't reach out to kiss my cheek or even shake my hand. He said he'd call in a day or two, and I said that sounded good. Despite that sinking feeling in my chest, I thought we had a really good time. I just didn't have that "end all, be all" feeling though. At least not yet.

He looked back one last time from his front door, and I was hoping that in a stealth-like manner he'd finesse his way back to the car and open my door in a style similar to James Bond. I hoped he'd grab me with one of his arms, spin me out of the car into his chest, and whisper, "I can't let you leave without knowing the taste of your lips," then passionately kiss me.

My knees became weak at the thought and for the first time in a while I was glad I was the driver and had the comfort of sitting in my car. Had roles been reversed and I was at my door, my legs might have buckled under me.

No, I didn't get my *Casablanca* kiss. Instead, he waved and that sinking feeling returned. As I drove home, I replayed every bit of the evening over and over in my head. I figured things were fine after the dinner incident because he paid for my movie ticket. More than that, he didn't make up an excuse not to go to the movie, which is something I did one time (I can't be blamed for that one though because that guy picked his nose in the middle of dinner).

So I decided it had to be something that happened from the time we sat down in the theater to the time I dropped him off. Something totally had to happen. I mean, what guy doesn't try to get a little something on the first date, right?

I guessed it had to be after the popcorn incident with the teens. Had he been upset with me, he wouldn't have defended me. Oh no! It was the horrible choice in movies. Of course! He must have hated that movie and would have preferred to watch *Lassie* over the terrible movie we just saw. Even the teens walked out halfway through it.

I should have realized what was happening. As soon as the blind woman started making out with her dog thinking it was the guy, I should have aborted the mission. But it was way too hard to read his expression in a dark theater without having to completely turn my head and stare at him. Ugh, I was so caught up in daydreaming about how I could get him to pass tests that

I wasn't concerned with how bad the movie was. I probably flunked whatever test he was scoring me on.

Deflated, I pulled into my driveway and parked. I took a deep breath and opened the door to get out. The door was heavier than I had remembered, and by the time I reached my front door, I was convinced I would never hear from Richard again. I flopped on my bed in a full X position as if to say, "God...just take me now." Who knows how long I was lying there when I finally realized it was time to kick off my shoes, get out of the Halloween outfit, fling off my bra, and get ready for bed.

Chapter 12

I tossed and turned all night and in the morning was grateful that my alarm was not going to wake me. It must have been around 9:00 a.m. when I realized I had to pee really badly. When I was done alleviating my bladder, I decided to check my answering machine on the off chance he called me between midnight and 8:00 a.m., and I just so happened to miss it. Naturally, there wasn't a message.

I managed to get myself together quickly enough to make it to ten o'clock mass. As I slid into the pew and pulled down the kneeler, I decided I was going to be very candid with God. "God," I said to myself...well...to Him, "I'm asking for some help here today. Please help me find someone who will love me because going to the movies alone sucks. Wait," I retracted, "sorry...I didn't mean to say, 'suck.' Ugh, sorry, I said it again. I shouldn't say that to you," I rambled in my head. "Just, please... um, well...you know what I mean. You're God. Please help. Thank you," I finally ended.

Normally I'm very engaged during mass, but after the sleepless night I had, I was finding it difficult to concentrate. Feeling rejected, afraid, tired, and overwhelmed, I began making a deal with God again, asking him to help me get through my loneliness.

As if on cue, music began playing, and I heard the most beautiful sounding words, "You who dwell in the shelter of the Lord, who abide in His shadow for life. Say to the Lord, 'my refuge, my rock in whom I trust.' And He will raise you up on eagles' wings, bear you on the breath of dawn, make you to shine like the sun and hold you in the palm of His hand."

I looked up past the altar and saw the most amazing light coming through the stain glass windows. Suddenly, the heavy burden I had been unintentionally carrying lifted from me, and I knew that I would be okay. When it came time to offer a sign of peace to the other parishioners, I hoped the calmness I was now feeling on the inside would pass to others through my handshake.

As I left the church, I was in a much better place than I had been a mere forty-five minutes earlier. If Richard didn't want to be with me, that was fine. God would hold me in the palm of His hand and not for nothing...no man could protect me quite as well.

The weather was really nice, so I decided to go for a drive. I turned the radio on to my favorite station and started singing along. Richard was a distant memory until the Goo Goo Dolls started singing that they'd "give up forever to touch you." And suddenly, I decided to stalk the distant memory.

I'm not even sure I intentionally drove to his house. Truth be told, I don't even remember getting there, which was becoming a habit at that point, but when I was about a block away, I snapped out of my haze and realized I was in dangerous territory. I started looking around for stores that I could say I was visiting if by chance I bumped into him.

On a day like today, I could imagine he was outside, working under the hood of his car, all sweaty and hunky-like. He'd look up just as I drove by and he'd be wiping his forehead with a red paisley bandana and that's when I'd notice his shirt was off and his chest was tan and much better than his outfit alluded to the night before. My thoughts quickly vanished when I remembered he didn't have a car. Thankfully, that wake-up call was enough to turn my car around and go home.

Chapter 13

When I pulled into the driveway and took the key out of the ignition, it was like turning on a "heart palpitation" switch. Seriously, the anticipation of seeing a blinking light on my answering machine was too much for me to take. I had to count to ten and pep talk my way out of the car ("C'mon, Lani, just pull the handle and get some fresh air," I chanted).

After getting the door open and swinging my left leg out, my right leg took a defiant stance and stayed still. It was honestly the most awkward disagreement I had ever been in. Just as I began chatting to myself again ("Listen, stupid leg..."), I was startled when a man asked, "Are you okay?"

I jumped in my seat, which was actually a good thing because my right leg finally moved. A hand reached toward me, so I took it and was pleasantly surprised how much easier it was to get out of the car with a little help.

When I was fully out of the car and smoothing down my outfit, I realized the "man" was my neighbor, Billy. Billy was an interesting character. He was kind of awkward with a slight limp. I think he was younger than me because I remember seeing him in high school, and he was so scrawny that he must have been a freshman when I was getting ready to move on to campus life.

Anyway, we never really talked much despite our close proximity, but I remembered he chased my garbage can cover down the block on a windy day for me. That was pretty cool. It's a shame he didn't seem to blossom much from high school.

I tried to picture him under the hood of a car, and it just didn't work for me.

"You okay?" he asked, pulling me out of my trance.

"Oh, yeah, I'm fine," I flubbed.

"Okay, cause you were saying some weird things."

"Oh...you heard me?" I questioned.

"Yeah, you were shouting something about your leg. I thought you might have hurt it."

And at that moment, I would have given anything to have hurt it, so I did the next best thing. I pretended I did.

"Actually, yes...I twisted it in a weird way, and now I have this stupid limp," I said a second before I realized that I just insulted the kid with the slight limp. "Not that limps are stupid. I mean...yours isn't," I rambled.

"It's okay," he urged. "It is stupid. But it doesn't stop me from chasing down flying garbage cans," he added.

I had to give it to Billy. He knew how to make the best out of a bad situation. "Well, listen," he said, "I need to get going. I'm sorry about your leg. Hope it's better soon."

"Thanks, Billy," I replied and then wondered how on earth I was going to fake a limp and for how long I was supposed to fake it. And why was he just standing there all "gentleman" like? That makes the whole limping thing a lot harder.

"See you later, Billy," I implied.

"Well, I just wanted to make sure you got up the stairs okay," he responded.

"Billy?"

"Yes?"

"I don't really have a limp," I confessed. "I just felt dumb that you caught me."

"I know," he replied and then he hobbled off.

Flustered by his calling me out on my fake limp, I made it up to the house completely forgetting about Richard until I heard the beeping sound on my answering machine. I was so excited that he actually called that I almost broke the Play button. When I heard, "Hurry up and call because we want to give you a free cruise," spewing from my phone though, I dropped to my knees and realized I blew it big time.

At that point, I did what any respectable, single, heartbroken girl would do. I opened my freezer and found comfort in my girlfriend Dolley Madison (given my life, it's not surprising that my favorite is plain vanilla). Grabbing a spoon and a napkin, I plopped my pathetic butt on the couch, flicked on the "E!" channel, and savored bite after precious bite while finding out the "True Hollywood Story" of Jack, Chrissy, and Janet of *Three's Company*.

It was a fitting show to watch considering I began feeling like a third wheel recently when hanging out with friends. It always seemed like my girlfriends could walk into a bar and pick up a guy every single time. Me, I was looking for quality, not quantity.

At some point, I dozed off and woke up when I felt something cold on my leg. Apparently, the ice cream lid slid off of the arm of the couch and onto me. What was with my legs both literally and figuratively freezing on me today?

I managed to sop up the majority of the mess with the one measly napkin I brought into the living room with me. The clock told me it was ten after nine, and I sulked the whole time I changed out of my Dolley Madison stained clothes and into my pajamas. A whole day had gone by, and he hadn't called.

Chapter 14

When the alarm went off on Monday morning, I wanted no part of it. I hit the snooze button three times before I remembered it was my review day. I had been with the publishing company for three months, and it was time for my ninety-day review. This was definitely not the time to arrive late.

I sprang out of bed, checked the answering machine (just in case), and ran into the bathroom. I wasted about five minutes holding my hair in all different poses seeing if I could get away without washing it. As I said, washing it is incredibly annoying for a person with curls. All that mousse, gel and hairspray is tiring, but you need to go through the ritual on important days. And if you do it right, that regimen definitely takes you through the next day, and if you're really lucky, you can get a third day out of it.

Since Saturday was my date night, I had gone all out, which meant it was fine on Sunday, but today luck really needed to be on my side. Unfortunately, it wasn't. All those beautiful curls that were bouncy just yesterday now looked like a brillo pad went haywire. It had to be washed.

I skipped the shampoo and went straight for conditioner. I scrubbed my body with the loofah giving the conditioner a chance to...well...condition. When I was all soaped up, I grabbed my shower comb (yes, women with curly hair have shower combs because it's the only time you can get one through your hair) and quickly proceeded to get the knots out.

I moved so fast that my hair didn't have time to...well... condition, and by the time I was done, I had ripped out so much hair that it looked like a wet kitten was in the shower with me. I hosed myself off, tossed the wet cat into the garbage, and in the interest of time chose to only throw mousse into my hair. I added some eyeshadow and eyeliner to compensate for the hair. Since I hardly wear makeup, ever, I figured the added accent would show initiative.

I threw on the first outfit I saw and ran like a bat out of hell to my car. I prayed and prayed I would get a parking spot at the train station and, thank you God, I did. I hustled down the stairs in the subway and rubbed the sleepies away from my eyes.

I caught a quick glimpse of myself in the reflection of a poster behind a plastic case. My hair was frizzing up, and I had water marks all over my shirt from my wet hair. On top of it, I had forgotten I was wearing makeup when I rubbed my eyes and now I resembled a raccoon.

There was no turning back though. If I got on the train in the next minute or two, I might have a chance to go to the ladies' room before the meeting. I hurried through the turnstile and thanked God for my good fortune once more. The train pulled into the station as I reached the platform.

As the doors opened, someone from behind pushed me, and I stumbled into the car and into the back of someone. That "someone" turned around and I was horrified. It was Richard.

I couldn't understand the cruel joke that God was playing with me. The parking space, the train pulling in right away, and the odds that Richard would be in exactly the same car I was bullied into by an inconsiderate commuter.

"Oh...hey...Lani. How are you?" he asked. "Looks like you had a rough night."

(Nervous laugh) "Yeah, I...um...yeah. It was definitely rough," I mustered.

"You must have had some time with your friends by the look of you," he continued. If only he knew my friend was a tub of ice cream.

I decided that in this instance, honesty was not the best policy. "Well, you know, get a few friends together and you never know what kind of trouble you can get into."

"Hmmm...sounds like fun," he said, "I'd like to meet them someday."

"Wha...what?" I fumbled.

"I'd like to meet your friends someday. If they're half as interesting as you, I'm sure I'll like them," he continued. "And by the way, I'm sorry I didn't call you yesterday. My buddy got tickets to the baseball game and his girlfriend couldn't go, so I lucked out and went with him. Well, the next stop is mine, I'll call you later," he finished.

And just like that, the doors opened and closed, and he was gone again and I wondered if I dreamt the whole thing. He said he was going to call me, he said he wanted to meet my friends. Luckily "Mr. Inconsiderate" bumped into me two stops later because otherwise I would have missed my stop.

My ascent out of the train station was quite the opposite of my descent. As I replayed the words, "I'd like to meet them someday," I fluttered through the turnstile and floated up the stairs and out into the bright sun. I was lighter than air and felt no pain until I swiped through the doors of my job right into (you guessed it) my boss.

"Oh, great, Lani, you're here," he said and then took a good look at me. "Dear God, woman, are you okay?" he continued. "Was the air conditioning off on the train?"

Another opportunity where the truth wasn't going to help me. "Yes, can you believe it?" I lied. "And the smell was God-awful," I added (for effect). "Would you be incredibly inconvenienced if I took five minutes to straighten myself up before we met?" I asked.

"Take ten," he retorted.

I wasn't sure if I should be insulted by that comment or happy I pulled off the white lie. I settled on the latter until I looked in the mirror. It was as bad as he alluded, and Richard saw me. UGH.

But...there was no time to dwell on that. I needed to focus on the task; be presentable for my review. I found a pony in my pocketbook that I immediately used to tie the frizz into a bun. Next, I wet a piece of the sandpapery hand towel and scrubbed at the black rings around my eyes. The good news is the black was coming off, but the bad news was I replaced it with red rings. Que sera, sera.

Ten minutes must have passed by the time I decided to just grin and bear it. I dropped my purse at my desk and picked up a pad and paper. My boss was sitting in his office waiting and relief rushed over me as he said, "Much better."

He invited me to sit down with a grand hand gesture I came to expect. Luckily, on day one, someone was kind enough to warn me that my boss was a bit like Johnny Carson whereby you didn't sit down unless you were asked to. So whenever I met with him, I had to wait for him to raise his right arm, fan his hand up high, then swoop it down low, and pull it back to his side. It never looked like he tired of that gesture even though I certainly was bored of the routine after time number three.

The conversation went as well as I expected. I was hired as a proofreader, but my first thirty days was spent learning the systems, which were extremely antiquated and getting my paperwork in order. Their HR department was outsourced, so getting anything done in a timely matter was a joke. My second thirty days was spent out in the field meeting our authors at different book signing and book reading events.

Although I loved being out and about with the authors, I wasn't really doing the job I was hired to do. So, sitting in front of my boss at ninety days (not having much "proofreading" under my belt) was a bit daunting.

"Lani," he started, "the people in the office really like you. That one author, Jamie Allen, had nice things to say," he finished.

"Jamie Allen?" I inquired.

"Yeah, you know, the one you met with last month at Branden's Bookstore," he prompted.

"Oh...do you mean James Alex?" I asked.

"Yes, isn't that what I said?" he insinuated.

"Of course it is. My bad," I admitted. (It was my review for Pete's sake. I wasn't going to call the man out on it.)

"Anyway," he continued, "we'll keep you on. Just try to keep your makeup in the right spots."

"Yes, sir. Thank you for the opportunity to work for such a great company," I added.

I sat there awkwardly for a moment wondering if that was the end of my review. It seemed kind of short for having been there ninety days. Was he really not able to cite anything else from 720 hours of me working there? It took me longer to put myself back together in the bathroom; surely there was more to this interview.

When he cleared his throat and gave me the "one eyebrow up, chin swoop down to tilt his raised brow toward me" move, I took it as my cue to go. I thanked him again while pushing in my chair and was escorted out by a dramatic flair of his arm, flick of his wrist, and extension of pointer and middle fingers. If I listened hard enough, I'm sure I could have heard the sound of trumpets.

Relieved to have gotten through that, I headed back to my desk where I pondered if he seriously had considered not "keeping me." Since he said he would, I decided it was best not to wrack my brain over it too much.

Chapter 15

The book on my desk was calling to me and had been for a couple of days. Truth be told, I love reading books, but this one just didn't do it for me. The story is about a cat that turns into a human for one week. In that time, he rescues a dog from a shelter and decides the rivalry between cats and dogs has to end. I honestly don't know how my company stays in business publishing stuff like this. My guess...it had to be a favor.

Knowing that inevitably I was going to have to read it at some point anyway, I dove into it. "Jasper was a tuxedo cat, mostly black with white paws. He longed for something more in his life..." Snooze fest. I put the book down a few pages later when the author vividly describes Jasper's self-cleaning regimen.

Sorting through the other works on my desk, I came across an interesting one called *Love Happens When It Happens*. Without hesitation, I walked into one of the "quiet rooms" so I could focus on the story uninterrupted. By lunchtime, I had read over a hundred pages and would have gone on longer if I didn't have plans with Doris, our sales manager.

Doris was an older woman who had been with the company for twenty years. She loved to tell me how she started as a temp and worked her way up year after year with a strong work ethic and "impenetrable integrity." Doris became my informal mentor and was the one who warned me about my "Heeeeere's Johnny" boss. She cautioned me to stay away from the office gossip, Sarah, and to turn a blind eye to the blatant affair the editor and his assistant were having.

"Well," she jumped in, "how was your date?"

"You remembered," I responded (in the back of my mind wondering how someone her age could have such a stellar memory when I can't even remember from Friday to Monday that I have a review).

"It was okay."

"Just okay?" she prodded, and I was forced to rehash everything. The good (he called), the bad (no kiss), and the ugly (yes, I had to relive the oyster story, and it took her a good five minutes to stop laughing).

Lunch ended with her patting me on the shoulder and telling me it would all be okay. Given her age and her background, I knew there was wisdom in her words and smiled the most genuine smile I had since Saturday night when Richard got into my car.

Chapter 16

Over the course of my three months with the company, Doris shared some of her personal pain with me. She was an excellent judge of character and knew I had a strong sense of loyalty and discretion. Unlike Sarah, I respected those who respected me enough with their innermost secrets.

She shared with me that she fell in love with Jack, a high school football player when he was eighteen and she was seventeen. He was a star athlete in his senior year with scholarships to three universities. She was a junior with a passion for home economics, wanting nothing more than to be a doting wife and a devoted mother.

When she turned eighteen years old, they ran away and got married because she was pregnant. Jack was a wonderful husband, and they were beyond happy with the prospect of becoming parents.

Jack gave up his scholarships and took a job in a factory. He brought her hand-picked flowers and rubbed her feet when they were sore. When she went to the hospital to give birth, she could hear him through the door shouting, "You can do this, Doris. You are going to be the best mom ever."

She likes to think she was. When Jack would go off to work, Doris would sit and read story after story with Jack Jr. She would sing to him as she washed dishes and folded laundry. If his diaper was "ripe for the pickin'," she would tickle his belly when the new diaper was fastened.

Watching Jack and his namesake play after work was one of her favorite hobbies. She'd sit on the porch and watch her husband toss her bundle of joy up in the air and catch him with as much ease as the footballs he once held; all the while Jack Jr. was giggling for more.

Doris imagined the pride Jack would feel when he could finally teach his son how to play football, and Doris was hopeful that the baby she was currently pregnant with would be a girl so she could teach her how to cook and sew.

On the way home from a family picnic, "the kind with a red and white checkered blanket," her dreams were crushed when a truck driver fell asleep at the wheel and crashed into their car.

Jack and Jack Jr., who was only two at the time, were killed instantly. Doris was rushed to the hospital where she spent a month in a coma. When she finally woke up, she was told the news about her husband and son. She also learned she lost the daughter she was carrying. Doris was barely twenty-one years old, and she stayed single the rest of her life.

She took a couple of odd end jobs (mostly secretarial work) to make ends meet, but she hated the "grab your secretary on the ass anytime you want to" environments, so it wasn't long before she returned home. Living with "I told you so" felt safer than working with horny men.

As fate would have it, her father died shortly after her return and her mother was diagnosed with cancer. Instead of a doting wife, she was forced to be the doting daughter, nursing her mother through her final years.

At the age of twenty-nine, she was not just a widow and a childless mother, she was officially an orphan. With no other siblings, the childhood home was now hers, and although there was no rent to pay, there were bills and so she had to go back to the environment she ran from.

Doris found a temp agency that placed her in "fill-in" roles. If someone was out on vacation or any sort of leave, she would "fill in." She liked this type of work because it didn't allow any bosses to get comfortable enough to start groping.

She worked in this manner for some years when she became a temp for a secretary who wanted to spend more time with her children. It was difficult when Doris sat down at her temporary desk for the first time. There were family photos everywhere; four people with no cares in the world. A husband and wife with two babies in their arms; two children smiling in a pool and the one that did her in...a man tossing a small boy up in the air.

As the tears streamed down her face, Doris wanted nothing more than to pick up her purse and walk away. She might have done just that had an overly excited young man in a bow tie not walked up and exclaimed, "Darling...thank goodness you are here. There is so much for you to do."

She put her purse back down and asked the young man (who she now realized was wearing a pink belt hidden under his shirt) if she could have a minute in the ladies' room. His response was, "Take ten."

Doris was eternally grateful she didn't make a rash decision to leave the company that day. It turned out the secretary never came back (except to pick up her family pictures) and that eccentric young man never once hit on her. The two of them climbed the ladder of the publishing company together; her for twenty years and him for twenty-two.

They shared an unyielding bond of friendship and professionalism. On many occasions he saved her from an unrequited advance, and she repaid him by keeping his "nightlife transgressions" to herself. She was grateful to have a guardian, and he was indebted to her for being his sounding board.

Over the course of twenty years, times changed, and he no longer had to hide who he truly was. As for her, the older she got, the less she was hit on and that was fine by her. There was only one love of her life.

Chapter 17

I raced back to my desk to pick up where I left off with *Love Happens When It Happens*, but it didn't happen as I wanted it to happen. When I got to my desk, someone was sitting in my chair. He was thumbing through the cat book.

"Hello, can I help you?" I asked.

"Why yes, you can tell me what you think of my masterpiece," he said as he turned the chair to face me, and I almost dropped to the floor.

It was "Mr. Inconsiderate" from the subway who couldn't control bumping into me. What on earth was he doing in my seat, and more importantly, why was he leaving coffee rings on my desk? Ewww, get a napkin.

"I'm sorry," I managed to get out, "what do I think of what masterpiece?"

"Allow me to introduce myself. Jasper Nicholas, the author of *Jasper, the Human Cat*, the next book to hit the best seller list," he said, extending his hand to me.

Good God, I thought. *Obnoxious, arrogant, and a terrible author.* With no other choice, I reciprocated the handshake. "Hi, I'm Lani."

"Excellent, Lani…What do you think of the book?"

"I…um…I haven't quite finished it yet," I admitted.

"Well, that's preposterous. Why not? Please don't tell me you've chosen some gushy, chick lit to read first," he chided. "My book next or I'll have a talk with management." And as if on cue, my boss came out (literally and figuratively) in the most dramatic fashion I ever saw.

With arms raising slowly in a V shape and inhaling the breath of a lifetime, he exhaled, "Jasper," as flamboyantly as I had ever seen in my life. Jasper returned the enthusiasm with a grandiose, "Sweetie," and the two embraced as if they were they were becoming one. I turned away to give them space and glanced back in time to see Jasper "discretely" grazing my boss's backside and all at once the favor was revealed. The two went off to lunch, and I realized I had no choice but to stop reading the *Happens* book and go back to Jasper.

It was very difficult to get back into the Jasper book. This time it wasn't about the content though. I couldn't stop wondering if "Sweetie" and Jasper were really having lunch or if they went off to some hotel for some "afternoon delight."

I knew that my love life wasn't what I wanted, but I couldn't imagine having to hide who I truly was. It saddened me to think about my boss trying to navigate his way all those years ago. With everyone...well...in the closet so to speak, how did he even figure out who he could talk to? And did he ever choose the wrong person and get beat up? You still hear about that happening now. I'm sure it must have been worse decades ago. Poor man. I vowed that however difficult it was going to be, I would not let him down like many others had.

With a newfound purpose, I once again picked up the book. To my surprise, it got better. Not better in the "best seller" sense, but better in the, "so this has a point after all sense." Once I got past the cheesiness (when Jasper becomes human, he dresses in all black except for white shoes), there was an actual moral.

Jasper, the Human Cat, the story about a cat that becomes human for one week and wants to end the rivalry between cats and dogs, was about loving someone the world expects you to run from. Well played, "Sweetie," well played.

Suddenly, I found myself wondering how on earth I could be so upset with my love life when others had to hide theirs.

How selfish had I been all these years, especially when I passed on a guy or two because they were quirky in some small way. I bet my boss would have given anything to openly date a guy who might pick (pun intended) a terrible time to explore the inside of his nose or another who wore too much cologne hoping the smell was so enticing that he could place his hands wherever he wanted. Yes, I was being ungrateful for all the opportunities I had in love and probably a bit too picky too.

I wasn't owed anything in this life. If my love life ended today, I could relish in the fact that I had more public affection than my boss did. And while he had no clue he was in a competition with me, it felt good to be a winner.

When their "afternoon delight" was over, Jasper didn't return with my boss. Not physically at least. He was there in spirit. I could see it in the way my boss took a twirl in his office when he thought no one was looking.

"Lani?" he called out from his office.

"Yes," I replied.

"Do be sure to finish Jasper's book this week please."

"No problem."

Chapter 18

I called it a day somewhere in the middle of the book and was sure to check myself out in the ladies' room before leaving the building on the off-chance Richard was waiting for me to bump into his arms again. Turns out he wasn't there, but it's better that way. Although I fixed myself up rather well, I still wasn't "honeymoon stage" ready.

The train took forever to arrive at our station. Seems there was a jumper a few stops ahead of mine. Again, God sent me a sign that I should be grateful for what I have. Times were tough, but nowhere near as tough as others have it.

When I got home, over two hours later than usual, Billy was putting the garbage cans out for pick up the next day. I thought about Jasper the cat and wondered if perhaps I was running from something I shouldn't be.

"Hi, Billy, how are you?" I figured it couldn't hurt to see if my feelings had changed since the weekend.

"Hey, Lani, I'm good. How about yourself?" he responded.

"Oh, I'm good. Got stuck waiting for my train," I explained. "Can you believe someone jumped in front of it?"

"Wow, you got stuck in that mess? I saw it on the news. A woman jumped after her boyfriend broke up with her. Crazy, huh?" he informed.

"Yikes," I said and suddenly I wondered if I could be crazy enough to jump if I finally thought I found "the one" and was dumped by him. I know I had so much to be grateful for (especially after my whole pep talk earlier in the day), but I was getting desperate. As my sister often reminded me, my biological time clock was ticking.

Oh man, what would my sister say when she found out I was splattered on the number 2 train? Would she even realize she was part of the problem? Mom...my poor mom. She wouldn't be able to have an open casket for me. Okay...I can't jump in front of a train or bus or off a building for that matter.

If I'm going to kill myself over a love gone wrong, I'd have to be more Romeo about it. I'd drink poison so my body would be "open casket" worthy, and I'd look exactly the way I did just the day before. Mom wouldn't have to hear the whispers about how bad it must have been to scrape me from the windshield. No...poison (or pills) would be the way out.

"Lani?" Billy startled the crap out of me. As I was dreaming about the right way to off myself, I'd completely forgotten I was running recon on Billy.

"Oh, sorry, I was daydreaming."

"Everything okay? You seem out of sorts lately," he asked.

"Yeah...I'm fine. I just...I've just had some things going on. I'm sorry. I didn't mean to be rude."

"It's okay," he ended. And just like that, my recon was done. Thinking of my body splattered across the train left no room for dreaming of Billy sitting across from me in a restaurant or, better yet, walking naked through my apartment. It just wasn't happening.

"Well, have a good night," I encouraged, "and thanks for handling my cans."

"I haven't touched your cans. I'm a gentleman."

"Wait, what?" I was so confused. I thought because he was taking out my garbage, that made him a gentleman.

"Bad joke," he admitted. "Forget it." And that's when it hit me...Billy was making a joke about my boobs.

"Oh my gosh," I blurted, "I'm so sorry. It actually wasn't a bad joke, it's just with all the blood I've been picturing—"

"Blood?" he questioned rather confusedly.

"Sorry...I have to go," and I ran up my stairs faster than I ever had in my life. I was actually quite impressed.

Knowing Billy was probably staring at me from behind, I fumbled getting my key in the lock and stumbled through the door when it finally opened. I stood against the closed door and took a deep breath.

A man noticed my "cans." He wasn't a dreamy, "under the hood" kind of man, but he was a man nonetheless. I couldn't help but wonder if he liked me. Maybe I could settle for him. His limp could be an asset in the, "Wow, she overlooked his flaw" sort of way. Oh my gosh. Did that sound as callous as I thought? I totally don't deserve a man.

And that's when I heard it. It was faint at first, so I had to wait a full thirty seconds to verify it, but after what seemed like forever, it was there again; the beep on my answering machine.

As if I was adhered by Velcro to the door, I slowly peeled myself off. I started with my butt, then a slow roll up my spine and finally, the tug of my head which felt much heavier than mere moments ago.

How I made it to the answering machine with my legs wobbling as hard as they were was beyond me. My hand trembled as I reached for the Play button; that triangle flag symbol looking more ominous than before, the number 1 flashing at the same quick pace of my heart.

"You got this, Lani," I coached. "This is your moment. Hit the button." So I did.

"Hey, Lani, it's Richard," he started. "It's so funny that we ran into each other this morning, and I hope you are recovering from your night out!" How bad had I really looked that he remembered to bring it up? "Anyway, give me a call before 8:00 p.m. if you can, I'll be out of commission after then. If it doesn't work tonight, give me a call tomorrow," he finished.

A quick look at the clock, and I knew I was too late; it read 8:05 p.m. A mere five minutes cost me twenty-four hours. UGH. Why on earth did I spend all that time daydreaming about my suicide? Loser.

At that point, my stomach reminded me that I hadn't eaten since my lunch with Doris. I wondered what she was up to right now. A part of me wished our friendship continued outside of work, but I felt asking her if she wanted to go out to dinner would be too presumptuous of me. She was a pretty secretive person at work, and I'm sure that carried into her home life as well.

Wherever Doris was, I hoped she didn't feel too alone. I hope she realized that somewhere, someone (namely me) was spreading peanut butter on a slice of bread, wishing her well and wanting nothing more than for her to be happy. I lifted my head up to God and told him I'd sacrifice my love life (just a little), if He would show her a bit of kindness.

In my fog, I hadn't realized that the peanut butter was destroying my bread by not gliding off the knife the way it does in the commercials. "Can I sue for false advertising?" I wondered. At that point I didn't want to add any jelly because it would just fall into the pot holes and truth be told, no one really likes the jelly in their sandwich. It's there strictly so you don't choke to death when the peanut butter clogs your throat. If you can't get a smooth jelly surface, you might wind up with a gob of goo in one bite and that texture is toxic.

No sooner did I take the first bite when my phone rang. Without hesitation, I picked up the phone and muffled, "Hello?"

"Hey, Lani, it's Richard," replied the voice on the other end.

With that, I did the most logical thing I could think of to be clearer in my speech; I swallowed the remnants of my PB&J sandwich which at this point was only PB, and I was quickly reminded of the importance of the J when I started choking.

"Are you okay?" he asked.

Desperately trying to clear my throat, I managed an "um hm" and continued coughing in the hopes the mangled up, pothole infested bite would come back up, and I could gracefully spit it out.

Meanwhile, I managed to get my glass of water and with tears streaming down my face and Richard repeatedly inquiring about my well-being, I took a gulp. It was a delicate one at first to make sure the water would penetrate the blockage; and when I was confident all would be right in the world, I took a bigger gulp and the sandwich was washed down as if it had never been there.

"Hey, hi, I...um...wow. I'm sorry. I don't know what it is, but when I'm around you, I can't seem to swallow." OH MY GOD! I just told him I can't swallow. Did he hear it the way I just played it back in my head?

"Wow, I thought I was going to have to call 911. You sure you're okay?"

"Yes, yes, I'm sorry. I had just taken a bite of a sandwich, and it went down the wrong way, but I'm okay. I wasn't expecting your call. It's after 8:00 p.m." I was hoping that was enough to change the subject.

"Yeah, well, my buddy bailed on me, so I thought I'd try you again."

This was interesting to me. If a girl left a message for a guy and then decided to call back within a couple of hours, she'd be seen as somewhat stalker-ish. The guy would start thinking she was clingy and probably create some distance between the two of them. But when Richard did it (besides almost choking to death), I didn't see a problem.

What if it was though? Oh no! What if this was red flag number one that he was actually more desperate than I was? Was it possible that he was a stage five clinger? Why did everything have to be so complicated in my life?

"You there, Lani?" he asked interrupting my inner dialogue.

"Shit...sorry." OMG I totally just said "shit" to him.

"Is now a bad time? I can call you tomorrow," he offered.

"No, no, no. I'm sorry, I just wasn't expecting you to call, and I was in the middle of something, but I can put it aside and talk to you."

"Awesome," he said.

And then it happened..."You're not a psycho or anything, right?" I blurted out.

"Um...no, I don't think so. Some of my exes might though."

How I could be so dumb as to let those words escape my lips, I'll never know. I was so grateful that he let me off the hook so easily. I couldn't help but keep the subject going though.

"Why would they think that? Should I be worried?"

"I guess you'd have to ask them, but my assumption is all women think their exes are psycho. It makes them feel better about the breakup. If the guy is a psycho, then you're better off without him, right?"

Hmmm...that was a really valid argument, and I told him as much. We spent about an hour on the phone talking about his job, my job, my meddling sister and her friend, and just when I thought we were starting to find our groove, he said his mom needed the phone. Before hanging up, he asked if I would like to go to dinner again on Wednesday night ("no oysters, I promise") and I agreed.

Going to bed that night was not easy. I tossed and turned thinking of the possibilities, replaying our discussion over and over. He had been with his company for five years, and he liked what he did. Personally, I couldn't remember exactly what it was, but I know it had to do with analyzing numbers for a financial company. He started as a summer intern and worked his way up. It was still unreal to him because he didn't think he'd make it through the second month. Turns out when he was an intern, he started dating another intern who happened to be the daughter of a very influential executive vice president. He had absolutely no idea who she was and only found out when the EVP paid him a visit. She was apparently very needy ("and a daddy's girl to boot") and required the best of the best. When Richard couldn't keep up with her fancy tastes, he broke up with her...in a letter.

This did not sit well with said diva who went straight to Daddy, and unbelievably, he showed no decorum at work. He went to the floor where Richard worked and marched right up to him and demanded to know why his daughter was treated so poorly. Richard said he mumbled something like, "She's too good for me," and that seemed to assuage him.

Richard was sure he would be terminated within the week, but by Friday, he was still there. Before leaving for the weekend, he stopped in to say goodbye to his manager who informed him that the EVP had never been on that floor before, and he was taken aback that Richard was the reason for his visit. At that point, Richard felt the hammer coming down, but instead of being fired, the manager shook his hand and said, "Good thing you got out before he became your father-in-law." That was the last time Richard dated a coworker.

I wished I would stop trying to put a face to "Daddy's Girl" as I dubbed her. I was torturing myself trying to figure out if they slept with each other. Two months was more than enough time, but if they didn't start dating on day one, then perhaps they hadn't, or maybe they had and she was really good, which is why he stuck around as long as he did, and I wondered if she was better looking than me and if he would dump me over email.

My brain would not shut off at all, so I did the next best thing. I thought about another story he told me. The one where he met my sister's friend. It seems that he was at a bar watching some playoff game when a couple of girls pull up next to his stool. In his opinion, they were "three sheets to the wind," and totally obnoxious in the way they were catcalling the bartender.

When the bartender finally came over to them, they didn't even know what they wanted, so he walked away to help other customers. When they started berating the bartender, Richard jumped in and told them they probably had enough to drink already, and they should order water.

Just as one of them was about to dump the ice from their otherwise empty glass on his lap, a more rational friend stepped in and stopped her. She apologized for her sloppy friends and offered to buy him a drink. He declined saying he had an early morning and left.

Two nights later, he went back to watch the next game in the series and there was the "rational" friend again. They started talking and formed an informal "we see each other at the bar all the time now" friendship, and one day she handed him a number and told him to call. I asked him how long he had my number before he called and he said a couple of days. His fear was that I was one of the obnoxious girls.

He was actually supposed to go to that same bar to watch a game, but a different friend cancelled on him so he called me instead. "Prayers work," I reminded myself.

We talked a bit about my job and my review. I told him about the silly story of Jasper which, thinking about it, might have been a dumb thing to do since Richard didn't sign a non-disclosure agreement and could divulge the information to our competitors. What are the odds of that though? I hoped slim to none.

I was hoping he'd ask me some questions so I'd see just how into me he was, but his mother had to interrupt. At least we got our date booked!

Chapter 19

The next day at work, Doris noticed that I couldn't stop yawning. "You okay, Sleeping Beauty?" she asked.

Rubbing the sleepies out of my eyes, I told her I was fine in a yawn-like way. I must have sounded like a humpback whale though and a few of my colleagues turned to look at orca.

"I don't think I'm going to last the day," I confessed. "Are you at all interested in taking a stroll around the building? I'm sure the fresh air will help."

"Sure," she said, "I'll just grab my purse." I loved how she used the word *purse*. Most women called it a "pocketbook" but not Doris. For me, there was something so endearing about that. It brought me back to when my grandmother was still alive, and I would take her grocery shopping.

"Lani, just give me a minute, I have to get my cane and my purse," she'd holler. "No problem, Grandma," I'd call back. We'd get to the grocery store and she'd unzip that purse and pull out her list and her pen. I'd walk the first two aisles with her and decide it was taking much longer than it needed to, so I'd look at the list and speed ahead to pick up two or three items. I'd continue this way until the list was complete.

It cut the time in half, and I felt awesome that I didn't have to spend another minute in that bright, yet somehow dreary, fluorescent light with aisles and aisles of items radiating "buy me" from their bar codes.

In hindsight, I should have walked every aisle with her. I should have let the moments I had left with her last as long as possible. I should have valued what was right in front of me. No, I didn't have that precious time with my grandmother anymore, but I certainly wasn't going to forget the time we did have and anytime Doris said "purse," my heart got all fuzzy.

"Ready?" Doris asked.

"Yes, ma'am."

As we waited for the elevator to arrive, Doris nudged me with her purse. I looked up at her, and she nodded to her right. Standing there was our really good-looking mail clerk to whom Doris said I should introduce myself on more than one occasion.

I gave her the open-eyed, "there's no way I'm going to say, 'hi' here" look at the exact moment the bell rang indicating the elevator was there. Naturally the hot clerk looked up just in time to see my distorted, eyes-bulging-out face. Doris giggled slightly, and he extended his tan, muscular arm across the threshold and casually, in a really hot way, said, "Ladies' first."

"My, aren't you a gentleman?" Doris complimented.

"I try," he teased.

"This is Lani," she said. Wait...what? Had she really just introduced me like a debutante on parade?

"Oh...well...HI, Lani. I like that name," he said as he reached out to shake my hand.

I could have killed Doris as I extended what I prayed wasn't a limp noodle hand to him as he said his name was Matt. "Nice to meet you, Matt."

"So where are you ladies off to?" he inquired.

"Well, Lani and I are off for a late morning stroll. She's having a hard time staying awake after her date last night," she told him. And if that wasn't bad enough, she winked at the end of it.

Thank God the doors opened when they did or I was going to die of embarrassment. He held the door again and wished us a good walk.

"Doris," I chided, "why on earth did you tell him that? I wasn't on a date last night."

"Well, he doesn't have to know that, and besides, from the stories I hear, a woman with a man is more desirable than one who doesn't have one."

"My love life is not a job search. That's when it's best to have one to get one," I informed her. "You know, for someone who cut love out of her life completely, you sure try hard with mine."

"Well, my dear, I want you to be happy."

"Thanks, Doris."

The two of us walked quietly for a bit, and she broke the silence by asking why I was so tired. I explained the late-night call with Richard, and she said he sounded like a nice guy and wanted to know where we were going on our next date and what I was planning to wear. I was having enough trouble sleeping at night that I didn't need the added pressure of figuring out my wardrobe.

Stepping through the revolving door was the way I imagined Dorothy felt when she stepped out of her black and white house and into the colorful world of Oz. I always knew my office was dank and dreary, but today as I entered into that beautifully bright sun, I realized I was like a delicate flower that was wilting away in the darkness. My life was nowhere near as happy as I thought it should be.

Doris was smart enough to have sunglasses, so she led me for the first minute or two until my eyes properly adjusted to the light. She had errands to run, and I was just happy to not be confined to a cube that I followed blindly. It was way too late to turn back when I realize she led me right into Victoria's Secret.

"Doris...you shop here?" I asked credulously.

"Now I do. What is your size, young lady?"

"Uh, huh...um...wha...what?"

"Your size?" she repeated.

"Large or extra-large I guess, depending on the fit," I explained.

"No dear. Your bra size. What size do you wear?" she nudged.

"Oh...I don't even remember. I haven't bought a bra in for-ever," I confessed.

"I had a feeling," she surmised. On her tip toes, she began looking for something...or someone. "Miss, miss, could you assist us please?"

"Sure, just a moment, ladies," the salesperson responded.

"What do we need her for?" I asked.

"Well, dear...she's going to measure you so we know your size."

"How on earth does she do that?"

Doris went on to explain that the woman will take me into a dressing room and measure me with a tape measure. "It's very discreet, Lani, don't worry about it."

When the salesperson, "Janet" (according to her name tag), arrived, Doris politely explained that we were shopping for a bra, "something uplifting," and we needed to know my size.

Janet escorted me into a dressing room and asked me to take off my shirt. I obliged and nearly died when I realized the bra I was wearing was all but disintegrated. Janet was either oblivious or took pity on me because she said nothing. Instead, she stood in front of me, told me to lift my arms, and with the tape measurer in one hand, put both her arms around me and I did the most natural thing I could do...I hugged her back. Except...it wasn't natural. She sort of pulled back slightly, and I did a weird weave and bob with my head trying to figure out what side she wanted my chin to land on. It was extremely awkward. Finally, she just said, "Okay, sweetie. You stay still. I'll do all the work."

She put her arms back around me and this time brought both sides of the tape measurer to the front on my boobs. Hugging was definitely not her objective, and I felt like a complete moron when I realized she was just trying to get the measurer completely around me.

Janet advised that she wanted me to try on a 38D. All this time, I thought D cups were reserved for porn stars and there

I was, a D. She told me to hold tight, and she'd get me some to try on.

While I was waiting, I couldn't help but notice just how saggy my boobs really were. They looked like two bald guys who were perpetually staring at my belly button. Even with the "D" cup, I was not even close to porn star material. But at least now I had an explanation for not getting that gray dress over my head.

When Janet came back, she presented me with three bras. The first one she held up was gigantic. It was a "full cup for full support" style in black. She handed it to me and stood there as I wondered why on earth she wasn't leaving the dressing room so I could remove the decomposing bra.

"How's it going?" Doris inquired.

Janet responded for me by saying I was just about to try on the first bra. Apparently, Janet was waiting for a peep show. After the gray dress fiasco, I was sure I could get through this, and I took off my old, reliable, crumbling bra.

I slipped my arms into the new bra and did the "behind the back" reach around to get both sides of the fastener. Usually it's a breeze with my "old faithful" bra, but this one...my hands were flopping around like fish out of water. Finally, Janet took pity on me and assisted by fastening them for me.

"See how amazing your breasts look right now?" she gushed.

"Um, yeah...I guess," I said only to be polite. Truth is, it looked like I had two large coin sacks draped around my neck and hanging over my chest. Seriously, if those sacks had been filled with actually coins, I'm sure there'd be thousands of dollars in them.

"Do you think we can try on another one?" I suggested.

"Sure. The next one I brought you is a 'Demi cup.'"

Hmmm...now this one looked a bit more youthful and stylish. It was a cute black and white stripe and was only half the size of the other one. I got out of the coin sacks (courtesy of Janet) and slipped into the new one. Janet immediately grabbed for the fasteners and hooked me in. She told me I had to pull each boob up while pulling the wire down which I did. She then turned me around to face the mirror and wowzah!

My breath was taken from me. I couldn't believe how beautiful...dare I say "sexy" I looked. With this bra, I might very well have pulled off porn queen. Janet stood there admiring her work. She knew she just pulled off a Hail Mary.

"This bra is amazing!" I exclaimed.

"Yes, it is part of our new line. You'd be one of the first to purchase it."

I couldn't stop staring at myself in the mirror. I was becoming smitten with my image. I turned to the side, propped myself up on my tippy toes in a very coquettish way, and chose to ignore the obvious rolls that formed on top of the strap. No one was going to be looking at my back while I had these beauties in the front.

"I absolutely love it. How much is it?"

She looked at the tag and informed me it was $89. And just like that, I knew I wasn't rich enough to be sexy. My heart sank, and I told her I had to think about it. "What is there to think about?" she quizzed me. "You look and feel fantastic. This is a no-brainer."

I agreed with her that I loved it, but didn't think I could justify spending the money. Janet was not happy with this decision. Although she tried to remain professional, I could tell she was irritated with the amount of time she spent on me, and it wasn't ending with a sale.

She quickly unfastened the bra, slid it off my arms, and left the dressing room. I stood in front of the mirror ashamed and lost. Doris asked me how I was doing, and I explained that I'd only be another minute or two and that it was a little pricey. "Maybe I'll pick it up on payday."

Fastening my "old faithful" bra, which served me just fine up until that very moment, I realized that I was going to have to find someone to love me for me, not my looks, because being sexy is too expensive for my bank account. For a brief moment

I imagined what it would be like to marry a rich man. I would spend all day at the gym, getting massages, and treating myself to manicures and pedicures weekly. Who was I kidding? I wouldn't get past date number two if the rich man got a glimpse of "old faithful."

When I finally emerged from the dressing room, it took me a while to find Doris. She was over by the exit fiddling with her purse and waved me over when our eyes locked. I held the door open for her and was happy to be back in the bright sun.

"So, how'd that go?" she asked.

"Not very good," I admitted.

"Oh. Sorry."

Chapter 20

We walked around the block quietly just soaking in the sounds of the city. Cars honking, people chatting, an occasional siren in the distance. It's amazing how so much noise can actually transport you to a calm place (at least in your head). Had it not been for an impatient pedestrian pushing by me and waking me from my trance, I might have missed a really beautiful exchange.

Matt, the hot mail room guy, was leaning down and speaking to a homeless man. By the looks of it, he had just given him a hot dog and a bottle of water. The homeless man was thanking him, and Matt patted him on the shoulder and said something to him. I wished I heard what he said because that man was beaming as Matt walked away.

Doris and I were rapidly approaching Matt who was now heading toward us. I was just about to ask Doris to go into the store that was to our left when I hear her say, "Matt! Isn't this a coincidence?"

"Ladies, did you enjoy your stroll?"

"We sure did, didn't we, Lani?"

"Yes, it's beautiful out and you're beautiful...I mean...what you just did for that man was beautiful." That didn't go exactly how I planned it.

"Oh, that's Freddy. He's been out here for as long as I can remember. He fell on hard times and his wife left him. She wasn't happy when he lost his job and immediately recanted the 'in good times and bad' part of their vows. It's a shame. We live in a throwaway society. You don't like something...you just throw it away and replace it.

"He seems like a nice enough guy. He used to work on Wall Street and make loads of cash, buy his wife whatever she wanted, but as soon as the well dried up, she was out. I wish I could do more for him but I can't.

"Anyway...you ladies probably have to get back to work and so do I. Mind if I escort you?"

"No, we'd like that, right, Doris?" I surprisingly said.

"You bet!"

Like the true gentlemen he proved to be during our first encounter, Matt opened every door from the entrance to the building to the door leading to our floor. He told us he enjoyed the chat and hoped we could meet up again another time.

Not going to lie...Matt...he was totally worth an $89 bra, and I made a mental note that if I ever wanted to be with a guy of his caliber, I probably needed to make the purchase. My mind started wandering (which is never a good thing), and I tried to imagine why on earth he worked in the mail room. Stereotypically, most mail room associates aren't overachievers but Matt...he was smart and kind and super-hot.

Maybe he was an ex-con and that was the only job he could get. Ugh...suddenly he wasn't as hot as I imagined, and God forgive me, but I was praying he washed his hands before touching the mail. I'm sure Freddy appreciated the human contact very much, but who knows what germs might be on him. Oh God! I know that sounded so callous. I hoped that by praying for Freddy every night moving forward, I could somehow erase that comment from my mind. I knew that wasn't likely to happen, but I'm sure Freddy would appreciate the prayers anyway.

Doris startled me from behind and handed me a manila envelope that was overstuffed. She put her pointer finger to her lips to signal that this was top secret. She then discretely slipped away.

I made sure no one else was around my cube and slowly opened up the package. Like a schoolgirl who has been passed a note, I had to be extra careful for fear the boss would take it from me and hold it up for the world to see. When I broke the seal, I could have cried.

Doris bought me the bra. I opened the package wide enough to see a slip of paper. "Every woman deserves to feel pretty."

Not wanting to seem ungrateful, but knowing how much she spent, I closed the envelope as best as I could and walked over to her desk.

"Doris, I appreciate this more than you will ever know, but I can't accept this."

"Oh yes you can."

"Doris, I—"

"Lani," she began, "you are the closest thing to a daughter I have ever known. You have invited me into your little world and gave me a true glimpse into what being a mom is like. I have enjoyed your stories and friendship like no one else's, and it gives me pleasure to help you where I can."

Her eyes began welling up with tears, and I knew I had to accept the gift. I didn't care who was watching, I bent down to her level and gave her a huge hug. Janet could have had an awesome hug like that; she was just too concerned about measuring my boobs though.

I wiped away the tears from my eyes, took my package, and walked back to my cube. My manager stepped out of his office as I was approaching and reaching for the envelope said, "Oh, great, is that the new novel? I've been waiting for it."

Before he could grab it, I pulled it away and advised that it wasn't, but I'd keep an eye out for it. In a weird way, I wondered what he'd think of the bra if he saw it. He did have an eye for fashion after all. It was so depressing to think that a man could probably dress me better than I could.

Chapter 21

Being I was in such a happy mood, I decided to finish the "Jasper" book while my spirits were up. Turns out Jasper meets Shaggy, a hairy, loveable, stocky man who...get this...is really a dog who turned human for a week to...get this...end the rivalry between dogs and cats. The two were so passionate about their cause that they formed an unbreakable bond that lasted when they were transformed back. As a dog and a cat, they were inseparable, even walking side by side with Jasper's tail hovering over Shaggy's back.

When people laughed at them, they ignored it. When teenagers threw garbage at them, they crossed the street. When old folks looked at them cross-eyed, they held their heads up. And finally, when a little girl "no more than three years old" hugged them simultaneously in front of a crowd, they got the respect they deserved, and from that day on, other brave cats and dogs hung out together. Jasper's mission was accomplished.

Amazingly, I found myself loving the book when just a week earlier I dreaded it. I compiled my notes and presented the package to my boss. His eyes lit up when he saw the cover; Jasper as a dapper man. I gave him the best, genuine smile I could muster and told him I loved how inspiring the book was. He thanked me and asked me to close his door on the way out.

From the other side of his office, I could hear him aggressively punching the numbers on his phone. At the risk of being caught, I stood there hoping to hear the first thing he said when the other party picked up. My wish came true.

"Jasper," he said excitedly, "your book is done, sweetie! And guess what? My proofreader said the very word we were looking for...*inspiring*. See you tonight to celebrate!"

Had anyone caught me at that door, I would have been mortified. There was no hiding the cheesy grin across my face. I ducked back into my cubicle before anyone had a chance to see me.

When my grin finally subsided, I picked up *Love Happens*, booked a quiet room and settled in. I skimmed through the first hundred pages to bring myself back into the heart of the book. As this was a quasi-self-help book, I didn't get as immersed as I usually do. A good fiction book can get me to transport so deeply that I imagine myself wearing the clothes, eating the food, and hanging in the same bars as the characters.

You know you have a hit on your hands when you are standing in a trench coat with a fedora on your head, shivering in the cold rain hoping you aren't seen peering behind the building feeling like you are moments away from catching the killer. Those books depress me the most when they end. It takes a good day to snap out of the funk of knowing that part of my life is over.

Nonetheless, I found myself enjoying page after wonderful page of inspiration. For instance, "Jill" was nineteen when she married her high school sweetheart, but her granddaughter didn't find "Mr. Right" until she was thirty-five. I was absorbing so much information for myself that for a while I completely forgot I was reading this for work. For me, that was another telltale sign a book is a hit.

Even though the book was short to begin with, I was shocked how quickly I got through it. Being the pace was so fast, I decided I should reread it to make sure I did my job correctly. Truth be told, it was an excuse to get the reinforcement that love will happen when it happens.

Once out of the quiet room and back at my desk, my thoughts turned to Richard. After reading *Love Happens*, I knew it would probably take time. Secretly though I dreamt that love would happen on Wednesday.

"Hello, Lani" were the words that shook me from my stupor.

"Oh...hi, Matt." I blushed.

"Hey there. I have a package for you. Feels like another book. Do you ever get any other type of mail?" he asked.

"No, come to think of it. I can't even remember the last time I got a letter or a note."

"That's too bad. There's nothing like the anticipation of seeing what's inside an envelope."

"Yeah," I agreed. "There is certainly something nice about getting a handwritten letter."

"Oh, goody," my boss said stepping out of his office. "Is that my new book?"

"Let me see," and just like that, Matt slipped away from my cube as I opened the package, which was the anticipated "new book." I handed it off and plopped in my chair wishing our conversation hadn't been interrupted.

The rest of the day went by in a blur, and I purposefully held off rereading *Love Happens* until Wednesday so I'd be well prepared for my second date. "Second date." Just the thought of it gave me butterflies!

Chapter 22

When quitting time rolled around, I grabbed my things and headed out. Although I was excited about my second date, I realized I needed to keep my options open per chapter 3 in *Love Happens*.

Instead of walking with my head down, I kept it up today and was grateful I had. I saw Freddy sitting on the sidewalk singing "Amazing Grace." There was such passion in his voice that I was completely mesmerized. I stood listening for a moment or two, and when someone handed him a quarter, he thanked them like they just gave him a pot of gold.

"Thank you, sir. I hope God blesses you for all the good you've done."

The guy managed to mumble, "You're welcome," as he hurried off.

Freddy said, "Few more of these, and I'm gonna buy me a hot meal tonight," to no one in particular.

I found myself counting my blessings...a warm home, a car, a hot meal at my sister's. I couldn't imagine having to beg for quarters to eat.

When I stopped staring at Freddy, I saw that I was in front of a deli and instinctively jumped into action. I ordered the meat loaf special to go with mashed potatoes and peas. I was kind of proud of myself for considering he might not have a good set of teeth to chew anything hard like broccoli. A second later, I was scolding myself for possibly contributing to stereotypes. In the end, caution was better than giving the man food he couldn't eat. A bottle of water and a hot chocolate rounded off the meal.

Giving the food to Freddy was one of the greatest things I had ever done. "Here, Freddy...I bought you a hot meal."

In an extremely stealth-like way, more than I thought was humanly possible, Freddy jumped up, grabbed my hand, and pecked it in the most nonthreatening way. He thanked me, and I can't be sure, but I thought I saw a tear in his eye.

Truth be told, I didn't think my gesture was that grand and started to feel uncomfortable with the accolades. As I readied to leave, he said, "Darling, I hope someday I can make this up to you," and with that, I saw a glimpse of what Freddy must have been back in the day, and I pitied the wife who wouldn't see him through his hard times.

Walking away, I heard a faint, "Lani, is that you?"

I turned my head and saw Matt just as he caught up to me.

"Hey...where you heading?" he asked.

"Oh, just heading to the train."

"Matt...Matt...do you know this angel?" I had forgotten about Freddy although I made it no more than ten steps away from him.

"Freddy...my man. Yes, yes, I know her. Why? Is she causing you any trouble?"

"No, man. As a matter of fact, she just made my day." That's when Freddy lifted his container of food up to his nose and sniffed it. "And by the smell of it, she made my night too."

"Well, well, well, Lani. That's very nice of you."

"It was the least I could do," I said shyly. "If you don't mind though, I really have to get to the train," I lied. I had nowhere to be, but seriously, I was not used to so much gratitude, and I was starting to get embarrassed.

"Okay, okay, we get the hint," Matt joked and I couldn't be sure, but it seemed like he wanted to say something else but stopped himself.

"Well, goodbye, gentlemen!" And off I went.

Before I was out of earshot though, I heard Freddy ask Matt if he wanted some of the food. Matt naturally said no, but I was completely humbled by Freddy's gesture. He was never sure where his next meal was coming from, but he was willing to share whatever he had. I hoped Richard was just as generous.

Chapter 23

My night was uneventful, but in the morning when I got to work, I was greeted with an unexpected envelope on my desk. My name was handwritten in a "this could be the work of a doctor who decided to become a school teacher" style. It was messy, but legible, and I was completely intrigued.

As I slid the piece of paper from the envelope, I was overcome with butterflies in my stomach as I reverted back to my high school years when getting a note in school was major news.

After carefully unfolding the letter, I read it and then read it again and again.

> Dear Lani,
>
> What you did for Freddy was remarkable, and I'd like to repay you by taking you to lunch someday.
>
> If you will indulge me with your presence, I would appreciate a handwritten response that you can leave in your mailbox. I'll be sure to find it.
>
> With complete sincerity,
>
> Matt

All I wanted to do was jump up and down like the schoolgirl I used to be, but all I could do was silently giggle otherwise my coworkers would have thought I was crazy. There were so many amazing things about this letter.

For starters, he remembered our conversation about hand-written letters. Hello? Men never remember things, but Matt did! Secondly, he wanted to go out to lunch with me...me! Third, a good deed was being rewarded. Karma works for good things too!

I knew I had to address his request, but I wasn't sure what I wanted to do. I mean, I wanted to focus all my energy into Richard, but man...Matt was gaining traction. After a minute or two, I got a pen and a piece of paper.

> Dear Matt,
>
> Thank you so much for your generous offer. While I appreciate it, I really didn't buy Freddy food to be rewarded, so I do not think I can take you up on your offer. I just wouldn't feel right about it.
>
> I hope you understand.
>
> Lani

And just like that...I made a decision to work on one relationship at a time and seeing Richard beat Matt to the punch, he won. I hoped I chose correctly!

Chapter 24

When I got home from work on Wednesday night, I jumped in the shower to ensure my hair was going to be way more fabulous than it had been on the train when I bumped into Richard. After applying all the necessary hair products, I grabbed my "miracle bra" and slid my arms into the straps.

As the straps glided up my arms, I could feel myself transforming into a voluptuous vixen about to take on the world. As I slipped each breast into the cup, I became more and more confident that Richard was going to find me irresistible, and I'd get my good night kiss for sure.

While gazing in the mirror admiring the masterpiece that was me, I reached behind and grasped the two bra fasteners. Just as quickly as the voluptuous vixen appeared before me, Petunia Pig wrestling to free herself from imaginary handcuffs took over the mirror. I twisted, I turned, I wriggled (not giggled), and mustered up every prayer I knew to get the bra fastened.

All my efforts were in vain. I couldn't get that damn thing on. I wished Janet was there; she would have definitely fastened me in. I went through the rolodex of people I could call, but in the end, I would have been mortified to ask for help.

I took the bra off and threw it on the bed like it was on fire. Shaking my arms and stretching my neck like I was getting ready to run a race, I paced back and forth a few times willing myself to try again.

Just when I thought I had enough courage to try again, I'd look at the bra, and I swear I heard it mocking me. After three deep breaths and a new strategy, I picked up the bra. This time, I didn't put my arms in the straps. Instead, I put the bra on backwards and fastened it in the front. Step one accomplished.

Next, I began the arduous process of twisting the bra into the correct position. Centimeter by centimeter, ever so gently, I twisted that thing until alas...I was halfway there. I couldn't help but throw my hands in the air and laugh at the spectacle before me.

I looked like one of those trees that has two awkward knots jutting out from the side of it. And the tree that was me had an awkward branch hovering over the knots because I couldn't put my arm down for fear of squishing the perfectly shaped bra cups.

Another deep breath and I continued the agonizing journey of perfect cleavage. Grab and twist, grab and twist, grab and...ugh. I finally hit a boob. Now I had to maneuver the cups around although it was different to see myself with what looked like three boobs. Even odder that one was uncovered, one looked perfect, and one was under my armpit.

Finally, when my trial was over, I had the bra on and despite the sweat beading on my brow, I thought it looked pretty darn good. After splashing some water on my face, I quickly threw on the rest of my ensemble and put on my makeup.

For some reason I was less concerned about what I was wearing this time around. Maybe it had to do with my confidence under my clothes. Whatever it was, it didn't really matter. I was just happy I got out of the house on time!

Richard was waiting for me when I pulled up, so I didn't even have time to think about whether or not I had to get out of the car to greet him. He slid into the passenger seat and gave me a big smile and an upbeat, "Hello."

There was something about the way his teeth peeked through his lips that made my heart skip a beat. Had a casting director for a toothpaste commercial been nearby, I'm sure Richard would have been selected as the spokesperson. How could he not? His tooth sparkled when he looked at me.

"You all right?" Richard asked. "If tonight isn't good anymore, we can reschedule."

Shaking my head to get out of my daydream, I said, "Um... oh gosh...no, I'm fine. Hi!"

"Okay, good. You got me a bit nervous for a second."

"No...I'm sorry. Just my usual flighty self." Oh great. I had just led him to believe I was "flighty," which was truly not the case. In fact, I was so in tune I was caught up with how devilishly handsome his smile was that I appeared flighty...

"Lani?" he interrupted. Ugh...I zoned off again.

"Yes? Where are we going tonight, sir?" I was hoping that jumping into a cute chauffeur role would make Richard forget my "flightiness."

"Well, I thought I'd let you decide," he said. *Wait...what?* I wasn't prepared for this. How did he not give me advance notice of such an undertaking? My restaurant selection consists of kid meals with greasy French fries. How on earth could I make that decision?

"Oh, Richard...that is mighty kind of you, but..." "But" nothing. Who the hell did I channel that says "mighty kind of you?" I was blowing it big time.

"What I'm trying to say is, I appreciate you letting me chose, but I'd love to go somewhere I haven't been, so I'd like it if you chose this time." Whew...totally back on track and made a mental note to research some places so I'd have a suggestion if asked again.

"Hmmm...well...do you like Chinese?" he quizzed.

Now, my instinct was to shout out, "Heck yes, who doesn't like Chinese?" but I channeled that Southern Belle again and replied, "Why yes...yes I do."

"Okay then, go to the corner and make a left."

About ten minutes later, we arrived at Mr. Chang's House of Goodness (Richard assured me I shouldn't judge it by its name). Like a true gentleman, Richard held the door open for me. I walked into what I can only describe as an "Alice in Wonderland has been hiding out in the forest for years" scene.

Green booths, green rugs, and green walls were adorned with hanging gold and red lanterns, gigantic silk artwork of people drinking tea, and dangling cats (thankfully brightly colored, ceramic ones). Richard once again assured me I shouldn't judge it by its décor as we were escorted to a quiet booth in the back.

"I know, I know," he began, "it isn't much to look at, but trust me, the egg rolls are to die for."

"Sounds good."

As I slid into the booth, I couldn't help but notice all the gunk on the menu. I was second-guessing not choosing BurgerPalace, at least their menu doesn't have stains on it. But alas, I deferred to Richard so I had to commit.

"Well, this is nice," I said and took a sip of water.

"I agree. Do you want a PuPu Platter?"

And for the third time, I started choking around Richard. "A what?" I questioned after getting the water down.

"Don't tell me you never heard of a 'PuPu Platter.'"

"Okay, I won't tell you that, but can you tell me why it's called such a horrible name?" I asked.

"That's a great question. I just don't know the answer. Think of the seafood platter we had last week and substitute it with Chinese food. It's got a bit of everything minus the oysters."

"Well...that sounds good to me," and when the waiter came back, Richard ordered it and asked for more time to decide on our main dish.

"See anything you like, Lani?"

"Well," I said, rubbing grime from my thumb onto my pointer, "have you ever had the chicken with broccoli?"

"Chicken with broccoli?" he scoffed. "That's way too boring...do you like Szechuan chicken?"

What the hell was "Szechuan chicken"? I wondered. I quickly skimmed through the menu, found the dish, and read that it contained chili paste and responded, "Actually, not to sound completely boring, but I'm not a spice kind of girl."

"Oh, that's too bad," Richard responded. "I love spicy food."

All I could think was I just blew it until I was saved when a monument of sorts was placed in the middle of the table. It was wooden and tall and smelled fantastic. I still had no clue why it was called a "PooPoo" platter, but I had to admit, it looked a lot more appetizing than normal poo.

We gave the waiter our order (I stuck to my comfort zone with the chicken and broccoli), and when he walked away, Richard said, "Dig in Lani."

"It all looks so good. I don't know where to start."

Richard knew though. When I looked up, he was already gnawing on chicken on a stick, and I made a mental note that his teeth weren't quite as attractive when he was using them to rip apart food. "This is good, you should try it."

Quite frankly after watching him devour it, I decided I'd go for something a little more civilized; I chose an egg roll and hoped I wouldn't "die."

I took a petite bite just to establish a hole with which to pour my soy sauce. I may not be into spice, but I sure love salt. Once the soy sauce was applied and spread through the innards, I took a "bigger than I should have" bite just as Richard looked at me.

I could only imagine what he was thinking when he saw the girth of that egg roll jutting out of my lips. I am pretty sure I saw him adjust in his chair when he realized just how wide my mouth could get. At that point I decided to heed my earlier advice and commit. A little flirting could do a girl some good.

Seductively, I pulled the egg roll out of my mouth and said, "Wow...you were right...this is delicious. It just about melts in your mouth." And this time I know I saw it. Richard shifted in his chair and his hands tugged his pants down at the thighs; a move I surprisingly saw plenty of times before. It indicates the man has to pull the fabric that is bunching in his crotch. Go me!

He cleared his throat and said, "I'm *really* glad you enjoyed it." The fact that he stressed "really" wasn't lost on me.

We barely made it a quarter of the way through the platter when our main food arrived. I guess it was to be expected. When I order Chinese delivery, it seems the moment I hang up the phone, my doorbell rings.

The waiter pushed the monument aside and presented us with metal trays on pedestals. He removed the condensation-filled lids, and I was very impressed with how delicious my boring choice looked. Richard's Szechuan chicken looked amazing as well with its greasy, brownish-reddish sauce and picture perfect chili peppers.

"Bon appetite," he said and shoveled a spoonful of rice into his mouth. I had to agree that after a bite of my dish, I was completely hooked on the hole in the wall, bizarrely decorated place. The food was so good, I gave Richard a pardon on the way he scarfed down his food, alternating between main dish and PooPoo platter.

"So, Lani," he began, "tell me about your job."

"Well, I get to read books for a living. I'm the one who proofreads books."

"Wow...have you ever met any famous authors, like Stephen King?" he asked.

"No, no, definitely not. We are a smaller company, so we get the folks who are mostly just starting out. Needless to say, the books aren't always that great," I confessed. "I really like being a part of the process though. You never know when you are going to discover the next Nora Roberts. What about you? How's your job going?"

"Oh, not too bad. I sit in front of a computer all day crunching numbers. It gets kind of boring, but I'd rather do that than stand on top of a ladder fixing things all day."

I thought it was an odd reference, but I didn't say anything to him. I just silently wondered if in the past he had an "incident" with a ladder. I giggled slightly picturing him on top of a ladder gnawing on "chicken on a stick" and tumbling down without ever missing a bite.

"What?" he quizzed?

"'What,' what?" I responded.

"You're laughing. I'm trying to find out why."

"Oh..." Busted! "Nothing, nothing. I'm just enjoying myself, what about you? Are you having a good time?"

"I sure am. This chicken is awesome."

Okay, so I was hoping for more of a "this company is awesome" response, but admittedly, the food was "awesome."

I had eaten my fill of food and had plenty left over. I couldn't decide if it was tacky or not to ask for a doggie bag. Richard had finished most, if not all, of his food so I couldn't take a hint from him. Not wanting to be tacky, but really wanting to take home the food, I decided to feel him out.

"Oh boy...that was fantastic, but I don't think I can eat another bite."

"No?...You sure?"

"Yes. I mean...it's so good, it'd be a sin to waste it though."

"Well, I can help with that." And without a beat and in a very suave maneuver, he reached over and swiped up my plate and began nibbling at my boring chicken with broccoli. My plan completely backfired, and if Richard looked up, he might just have seen my bottom lip quiver.

The waiter came back just as Richard put the fork down and asked us if we'd like ice cream. Richard told the waiter that we had other plans for dessert, and we'd just like the check. I had completely forgotten the whole "check" ordeal from our last date until that moment and suddenly I had the urge to go to the ladies' room. Realizing it would look odd, I decided to stay.

When the waiter placed the bill down (with two fortune cookies), I was shocked by the total although I shouldn't have been because everyone knows Chinese food is cheap. The whole bill was just about $30, and Richard did not hesitate to grab it. That $30 was the price of one meal on our first date, and I was silently cursing that first waiter for putting me in a position where I had to pay.

Given how much I spent last time and how little Richard was spending this time, I didn't even consider asking if he wanted me to leave the tip. If he was testing me on my manners, I didn't care. As far as I was concerned, I was still ahead by a long shot.

Richard gave me first choice of fortune cookie, so I chose the one on the left. I carefully pulled out the paper and it read, "Even the tallest tree doesn't reach the sky." What the hell kind of fortune is that? It definitely wasn't inspiring in any way, shape, or form.

Richard's fortune was much brighter, "Good things will come your way." After he read it, he looked at me and said, "I think they already have," and escorted me out of the restaurant. My heart melted, and I could care less about tall trees and cheap checks.

I knew I had a prince in Richard when he walked over to the driver's side of the car, asked me for the key, and opened it for me. Apparently, there is etiquette when the woman drives, but it comes from the man.

He literally took my breath away with that move, and I quickly had to take a few short breaths to gain my composure as he walked around to his side. When he got in the car, he said, "Please tell me you like cheesecake."

I gave him a devilish smile and a flirty wink, and he responded with, "Perfect." He directed me to this quaint little dessert shop that had ten or more cheesecakes on display. When he asked me what I'd like, I was not really sure and asked his opinion.

"Well, if you like a chunky cheesecake, I would say the Oreo is really good, but if you like a more creamier cheesecake, I'd go for the peanut butter."

I couldn't help myself, he opened the door and I went right through it. "I love creamy...cheesecake, that is."

And with his own devilish grin, he said, "That's music to my ears."

He ordered the cheesecakes, and after what seemed like a five minute discussion on how I've never tried coffee before, he ordered a coffee and water. He paid without issue, and I was finally able to assure myself that he wasn't looking for a sugar mamma and that the first waiter screwed up everything.

The shop had bar tables and high stools and the lighting was dark and romantic. We took a table toward the back and waited for our desserts.

He asked me more about my job and what types of books I enjoyed. I decided it was best not to mention the whole *Love Happens When It Happens* obsession I was experiencing. Instead, I talked to him about some of the thrillers I read in the past and how I thought one or two could be adapted into a screenplay rather quickly.

That got us on the topic of the awful movie we saw last time. "I'm so sorry for that terrible movie I chose. I had no idea it would be that bad."

"Ah...don't worry about it. It's probably one of those movies that gets better when you watch it a second or even third time," he said.

"Well...you can let me know how that goes. I personally will not give it another try," I kidded as a young girl brought over two of the most delicious-looking cheesecakes and our drinks.

I was just about to put my fork into the peanut butter goodness that was in front of me when he said, "No...allow me." He gently took the fork from my hand, took a chunk from the cake, and said, "Close your eyes."

I did exactly as he asked and with my eyes closed, in a wonderfully sexy voice, he said, "Open your mouth." I totally obeyed and as he placed the fork in my mouth and my lips closed around it, I felt a warmth building up between my legs. I honestly couldn't tell you if it was him or the cake, but man oh man, I was in ecstasy.

"Mmmm," I moaned as I slowly opened my eyes and licked my lips.

"Aren't you glad you like cheesecake?" he asked.

"Yes...yes I am."

I contemplated returning the favor and thought better of it. He looked like he was perfectly capable of using the fork for his own eating, and truth be told, I wanted another taste of the creamy goodness as soon as possible.

In between bites, we talked about our personal interests, and he divulged he was an avid gamer and his true passion was video game developing. When he confessed, I could see he was concerned by what my reaction would be. Once I talked about my love of Space Invaders on Atari and Super Mario Brothers on Nintendo, he seemed to relax more. In a way, I would rather him play video games than admit he was addicted to coke.

"Do you play any sports?" he asked.

"Me?" I questioned (as if someone else had miraculously joined our table and he could be referring to them).

"Yeah...do you play any sports?" he repeated.

"Well...I liked tennis in high school, and I used to play Wiffle ball with the kids in the neighborhood. Sometimes I play paddle ball in the park."

"Paddle ball?" he said. "I haven't played that in so long. Recently, my friends and I have been playing two-hand touch."

I thought back to his feeding me cheesecake and thought I'd love to play "two-hand touch" with him.

"What?" he asked. OMG...did I say that out loud?

"Um...I didn't say anything."

"Oh...sorry...I thought I heard you say something under your breath."

"No...I'm good. Just like this cheesecake. Thank you so much for the suggestion although my waistline isn't happy."

"Your waistline is fine," he assured me and that's when I knew...he was a keeper.

Over the course of the next few weeks, we hung out quite frequently. We played paddle ball, went bike riding, the movies, all the things we were supposed to do. It was such a great feeling until the phone calls started.

"So did you do it yet?" (My sister was unbelievable).

"Uh, no," I replied. "We haven't even kissed yet. Leave me alone." This was actually the truth. It was okay at first until I started thinking he thought I was grotesque. (I mean seriously, what man doesn't try to hump every woman he sees. Unless...)

Surprising myself, I asked him about it the next day. "Are you gay, or are you just not attracted to me?" I had to know, "Are you really that nice of a guy? Why haven't you tried to kiss me?"

I should have asked sooner because right then and there, in my car, at a stop light, he planted the most amazing kiss on my lips. I'm telling you the birds were singing.

Hoooooonk (Stupid cars. Couldn't they tell I was falling in love? Geez.). Basking in the moment, we went back to his place and continued from where we left off. (Thank God his mother was playing bridge somewhere). Thirty-eight days I waited for a kiss, and it instantly turned into being locked in the throes of passion. Amazing...

Oh no! In the middle of our tryst, I was suddenly hit with thoughts I forgot about in the dating world: Will he think I'm a slut? I only waited thirty-eight days. Am I any good at this? Do I look fat from this angle? Is he going to dump me now?

But the worst question of all was: How am I going to handle my sister's questions?

"Staaaaahhhhp!" I screamed.

"What," he shouted, "am I hurting you?"

"No," I said, "we just can't do this."

"Why not?"

"You wouldn't understand" is all I could say.

While I gathered my clothes wondering how my bra wound up on his leg, I realized he really was going to dump me. But he didn't. The next day we hung out, and he didn't even bring it up. Bless his heart!

Chapter 25

"Looks like someone had a great weekend," Doris implied. "I guess things are going well for you and Richard."

"Yes. Yes they are. I'm really happy, Doris. He might just be 'the one.'"

Ever since that first run in with "the doctor," I had to upkeep my lip wax every two weeks or so. I never had that much hair before, and quite frankly, I was irritated (both literally and figuratively) that I had to keep it up. I thought about getting a class action lawsuit together to bring down the "we take away your hair but it will bring back more" vicious circle racket, but I doubted I could get enough women to speak publicly about their mustaches. So there I was slipping into a nail salon during lunch and holding back my yells (and tears) for the third time all in the name of vanity. Fortunately, the more I went, the less painful it was. Perhaps all my nerve endings were being damaged. Another great opportunity for a law suit that would never come to pass.

I bumped into Freddy on the way back, and he greeted me with an, "Are you okay, miss?" I told him I was great actually and asked why. He said, "Looks like you burned your mouth."

I assured him that it was not a big deal and asked how he was doing. He stated that God was good to him and that's all he needed in this life. I gave him a heartfelt, "Amen," and asked if he needed anything. He told me that he received many blessings that morning and maybe I could help another day.

"You got it, Freddy."

"Thank you, miss."

Back at my desk, I did my best to conceal my "burn" marks. After the last waxing, I bought a concealer thanks to Doris. "Doris, all this makeup...I have no clue what I need."

"Now don't worry yourself, Lani. This is what you need," she advised, and I made my purchase.

We snuck into the bathroom, and she helped me cover up the red bumps. It was a good job considering how bad the red was.

"Thanks, Doris."

"Anytime, dear."

Given it was lunch, I assumed that the women's bathroom would be occupied, so I pulled out a mirror and started "concealing" at my desk. I was careful to keep my head down low so as not to be seen.

That didn't work so well.

"Package for you, Lani," Matt announced.

OMG! I looked up at Matt with mirror in one hand, concealer sponge in the other, and a half red, half "concealed" lip.

He must have seen the horror in my eyes because he added, "Oh...you're just like my sister. I don't know why you girls are always trying to hide behind makeup. You're perfect the way you are."

"Thanks, Matt. Even though you're a liar."

"I'm not lying, Lani. Natural beauty is the best. Now, how about you sign for this package, so I leave you alone and you can get back to primping?"

I wanted nothing more, so I hurriedly scribbled my name and, as soon as he was gone, finished blotting my lip.

Chapter 26

Admittedly, I was caught up in my romance so much so that I was neglecting my sister and the mental note to help more. Since Richard was going to an office function, I thought it was a good time to stop by my sister's and see how things were.

"Hi, Aunt Lani."

"Hi, honey. Where's your mom?"

"She's in the back cleaning my room." (Was I experiencing déjà vu?)

"You still are making her clean your room? That's unacceptable. Let's go." With that, I took her arm and pulled her down the hall.

"Oh, hi, Lani," my sister said. "What are you doing here?"

"I came to see how you were doing, and I brought help." I presented her daughter to her and said, "She's going to continue where you left off."

"She is?" my sister said surprisingly.

"She sure is. Isn't that right?"

Perhaps it was the fear of her aunt being oddly aggressive with her, but for the first time ever, there was no arguing. My niece simply said, "Yes," and began putting her things away.

"Everything okay, Lani? We don't see you anymore since you started seeing Dick."

"Excuse me?"

"Dick...isn't that his nickname?"

"Ugh...you are so annoying. No...his name is Richard, and he goes by Richard."

"Too bad he isn't 'Rich,'" she added. "He could buy you a new wardrobe."

"What is that supposed to mean?"

"Why are you always so uptight?" she asked.

"I don't know...Why are you always picking on me?"

"I'm not picking on you, I'm teasing you. There's a difference."

"Really?" I asked. "I couldn't tell. Anyway...I'm glad I came here to see if you needed help with anything. Seems to have backfired on me. How's Paul's new role?"

"Well, the money is good, and he absolutely loves it."

"And...what about you?"

"Like I said, the money is good. I can't say I don't enjoy the pedicures I've been treating myself to. I just don't see him much, and I'm running around like a chicken with my head cut off once school lets out. But he's happy though, and he is helping when he does get home. I put him in charge of lunches."

"Well, that's good. Hopefully it's not always PB&J," I said with a chuckle.

"No...it's not. But that's because I make sure he has a supply of cold cuts. Otherwise, my daughter would probably get bread and butter every day. So," she continued, "how are things with *Richard*?" and I laughed at how she meticulously emphasized, "Richard."

"Things are going really well. We like the same things, we're both into our careers, and we make each other laugh."

"Do you make each other moan?" she kidded.

"Ugh...only when I think of your questions."

"Did you really come over to help?"

"Yes," I told her. "Why? You got something you need?"

She asked me if I knew anything about the planets. I knew it was a setup, but I was there to assist, so I told her I wasn't sure; it depended on the situation.

For the next two hours, I helped my niece hang painted Styrofoam balls in a shoebox, and I have to confess, I really enjoyed it. She told me a secret to remembering the order of the planets. "My Very Efficient Mother Just Sent Us Nine Pizzas." Quite frankly, it was a good system, but I thoroughly confused her when I asked how she remembered which "M" was which planet.

Chapter 27

Around 8:00 p.m. when the project was finally done, I excused myself and went home. I had spent so much time with Richard, that my house was significantly neglected. Even though we'd been together for over a month, he still hadn't been to my apartment. We spent so much time at the movies or parks and/or at work that we didn't need to hang at my house. Given our recent "discovery," though, I knew it was only a matter of time before we christened my bed.

That evening, I went through my bedroom with a fine-tooth comb. Not sure why I looked under the bed (I couldn't imagine any situation where Richard would wind up there), but I'm glad I did. Given my significant dry spell, I was completely shocked when I pulled out an old condom wrapper. I wracked my brain trying to figure where it came from; I even wondered if I loaned my bedroom to someone and forgot. Then it hit me.

Tony was a quiet guy, and I met him at my previous job. We worked on a project together, and I was obsessed with trying to get him out of his shell.

"So, Tony," I began, "do you like working here?"

"Yes."

"Great! What part do you like the best?" I'd pry.

"Editing."

"Me too," I lied, "why is that?"

"It's quiet."

That is how most of our conversations went. Each day I would try harder and harder to get more information, but I would inevitably be let down. The most I knew about him was he liked editing and turkey sandwiches (and I only knew that because we'd eat lunch while working on the project).

Things changed at the company Christmas party though. The employees were greeted with flutes of champagne, and I noticed Tony take his and gulp it down before the server could tell him to wait until the toast. She handed him a second one and was faster with the information.

I could tell Tony was uncomfortable in this environment. He fidgeted from side to side and kept his head down. Knowing he probably would be more comfortable if someone actually acknowledged him, I made my way over. Before I got there, the lady with the champagne tray walked by him, and I saw him gulp his and reach for another one.

"Hi, Tony, Merry Christmas!"

"Oh...um...thank you, Lani," and I swore that was the first time he said my name.

"Are you enjoying the party?"

"It's okay."

"Do you dance?" I asked, and with that, he swallowed his third glass of champagne.

"I think we're supposed to save the champagne until Mr. Mack gives his speech."

"Oh, well, I'll just grab another one. Be right back." That's when I realized two things. One, that was the most he ever said in one sentence, and two, he seemed a bit more...confident.

"There, that's better," he said as he took his place next to me, and before I could analyze my new found "is it me or is Tony kind of cute" feelings, Mr. Mack made his speech. At the end of the speech, Tony drank his flute and noticed I barely touched mine.

"Are you going to drink that?" he asked.

"No...I'm not much into alcohol."

"Do you mind?" And he gestured toward the cup. I surrendered it to him and watched him drink his fifth (or was it sixth?) glass.

When the music began playing, I could have sworn I saw his right foot tap, so I decided it was then or never to bring him out of his shell. I took his hand and dragged him to the dance floor before he even knew what was happening.

A couple of our other colleagues were already "cutting a rug" as they say and gave us the courtesy chin nod that gave us permission to use "their" dance floor.

In an instant, I realized the huge mistake I made. Tony's arms were flopping around like a dying fish, and he blurted out, "I like you, Lani."

In my quest to make him more comfortable, I made him too comfortable. I was probably the only woman who spoke to him, so naturally he would fall for me. He stopped flailing his arms for a moment, looked me straight in the eyes, and said, "You're really pretty," and all of a sudden my, "Holy cow, Tony is totally cute" radar went off.

"Thanks, Tony, I think you're special too." I didn't exactly lie. He was special in that he wasn't like any other regular guy I knew.

We hung out for about an hour (and I made sure he ate a little something to offset the champagne he continually consumed) when he said he wanted to leave...with me.

He was stumbling a bit, but I managed to get him to the cars the company provided for its employees to safely get home. Truth be told, I didn't want to "partake" in Tony when he was in this condition, but I didn't think there would be another situation where he'd be uninhibited, and I didn't think he had many notches on his belt. Call me crazy, but I wanted to help him out and quite frankly, in that hour, Tony started looking really good.

In the car, Tony grabbed my hand and started telling me how beautiful it was. I thought it was odd, but no part of me had been considered "beautiful" in so long that I overlooked it. He kissed it, and I was torn between "OMG, this is hot" and "please don't tell me I just felt a wet bottom lip."

Since it was so late at night (on a Wednesday no less), we got to my house pretty quickly. He grabbed the banister to help himself up, and I opened the door. I left the lights off (because I had no idea what condition the house was in) and prayed that the light from the street lamp seeping in the windows would be enough to lead us to my bedroom.

He stopped in the bathroom, and I should have timed how long he was in there. It sounded like a never-ending stream, and I took advantage by quickly flicking on my bedroom lights and straightening up before he came out. I was certain Tony would not have a condom, so I was glad when I remembered my sister gave me some as a gag gift for my last birthday. At the time I thought, "These are a waste," but now I was grateful for the opportunity.

When I heard the flush, I turned off the lights and met Tony by the bathroom door. Thankfully, I heard him wash his hands, and when he came out, I led him to my bedroom.

"Lani...I've been thinking about this moment for a really long time," he confessed.

"You have?"

"Yes."

"But you never said anything," and when we reached the bed, he fumbled but finally kicked off his shoes; I followed suit.

"Well, I don't like to mix business with pleasure," and he unbuttoned and unzipped his pants, and I instinctively squeezed my thighs together as I felt myself get warm at the sound.

He tossed his shirt over his head and...he was covered in hair. It was not the "I could have fun twirling my fingers in it" hair; it was the "I could lose my hand to a creature if I go in too deep" hair. But I was committed. He was a nice guy, and I wasn't going to judge him by his...well...shag carpet.

When I took my shirt off, he looked completely in awe of my boobs even in my "old faithful" bra. Apparently, dim lighting was flattering for me.

"Wow...they are amazing," and he sat down on the bed after taking off his pants and revealing "tighty-whities."

"Can I touch them?" he asked, and suddenly I wondered if this was his first encounter but didn't want to embarrass him by asking.

"Sure, let me just finish getting undressed," which I did and slid next to him.

The light was drawn directly to his white underwear, and I was completely turned on by the enormous boner beneath it.

"Would you like help taking those off?" And he nodded "yes" rapidly.

I seductively slid the underwear off, purposefully taking my time so he could bask in what might very well have been his first encounter. When I was done, I turned to get the condom. I tore the wrapper and pulled out the contents. Since I wasn't usually the one to do this part (and let's face it, I didn't get to that part often), I fumbled a bit with it before I turned back to him.

In an ironic twist of fate, Tony was sleeping, and I didn't know if I was more disappointed because I couldn't add another notch to my belt or because Tony never got to "touch them."

I decided this was divine intervention, and I was foolish to think I should have sex with a drunk coworker who wouldn't give me the time of day otherwise.

In the morning, Tony found me sleeping on the couch. He didn't remember how he wound up at my house and timidly asked if he had been an issue. In order to not ruin our work relationship, I explained that he had two glasses of champagne that didn't sit well with him. He wasn't able to give his address to the driver, so I took him home with me where I knew he'd be safe.

"Thank you, Lani. I have to go now."

"How will you get home?" I asked. "Do you want a ride?"

"No. I'll walk."

"Do you even know where you are?"

At that point, he had to concede, and I threw on some clothes and brought him to the train station. Our project ended a couple of days later and that was the end of our pseudo relationship. I liked Tony. I knew there was something deep-seated about him that contributed to his shyness. I'd never pry and I'd never tell anyone about him. I only wished that someday he'd find someone who could help him.

Chapter 28

When I was satisfied with how clean the house looked, I flicked on the TV, and there was that George Foreman again. It was willing me to buy it, but I just didn't think the time was right.

When my phone rang, it startled me, but seeing it was around 10:00 p.m., I assumed it had to be Richard and jumped up to answer it.

"Hello?"

"Are you in the house alone?" he said in a creepy voice.

"No. My 6'5", 350lb, body-builder husband is standing right here as a matter of fact."

"Oh...is that so? Put him on the phone then."

I changed my voice into a low, gravelly sound and played out a whole conversation as "body-builder man" with Richard the "serial killer" about how he'd never have a chance to harm Lani because he would be crushed before he ever reached her.

When he asked me how my night went, I explained it was really good. I told him about the planet project I helped my niece with and the George Foreman infomercial I was continually drawn to. He told me that his business meeting was a great success, and there was even talk of a promotion down the line.

As much as we both wanted to keep talking, after the third yawn of the conversation, we decided it was time to hang up.

The next day at work was a struggle. I was yawning when Matt delivered a new book to me, and I couldn't help but wonder how he timed every trip to my desk so perfectly to catch me in an awkward position.

"Rough night?" he teased.

"Not especially," I responded. "I just love my sleep, and I went to bed too late last night. Hey...can I ask you a question?"

"Sure, how can I be of service, milady?"

"Wow," I responded, "I didn't know I was royalty. Anyway...I'm just curious...I'm sure it's none of my business, but why on earth do you work in the mail room?"

"Well, Lani, that's a legitimate question, and I'll be happy to answer it for you over coffee. What do you say?"

"Matt...I...um..."

He cut me off and made it clear it was strictly two friends having coffee so I agreed. When my boss slipped away for his three o'clock appointment, I slipped away to Café Joe's with Matt.

"So...you want to know why such an educated, youthful, but too old to have an entry-level position guy who also happens to be extremely good-looking—if I do say myself—guy is working in the mail room?"

"Yes," I said, sipping on my hot chocolate, "I can't believe how modest you are as well. How does someone with all of your charismatic qualities work in the mail room?"

"Well, it's actually not that complicated."

"Do tell," I pried.

"Well, it's not my passion," he started, and I interjected with "Thank goodness for that." He went on to explain that he is a musician that is just on the brink of making it big, and in order to focus on his music, he can't have a job that requires too much attention. He's been at the company a while and every year he gets the most amazing reviews and the best bonus/salary increase they can give him. They actually want him to stay because no one has ever taken the role as seriously as he does. His management team is just as happy with the arrangement as he is.

"Wow...that's awesome. Do you play anywhere local?"

"Actually," he said, slipping his hand inside his jacket, "I have a show coming up this weekend," and he handed me a flyer. "I would love it if you could come."

"I will totally do my best to make it."

Matt picked up an extra coffee on the way out, and we walked a different path back to the office. The new path led us right past Freddy, and Matt handed him the coffee.

Freddy called out, "God bless you, brother," as we walked back.

"You really care about him, don't you?" I asked.

"Well, I sometimes think that could be me if my music career doesn't kick into high gear soon. The managers in the mail room are ready to promote me when I give them the word, but truthfully, I don't want to sell out and climb some imaginary corporate ladder.

"The problem is, I'm at a very high salary for a not-so-prestigious role. If there are cuts to be made, guess who's gonna go first?" I nodded my head completely understanding that those who make the most get picked off rather quickly.

He continued mostly to himself, "I really don't want to be in management." He looked at me and finished with, "I'd much rather be on my own schedule delivering happiness to beautiful people."

"You're too kind," I admitted, and we walked the rest of the way back to the office in silence that was broken when he held the door open for me.

"Thanks, Matt, you are a true gentlemen."

"My momma taught me right."

He walked me back to my desk where Doris happened to be standing while chatting with my boss. Suddenly, and without warrant, I felt like I had been busted with my hand in the cookie jar. Doris gave me the once-over and said, "Looks like you had a tasty lunch."

"It was just coffee, nosey," I teased her, and yet, I'd have been lying if I said I felt absolutely nothing. The moment he gave Freddy that coffee, I instinctively thought, "He's a keeper." Things were good with Richard though, so I let it leave my mind just as quickly as it entered.

"That must have been some coffee."

"Why? Wait...what do you mean?" I asked.

"Well, you have an...I don't know...call it a glow about you." Then she walked off and my phone rang, and by the time I was done talking an author off a cliff, I had forgotten our little exchange.

Chapter 29

That night I called Richard and explained, "My friend at work is in a band and he's having a show this weekend. Can we go?" He asked what type of music, and I had to be honest...I had no clue.

"Actually, I'm not really sure," I said with a chuckle.

"Wait...he's your friend and you don't know?"

"Well, we're not friend, friends," I admitted.

"Can you find out?"

"Sure...I...yeah...but does it really matter? I'd like to support him."

"Well, I hate country and death metal, I couldn't possibly sit through that."

In that moment, I felt something. I wasn't quite sure what it was; I just knew I didn't like the sinking feeling in my stomach, but I blew it off assuming Richard just had a bad day. I just hoped that if he was excited about supporting a friend my answer would be "yes" without hesitation.

The next day at work I kept an extra eye out for Matt. Every time I heard someone walk by, I popped my head up like a groundhog.

"Looking for someone?" Doris scared the hell out of me, so much so that I banged my knees on the bottom of my desk when I jumped.

"DORIS! Why are you spying on me?" I asked while rubbing my knees.

"I'm not spying, dear. I sit near you and keep catching you in my peripheral."

"Oh...your 'peripheral,' is that right?"

"Mmhmm. So...care to tell me what or who you are looking for?"

"Matt."

"Ooooh, I knew it," she said in a school girl sort of way.

"It's not like that. He told me about a show he's doing, and Richard wanted to know what type of music he plays before committing."

"Why?"

I hesitated a moment before answering. "Well...you know...I asked myself the same thing. Apparently, he doesn't like country or death metal."

"Talk about your opposite ends of the spectrum."

"Right? Anyway, I'm trying to find Matt so I can ask him."

She asked me what I would do if it turned out that he actually played country music. It was plausible considering his gentle-natured spirit.

"It's possible, but if he was truly that dedicated to his 'art' that he's working in a mail room, I'm thinking he'd be in Nashville if he was in a country band."

"Good point," and with that...Matt came whistling around the corner.

"What a way to start my morning off. Ladies, how are you?"

"We are great," Doris jumped in. "We were just talking about you."

"You were? I hope it wasn't anything bad?"

"No, of course not, Matt"—and I swear I heard her emphasize his name—"Lani was just telling me she was going to see you this weekend."

His eyes lit up like a kid at Christmas, "You are?"

"Well...I'm not entirely sure just yet. What type of music do you play?"

"Oh...," he said and with that...Christmas was deflated. "We play a cross between rock and pop. It's mostly a rock edge though. Truth be told, I can't stand the word *pop*."

"Then it's settled," Doris interrupted, "Lani will be there."

"Doris...I—"

"'Doris' nothing. Your friend is having a show, and you will be there."

"Well, Doris," Matt said with a devilish smile, "seems you are very interested in my work. Why don't you come too?" and he handed her a flyer.

She took a look at it and said, "You know what, young man? I'd be delighted."

And that was that. We were all going to the show.

Chapter 30

I picked Richard up about an hour ahead of the show so we could grab a bite to eat beforehand. I hadn't realized it at the time, but I guess I paid a lot of attention to how I looked.

"Wow, Lani, you are looking awesome tonight." It was then that I noticed I chose the same shirt I wore on my first date with Richard. My buttons were down, and my "cleavage bra" was in full effect.

"Thank you, Richard," and a twang of guilt hit me when I didn't know if I dressed for Richard or Matt.

Given we had been dating a few weeks, fast-food restaurants were no longer off the table. We slipped into a BurgerPalace and ordered. It was still a thrill that I didn't have to take out my wallet to pay (although I did offer every time).

I wondered if there would come a point where he did accept money. Would it happen after six months? A year? I had no idea, so I made sure to always have a way to pay just in case.

We sat down in as cozy of a spot as you can get which in this case was the spot farthest from the kid who was throwing French fries much to his mother's horror.

"So...who's this friend we're going to see?"

"Oh, he's a guy from the mail room."

"The mail room?"

"Um...that's not a dirty word you know. Without the mail room, I wouldn't get my books, which are my livelihood."

"Geez, why are you being so defensive? Most people aren't friends with the mailman, that's all."

I had to wonder why I was being so defensive, but I was afraid to think about it too deeply. I made a commitment to Richard and all other feelings were turned away.

"He's just a really nice person"—I was careful not to use the word *guy* for fear it would sound more personal—"and it sounded like you were making fun of him, that's all."

"Okay. Sorry...maybe I was."

A wave of relief rushed over me. Richard backed down. He knew he was wrong.

We finished dinner with thirty minutes to spare, and we headed to the club to try and get a parking space before all the good ones were taken up. When we pulled up to the club, there was already a line of people waiting to get in. Jealousy started creeping up when I realized the girls were at least ten years younger than me and looking really good in their short skirts and "hooker" boots. I was hoping Richard wouldn't notice, but given how much *I* was staring at them, I found it hard to believe he would miss them.

One person stood out from the hip crowd and a smile grew quickly on my face.

"Doris," I called out, "you made it. I didn't really think you would come."

"Well, my dear, my word is my bond." She gave a once-over of Richard, "so you are the one putting a smile on Lani's face?"

"Oh...yes...Richard, this is Doris, the woman I told you about. Doris...this is Richard...Isn't he cute?" I gushed.

"Yes, he is, Lani. Now...the two of you need to sneak under this rope and stand with me."

"I don't know, Doris, someone might get upset that we cut the line," I said worriedly.

"Oh...don't worry about them. I'll tell them you are my grandkids, and I forgot my cane, so I'm using you instead."

I shouldn't have been so surprised when no one said anything. Given our age, they must have thought we were the band's family.

It didn't take too long to get inside the club. Richard paid the cover charge for all three of us ("And a gentleman to boot," teased Doris) and once our eyes adjusted to the really dim lights, we found a cute little U-shaped booth off to the left of the stage and slid in.

After a thorough rundown of the club's house specials ("sex on the beach," "rock and roll over on top of someone," "guitar and feather yourself") Richard volunteered to fight the mob and went to the bar to get his beer, Doris' white wine, and my virgin strawberry daiquiri.

When he was out of earshot, I turned to Doris and asked her what she thought.

"Well, he definitely seems attentive, and I like his manners." She chuckled. "The important thing is that you're happy."

"I am," and with that, the lights went even dimmer (which I didn't think was possible) and the warm-up act took the stage.

After ten minutes, I went to find Richard who was missing in action. I fought my way through the youngsters who were shaking their heads back and forth bopping to the music. I met Richard halfway to the bar, and he was fighting just as hard to get back to the booth. I grabbed his beer as it seemed like the only thing I could easily slip from his hands that wouldn't make him drop the other two.

"Thank you, cutie," he said, and my stomach was full of butterflies.

"You're not so bad yourself" was all I could muster in reply.

When we finally reached the table, Doris said she was about to call in the coast guard. We explained that the sea of people who were in the club expanded into an ocean. We were all thankful to have had the seats although at times our view was completely obstructed.

Like any self-conscious woman, I began watching Richard to see if I could catch him looking at other girls. I'm not sure why I did it (or why other women do it for that matter). Intentionally looking for flaws in your mate usually doesn't turn out well. No matter how many times you tell yourself that you won't start a fight or ask what he's doing, the female ego takes over, and it comes out in one form or another.

The great part was he seemed to be enjoying the band. He didn't look away from the stage except once when he turned to me and asked me if I was having a good time. I told him I was and he said, "Good...I want you to." Cue the butterflies again.

Unfortunately, like most women, I couldn't be satisfied with his not looking at the women. I had to bait him. "Man...do you believe what these girls are wearing?"

"What do you mean?" he asked.

"Well, they're half-naked."

"Oh...I actually hadn't noticed," and I have to admit...I believed him.

Satisfied that he wasn't ogling other women, I turned to Doris.

"So...is this the type of music you listen to?"

I could barely hear her above the music but the gist was "Not really, but it isn't horrible."

Chapter 31

After about thirty minutes of the opening act, there seemed to be a commotion of sorts not too far from our booth. Young girls were pushing each other and oddly shifting toward us.

Suddenly, an older gentleman was pushed (or was it more "aggressively escorted") in front of our table, and he looked just as surprised as we were. But a moment later Matt, accompanied by an entourage of groupies, put his arm on the gentleman's shoulder and defeated looked at the booth.

I heard him yell, "Sorry, Pops" and start to turn away.

I yelled, "Matt!" as loud as I could to get his attention. Surprisingly, he heard me and leaned in to get a better look.

"Oh man! Lani...and Doris? Is that you?"

"It sure is, dear."

"I can't believe you guys came. This is great." As a "Matt obsessed" fan started pulling his arm, he called out, "This is my pops...Can he sit with you? He's dying by the bar."

"Sure," and I shuffled closer to Richard and grabbed Doris's arm to follow and make room for "Pops." As "Pops" slid in, Matt managed a quick handshake with Richard and then made his way back through the devoted fans.

As hard as we tried, we couldn't have a conversation with Pops to save our life until the opening band ended. When they left the stage, they were replaced with much lower sounding music to fill the dead air until Matt's band took the stage.

"Hi...I'm Lani. This is Doris and he's Richard."

"Oh, hi...I'm Matthew, Matt's pop."

"Well, Matthew, it's nice to meet you," I said, and I was so impressed when Richard offered to go through the crowd to get us all another round. He was really making quite the impression on my heart.

"So...what did you say your name is?" Matthew asked.

"Lani. I work with Matt. So does Doris."

"I thought that's what you said. You're the one Matt talks about." With that, Doris gave me a devilish look, and I'm sure I must have blushed because Doris giggled.

"So," Doris encouraged, "what does young Matt say about Lani?"

"Oh, not much. Just that he'd like to marry someone like her someday."

Confused more than ever, I got up. "I'm going to see if Richard needs any help." I looked back, and there was Doris giggling.

This time I got all the way to the bar, and Richard looked frustrated. "Hey. These teenyboppers are killing me."

"I'm sure."

Our drinks came shortly after I got there, and we fought our way back; Richard in the front parting the way for me, which I thought was incredibly chivalrous. At the table, Doris and Matthew were chatting it up quite a bit, and for a moment I wondered if Doris would allow herself to date again. I made a mental note to ask about it on Monday.

When the lights dimmed yet again (and I saw both Doris and Matthew squint), the teenyboppers were momentarily stunned into silence. Then one chord...just one chord on a guitar was played and all hell broke loose as blinding white lights filled the stage, Matt stepped forward in tight leather pants with a button-down shirt (whose buttons definitely weren't needed) and the girls went wild.

Doris instinctively covered her ears, Richard put his arm around me as if he thought I would rush the stage, and Matthew beamed with pride. Mail room Matt was a super-hot rock star, and he wanted to marry someone like me.

After the second song, Matt stepped up to the mic and over the drone of hysterical girls, I heard him say, "This next song is dedicated to my two favorite work ladies, Doris and Lani. Thanks for coming out tonight."

The song was amazing (although I couldn't understand most of it). It was the type of song that brought lighters out and the fans sang every word to.

At the end of the ninety-minute set, Matthew informed us that Matt told him to wait for at least twenty minutes and then he'd pick him up. Apparently, he needed to wait for the crowd to die down otherwise he'd never get out.

I asked Richard if he minded if we waited, and he said he didn't. The four of us talked about the set, and we all agreed that it was pretty awesome. It didn't escape me that Richard never took his arm off me. I liked the feeling of being "his."

When Matt finally got to our table (signing autographs along the way), he was sweaty and all buttoned up. Richard was the first to speak up. He pulled me close to him and said, "Great show, man. Lani and I enjoyed it."

"I'm so glad to hear it." Matt was interrupted when a strikingly good-looking blonde came up from behind him and wrapped her arms around his waist. I figured it was just a groupie until he turned around; he pulled her arms off of him, brought her to his side, and introduced her as "Michelle," then gave her a peck on the cheek. That is the first time I noticed Richard drop his arm from me. Can't say I blamed him. She was pretty hot. And somewhere deep down inside, I also noticed a pit in my stomach.

"So, Pops, what did you think?"

"I thought it was loud but the company was great," and he gave a little nod toward Doris. I wished the lights had been brighter because I'm sure it was her turn to blush.

"You ready to get out of here?" Richard asked as he slid his arm around my waist. The butterflies quickly twisted out of their slumber, and I responded with a peck on his cheek followed by a "yes."

I asked Doris if she would be okay, and Matthew assured me he would see her to her car. It was obvious where Matt got his manners from.

Matt shook Richard's hand and turned to me. I wasn't sure if I was supposed to shake his hand too, but when he opened his arms, I instinctively went in for the hug, completely ignoring the rock star sweat.

While embracing, he put his mouth really close to my ear and said, "Thanks for coming. It means a lot." I was getting a warm feeling between my legs, so I backed up and said, "Sure, no problem, pal."

"Pal?" What was I thinking saying that? Was I trying to draw the line in the sand for my boyfriend and his girl toy to see? And why did I call her a "girl toy" even if it was only in my mind? That was not very nice of me. I'm sure Michelle (or could it be Michele) is a great person; I don't see Matt dating losers.

Richard gave a general, "Good night, everyone," with a wave and then put out his hand for me to take. I gave my own final goodbye and slid my hand comfortably and wonderfully into his.

He escorted me outside and the fresh air and openness was welcomed. For the most part, the girls had scattered, but there were still a few puffing on their cigarettes no doubt waiting for Matt the rock star.

Richard opened the passenger door for me and walked around to the driver's side. We had been together long enough for me to trust him in the driver's seat, and quite frankly, I loved being driven around.

Chapter 32

"Where to?" Richard asked as he started the car. I hadn't expected the question, and when I looked at the clock it was too late to go anywhere formal, which meant one thing...the time had come to invite him "back to my place."

"Well..." And what I was hoping to sound seductive was anything but. The thought of finally having sex with Richard made my mouth go dry, and I started choking.

In the darkness of my car with only a few glimpses of street light, Richard turned to me and said in a soft whisper, "You know...you seem to get really choked up around me."

He leaned in close, put a hand on my thigh, and even more quietly whispered, "That's a shame because I've been fantasizing about something for a while that might be a big choking hazard for you," and a second later, our mouths were locked, and we were in full on make-out mode and all I could think about was going down on him and choking for all the right reasons.

As a car passed by, we broke apart and without hesitation, I said, "My place." I had to give him instructions since he'd never been there before but instead of "go left here" or "turn right there," the instructions were aggressive finger-pointing as I squirmed in my seat, and he adjusted his pants at the lights.

"There! There! Turn in there...That's my driveway!"

He pulled the key out of the ignition, and I opened my door. He pulled me back into the car though, and we started our make-out session all over again. His lips were soft and his

145

tongue was rough, willing mine to match his intensity. When he moved his hand from my back to my front and his fingers merely grazed the bottom of my breast, I stopped the session, opened the door, and gave him my most seductive look and said, "Give me a reason to choke."

I could only imagine what my words triggered because he bit his lower lip, clenched his hands into fists, and rolled his eyes up as his lids came down. He fumbled for a moment trying to get the keys that had fallen, but when he recovered, he was out of the car and at my heels walking up my stairs.

For a moment, I thought I wasn't going to make it because my legs were so weak from the anticipation, but Richard squeezed my hip and that jolted me up the remaining stairs.

I opened up the door, stepped inside, and the moment the door closed behind him, I turned and grabbed his face in my hands and started kissing him again.

His hands were all over me, and I loved every moment of it. Panic set in when he pushed me up against the wall behind me, and he grabbed the side of my thighs. He was about to pick me up in a "Fatal Attraction Glenn Close on the countertop" sort of way, and I had no idea if he could handle my weight. I decided it was better not to find out, so I did the one thing I knew would distract him...I slid down on my knees and went for his belt.

As I ripped the belt through the first part of his buckle, I looked up at him. His head was down leaning toward me, and when our eyes locked, I licked my lips and that's when his eyes closed, and his head leaned back in ecstasy.

I fumbled slightly trying to get the metal thingy (does anyone really know what that's called?) from the hole, and he must have sensed it because he sucked his stomach in. That did the trick, and I finished getting the belt off with a fervor I didn't know I possessed. Richard's pants quickly slid down, and I heard him moan.

I once thought seeing Tony's boner in his tighty-whities was hot. That sensation was nothing compared to kneeling submissively in front of Richard who was at complete attention. A small "You can do this, Lani" pep talk and I worked on Richard like he was the last man on earth.

When it was all said and done, Matt was a distant memory.

Chapter 33

When I rolled over in the morning and realized Richard was next to me, it took all I had not to shout out in childish jubilation. My excitement ended quickly and was replaced by fear that Richard would turn to me, and I would have horrific morning breath. As stealthily as I could, I slipped out of the bed, blushed when I saw my naked reflection in the mirror, and darted into the bathroom.

I hoped that I could pee and brush my teeth fast enough (and quiet enough) to slip back in the bed before Richard woke up and test if he was a cuddler or not. When I flushed the toilet, it seemed so much louder than it usually does but not flushing it would have been much worse.

I did a quick brushing of my teeth for fear that a full two minutes would give away my deceit. It definitely was too soon in the relationship to let him know that I am not immune to stinky breath.

While I was brushing though, I began wondering how long I had to keep the rouse up. And ugh...if bad breath was one thing, what about farting? I prayed I never was in a situation where I had to rip one when he was standing by. As if on cue, I heard a sound...a sound that sounded like it could have been a...wait a second...it happened again. OMG! Richard totally farted...in my bed...twice. Ahhhhhh! That was the most awesome sound ever! He was totally comfortable with me (granted he was sleeping), but hooray...that was the sound of commitment if ever I heard one. And there I was brushing my teeth still praying he never heard me fart. Friggin' double standards!

Now that the room was bright, I decided to cover up my nakedness and went for a cute nightie and left the undies off. Richard would obviously know I woke up, but he wouldn't know when, and I could always play it off that I was cold.

Sliding back into the bed, I carefully made my way close enough to him that if he moved in the slightest, he'd graze me but far enough away not to wake him. I then carefully staged my curls to frame my face and for added affect slid the spaghetti strap of my nightie off my shoulder slightly.

When I was completely satisfied that I would look desirable when he woke up, I closed my eyes and not wanting to wait any longer for him, took matters literally into my own hands by moving my left one enough to stir him.

He stirred slightly, and using my best acting chops, I yawned loud enough to wake him but low enough to sound demure.

"Good morning, beautiful," he said to me and came in for a kiss. While I loved the gesture, I didn't appreciate (or anticipate) *his* hideous morning breath. I gave him a quick pat on the lips and then darted off making an excuse that I had to use the ladies' room (as if I had one in my house. That's totally the girlie way of telling a guy she has to pee).

Since I didn't actually have to go, I spent my time trying to figure out a way to get his breath in check. Obviously, I couldn't say, "Hey...here's a spare toothbrush" or "I hear this new Listerine works well...want to try?" so I went to plan B.

"Hi, Richard. I'm going to grab myself some water. Would you like some?"

"No thanks, I'm good." Good grief!

Plan C was to wait it out in the kitchen for a little bit in the hopes he'd go to the bathroom and see my bottle of Listerine and try it out for himself. At some point though, I had to suck it up and go back in.

He was just walking out of the bathroom and said, "Oh...I hope you don't mind...I used your toothbrush."

My world completely spun around. I went from thinking, "Ewww, that's gross," to "Wow, he really digs me," to "I really hope I have a spare," to "No...really...wow...he is into me" in the span of five seconds.

"Sure...no problem."

"So, Lani?"

"Yes?"

"Did you enjoy yourself last night?"

"I sure did. How about you?" The moment it came out of my mouth I worried that he might not answer it the way I'd want.

"It was great. I'm glad I didn't make you choke." (Whew.)

"Want to try again?" I suggested, and he grabbed me and led me back into the bedroom, and that's pretty much where we stayed for the rest of the day.

As much as I didn't want to take him home, at 10:00 p.m. we decided it was time; we both had to get up early and tackle busy mornings. He asked me to wait for a minute before driving off since he had something for me.

He came out from his house carrying a large box. It was too dark for me to make out at first, but as he got closer, I couldn't believe it.

"You got me a George Foreman?"

"Yes, pop your trunk."

"But why? You didn't have to."

"I know. But you're my girl, Jenny."

When he saw how puzzled I was to be called by a different girl's name, he reminded me it was a famous line from *Forrest Gump*. I thought it was completely sweet. After carefully placing it into my trunk, he leaned into my window and kissed me again. Not only did he remember I wanted one, he actually got it for me. As I drove away from his house (seeing him wave in the review mirror), I looked up to the heavens and thanked God. I finally found someone.

Chapter 34

Weeks became months, and the months were amazing. We were a power couple. People envied us. He had a great job with a great income, and I had a good job with a good income but great flexibility.

We traveled to places I hadn't been. Sin City was one of our stops, and he spared no expense. We stayed at the Bellagio in their magnificent Salone Suite. The room screamed luxury and the views were so breathtaking I wanted to freeze time and stare out the window forever.

While he was off playing poker, I'd walk outside and watch the fountains dance and leap to the sounds of my favorite songs. It was exhilarating to soak up the atmosphere.

When the water display ended, I'd entertain myself at one of the five pools enjoying fruity drinks with little umbrellas in them. I'd wait in anticipation for Richard's arrival so I could tell him everything I saw, and he would brag about the stack of chips he walked away with. He did so well that I wound up going to "Cirque du Soleil" by myself because he qualified for a tournament. The show was fantastic, and when I got back to the room, Richard had rose petals on the bed with a note that said, "Love you and see you soon."

Doris was so happy for me and my instincts with Matthew were right. While I was being pampered by Richard, Doris was "enjoying time" with Matthew. They both had an interest in the arts so they'd go to museums or a show at the local college.

She and I would spend our lunches talking about how different our lives were from a year ago. Even Matt would join us occasionally and we'd quiz him about his music and encourage him to keep it up. We saw the way the fans couldn't get enough of him, and we knew it was only a matter of time before he made it big.

"So, Doris," Matt began over lunch one day, "my pops seems to be in a really great mood all the time. You wouldn't happen to know why that might be, do you?"

Doris blushed and for the first time I saw her stumble to find words. "Well...he...we...I mean...he's a very nice man, and we are enjoying our time together."

"Good, Doris, I'm glad. He was really down for a while there. Thank you for helping him get out of his slump."

"I do what I can," she said with a smile.

"I bet you do," I said with a devious wink.

"Oh, Lani," she chastised. "You are terrible," and she whacked my arm with her hand. We had a good laugh and went back to work.

Chapter 35

I felt bad that Richard and I couldn't support Matt at his next show. We had a cruise to the Bahamas planned, but I assured him we'd be at the next one. He completely understood and said that Doris and Pops would just have to cheer extra loudly.

Preparing for the cruise was not fun! I mean the prospect of being on the open water watching the sunset with Richard was very tantalizing. I just hated the whole packing thing. You needed to pack casual day wear but formal evening wear (and truthfully, I didn't even know what exactly constituted as "formal evening wear"). Your suitcase could only be a certain size, so how were you supposed to fit all your required attire in that one bag? The stress was crazy, but I eventually figured it all out especially when Richard said to just pack two or three shorts and wear them more than once. So, I focused on a bunch of shirts and two formal outfits I stole from my sister's closet.

The cruise itself was extravagant, and I had never felt as stress-free as I did for those five days. We feasted like royalty (my shorts can attest to that), saw Broadway-style shows, and he treated me to a spa day at sea while he checked out the beer tasting.

The spa day was something else. It started with a manicure and pedicure (which didn't affect me as much since I started getting them more regularly when Richard and I got more... well...intimate) and was followed up with a full body sea-salt scrub.

The scrub was exhilaratingly wonderful, and I have never felt so vulnerable and powerful all at once. The vulnerability came from getting completely naked except for a small pair of plastic underwear and a shower cap to protect your hair. The powerful part came from feeling like a woman worth a million dollars as the therapist rubbed sea-salt all over my body, scrubbing away dead skin. I went in and out of pleasure and pain as some parts felt like a massage and other parts felt like torture by sandpaper.

At the end of the scrub, she left the room and I went into the beautiful, glass shower and washed all the salt away. My body was glistening and smoother than the day I was born. And if I wasn't feeling regal enough, the icing on the cake was the one hour body massage with lotion (so it was only pleasurable).

Richard met me outside of the spa and laughed when he saw me.

"You okay? You look like a zombie."

"Yes, I've never felt better. I can't get my body to move any faster. Sorry."

"No...don't. I'm happy you are so relaxed. Do you want to go back to the room and take a nap?"

"No, it's been almost three hours since my last meal, let's get something to eat," and he escorted me on his arm to one of the many restaurants on the ship. There he excitedly told me about the friends he made at the beer tasting and how they made plans to meet up for a cigar on "Deck 12" later that night.

Since Richard wasn't keen on that night's featured movie, he planned to meet them while I watched the movie (since "we can't interact during the movie anyway"). He said he'd meet me at the exit doors, and we'd go for a nightcap after. So thoughtful!

As promised, he met me at the doors, and we went for a stroll. When we got to the front of the ship (I think it's called the aft or maybe it's the stern; who can remember all the terms when you're falling deeper in love?) he took my hand and kissed it. He then pulled me close to him and kissed me passionately.

It was almost the perfect scene except I hated the taste of his cigar mouth and pulled away.

"What?" he asked. "Is everything okay?"

"Oh...yes...sorry. It's just...well...you have cigar breath."

"Oh no. Sorry!" And we ran back to our room where he brushed his teeth, and when he came out of the bathroom, I was lying on the bed waiting.

"Well, hello there. Who let you into my room?" he questioned.

"I slipped housekeeping a twenty to let me in."

I sat up on the bed with my legs draped over and beckoned to him by calling him over seductively with my pointer finger. He awkwardly sashayed over to me, tripping slightly, which was odd considering there were no more than five steps between the bed and the bathroom.

When he reached me, he gently pushed me down on the bed, raised my legs, and slid my underwear off. Surprising me, he got down on his knees, spread my legs apart, and began teasing the fleshy part of my upper thighs with his tongue. I knew what was coming next, and to be honest, I wasn't happy about it.

As a female, you are taught that receiving oral sex is an amazing experience; that it is the ultimate way a man can please you. You grow up hearing stories about men with magical tongues who can touch your "G Spot" like no one else. Men who write the alphabet on your clitoris are the masters.

Well...I call "bullshit" on that. Perhaps my partners (albeit only a few) were completely illiterate, but truth be told, I have never enjoyed receiving oral sex in my life. I am too busy calculating how long it was since my shower, and if I exerted any energy that would leave me with that "not so fresh feeling." Additionally, I have to wrack my brain to remember if I passed gas close enough to the act where lingering odors might turn my suitor off. And if I had a bowel movement in the past twenty-four hours, I have to be quick on my feet to bait and switch so that I'm the one on my knees. So there I was, lying down, knowing what was about to happen and I couldn't think of anything to stop it, so I looked at the clock to gauge the start time. I figured I would give him two minutes before I started doing the "Oooh, that feels so good, but I need something bigger" plea, which makes him think he turned me on so much that I wanted more.

That usually works because it's great for a man's ego, but the problem with that maneuver is his face usually lines up with yours and seeing the glistening shine around his mouth and knowing what his breath probably smells like is flat out gross. I don't care that it's my "shine," it's gross and the thought of him wanting to kiss me is terrifying. Seriously, I don't know how men enjoy performing that act.

But at the two-minute mark, I tapped Richard on the shoulders, boosted his ego by pretending I would simply explode if he didn't stick his penis in me, and just as I suspected, I got an "Oh yeah? I'll give you something bigger."

We positioned ourselves better on the bed and he mounted me and that's when I saw it...the glistening shine. He came in for the kill with a kiss, and I turned my head to the side willing him to kiss my neck and making a mental note that I had to scrub that area extra good in the shower. I overplayed how much I enjoyed him nibbling on my ear (which is another move I don't care for) just to keep him there and avoid my mouth.

I cannot tell you the relief I felt when the act was over. I loved being intimate with Richard...as long as receiving oral was off the table.

The rest of the cruise was simply amazing, and I never wanted it to end. Unfortunately, it did, but Richard promised it wouldn't be our last.

Chapter 36

It is very rare to see me with a newspaper instead of a book, but for some reason, I picked up the paper that was in the lobby area and sat down to read it while I waited for Doris. Knowing I only had a few minutes, I quickly skimmed through and stopped on a page that caught my attention.

It was a picture of a man and a woman, and they looked very familiar. At first I couldn't place them, and so I read the caption "Edward and Phyllis Smith" circa 1980. I still didn't get it and widened my gaze toward the full page. It was the obituary section, and Edward Smith had died.

Still struggling to understand where I knew them from, I read the obituary, and it finally hit me when Phyllis was quoted as saying, "I'm going to miss my Ed."

Ed...from the laundromat. The most charming and wonderful couple I had ever known. They gave me hope that true love did exist. Poor Phyllis. I hadn't known her name until then, and I felt terrible I found it out the way I did.

"What's the matter?" Doris asked. I hadn't even noticed her approaching, and I wiped the tear away I hadn't even noticed made its way down my cheek.

I ripped out the obit and shoved it in my pocketbook. I wanted to look at it again and possibly visit Phyllis. "Oh...just saw that someone I once knew died."

"Oh, Lani, I'm so sorry for you."

I was about to tell her we weren't close, but thought the whole story would be too complicated. I didn't much feel like talking, so I just let it be with a heartfelt "thank you."

Luckily, it was a quick grab-and-go lunch. My appetite had died (bad pun, I know) and I wasn't up for much chitchat.

When I got back to my desk, I pulled out the paper and reread it. They had been high school sweethearts, and he died at the age of seventy-two. Seventy-two...so young. It did not have the details of his passing but did have the viewing information, and I decided I would go pay my respects.

Chapter 37

I was taken aback by the amount of people who were there. Most of them were gray-haired and wondered if Ed and Phyllis had lived in a retirement community. In my daily life, I never recalled seeing that many elderly people walking the streets. Perhaps they were always there, I just wasn't looking.

I felt very out of place and considered turning around when my eyes locked eyes with Phyllis, and she gave me a puzzled look. When I made it through the crowd, I put out my hand to take hers, and I realized I was trembling. My legs were weak as I said, "I don't know if you remember me or not…"

Before I could finish, she put a smile on her face and said, "Yes…from the laundromat, I remember you. Ed and I always wondered how that date went."

A rush of relief passed through me, and my legs regained their steadiness. "Wow, you have a great memory."

"Well…you don't forget the people you like."

A tear dripped down my face, and she turned me to the casket and said, "Would you like to see him?"

I nodded and she led me to Ed. "Ed, honey, remember our friend…I'm sorry, I'm not sure I ever got your name."

"Lani, my name is Lani."

"Ed, our friend Lani came to see you. You can find out how her date went after all." Then she turned to me and said, "I'll give you two a moment."

To say I was taken aback at how casual she made this "moment" seem is an understatement. It was as if he was in a

159

hospital bed, and I was paying a visit. Not wanting to embarrass her by walking away so soon, I threw normalcy to the wind and "spoke" to Ed.

"Um...hello, Ed. Hi. I...well...this is odd. I happened to read the newspaper and was compelled to see you. You and Phyllis... were...um...very inspiring. I left that laundromat wanting what you found. I was hoping that true love still existed."

Fifteen minutes later, when I was finally done "speaking" to Ed, I felt like the weight of the world was off my shoulders. I went from feeling totally awkward to pouring my heart out by disclosing my insecurities and fear of not finding what he and Phyllis did. I told him I was sorry he lost his son and that I am so glad we crossed paths. I said I would give Phyllis a hug for him, and when I finished embracing her and told her how good it felt to talk to him she said, "He was always a great listener."

Ed had been trying to put something away on a top shelf using a small step stool. He lost his balance and broke his hip. He was gone within a month. She was at his side the whole time, and they talked about how wonderful their life was and how they made it through the worst of times and best of times. They made their vow to meet again in heaven, and Ed teased her that if there are too many pretty girls, he might not be able to wait. They both chuckled and in a beautiful moment Ed told her that "he'd wait for her forever, and she should live happily, knowing he was enjoying being her guardian angel."

By the end of the conversation, Phyllis and I were in tears, and she lightened the mood by asking me about my date.

"Well, things have been really good," I said and left it at that because I never knew how happy you could be when you were at a wake. It's an awkward balance of being solemn to show you understand the gravity of the situation, but cheerful to try and make the grieved feel better.

"Phyllis...can I ask you something personal?"

"Sure, Lani."

"How did your relationship last so long and how on earth were the two of you so happy?"

With a chuckle, Phyllis explained that it wasn't always easy, and they weren't always happy. There was a time she thought she'd go crazy with her son when Ed was out fighting for our country. Her son had been a handful, and she questioned everything she did as a mother. Just when she figured it out, Ed came home and suffered from PTSD. That threw everything out of whack, but spending time with his son made him the man she remembered.

When their son died, they only had each other. They stayed in bed holding each other and crying until they fell asleep. They once considered a suicide pact but knew their son would be terribly disappointed in them; they had a lot of life left to live.

"Let me tell you something, Lani. When you love someone...I mean really love someone, you stick with it in thick and thin. You take the good with the bad and you work hard. Marriage is one of the toughest things to maintain, but if you have someone who is worth it, everything eventually falls into place. The most important thing is to have trust. If you do not have trust for your partner, nothing else will work. My Eddie would have moved heaven and earth for me, and I trusted everything he told me."

I hugged Phyllis and thanked her for her guidance. She gave me her phone number and said, "Any time." I made a mental note to call her for lunch one day soon.

Chapter 38

Richard was the first person I called after leaving the wake. I spoke to him for at least an hour detailing how I met Ed and Phyllis at the laundromat. "Wow," he said, "I can't believe you put that much effort into impressing me. I never would have known if your pants were dirty or not. I think I just pulled stuff from my closet and threw it on."

"Really?"

"Yes, men don't think about those things."

We went on to discuss how wonderful their love had been and how it restored my faith in true love. Richard responded that "Fairytales happen every day," and as if he got distracted by something, he quickly ended the call. I was slightly disappointed but assumed his mom needed the phone or something.

The next day (which was a Thursday), he called me to say I needed to pack a bag and ask for Monday off because we were going to go someplace "magical" for the weekend. No matter how hard I tried, I could not get him to spill the beans.

"Well, do I pack for warm or cold weather?"

"Pack for both," he replied.

"Okay...do I need a bathing suit?"

"Sure...pack it. Just don't know if you will use it."

"Do I need to pack something fancy or casual?" I pried.

"You should probably go with a little of each.

"Geez...not even one hint?

"Nope!"

When we got to the airport terminal, I was like a kid knowing that any moment I would find out where we were headed. As we approached the gate, I saw all these little kids running around, and I looked at our destination, "Orlando."

"Oh my God!" I started. "The most magical place is Disney. Are you taking me to Disney World?"

"Yes. I hope you don't mind."

"Not only don't I mind...this is the best surprise ever!" And I hugged him like no one was watching.

He booked us two first-class tickets and three nights at the BoardWalk Inn. The rooms were enormous compared to the value resorts my budget had me at. Not even ten minutes into the trip and I was already swept off my feet. As he unzipped his suitcase, he told me he had a surprise for me.

Like a child, I waited with baited breath when all of a sudden, he pulled out a pair of his underwear. HUH?

"Oh, sorry, it got stuck," he said. Then he shook his hand so hard that the underwear came flying in my direction, and I couldn't help but notice the discoloration around the butt area. Ewww.

But when I looked up at him, he was holding a pair of Minnie Mouse ears. Immediately any thought of skid mark underwear was completely erased by his ear-dorable gesture. I ran over to him and hugged him.

He put them on my head (and not in the most gentle of ways) and told me how cute I looked. I asked him if he had a pair for himself, and he said he wouldn't be caught dead in them. *Oh well*, I thought, *he is a pretty masculine guy.* Within ten minutes, we were out of our room heading to Epcot Center. One of the things I love about the BoardWalk is you can walk right to Epcot from it. Unfortunately, Richard was a little jet-lagged, so we hopped on the ferry instead.

That night after the boat ride in Mexico, we walked hand and hand through the countries where he insisted we try a snack from each one. By the time we got to Italy, the fifth country on our walk, I couldn't even think of taking a bite of the gelato, so Richard gladly enjoyed it alone. He skipped a snack in America because, "every snack outside of world showcase is American." He picked back up in Japan with a green tea cheese-cake then moved on to baklava, a baguette, and fish and chips. Thankfully, Canada had nothing to eat.

He made it a point to make sure we scouted out the best area to watch the fireworks. We found a bench overlooking the lagoon and sat there for a good hour, so we didn't lose the prime viewing spot.

We talked about all the different types of people walking around. From new families with babies strapped to their backs to old couples strolling along without a care in the world and everything in between; Disney was a magical place indeed.

When the street lamps dimmed down and the music piped in from speakers, I grabbed Richard's arm and snuggled into him. As the fireworks burst into the sky, he turned to me and took my hand in his.

"Lani?"

"Yes?"

"Are you happy?"

"Oh my gosh...yes. This is amazing. Thank you so much."

He leaned in and kissed me then whispered in my ear, "I love you."

I pulled my head back from him and saw a burst of color in the sky. Everything was so completely perfect how could I not be in love?

"Oh Richard, I love you too. Thank you for coming into my life. I have never been so happy." We spent the rest of the night hand in hand strolling through Disney.

The next morning while eating Mickey waffles as Cinderella greeted her guests, Richard made a suggestion.

"So...did you really mean it when you said you loved me?"

"Of course I did." OH NO..."Did you?"

"Yes, I wouldn't have said it if I didn't mean it." Thank goodness. Crisis averted!

"Well then," he began, "what do you think about moving in together?" That's when the choking began again. And to think I was on a streak.

He leaned over to me and patted me on the back, "I'm sorry, Lani...if you think it's too soon..."

"No, no, no," I managed to get out while trying to compose myself. "It's not that at all. I'm just excited and didn't expect that."

"What about your mom?"

"What about her?" he asked.

"How will she get along without you?"

"My mom will be fine. We have other family that can help her. I can still help as needed. I just will take a little bit to get to her."

"Well...then...it's settled I guess."

Chapter 39

Since I had my own place I was completely happy with, we thought it would be most economical for him to move in with me. The move went very smoothly since we didn't have to prime a new place, and he didn't have to move all his belongings from his mother's place at once.

I barely slept the first night he was there. We had been in bed next to each other so many other times before, but this was completely different. I was lying in bed with a man who just made a commitment to sleep next to me with no end date. That amount of time could be forever, and it got me thinking that someday I could be sleeping next to him as his wife.

Normally when I can't sleep, I turn on the TV, but when you have another person to consider, you can't do that so easily. Knowing I was just going to be awake for most of the night, I tried to slide out to go to the living room and watch it, but the moment I started sliding, Richard's big arm came rolling over me like one of those barriers at a toll booth.

Apparently, his sixth sense went off, and he knew I was trying to escape. It felt amazing to be wanted, and I snuggled into him and fell asleep. It was a good thing too because it was four o'clock in the morning. Other than that, life couldn't have been better.

In the morning, I woke up to the phone ringing. "C'mon, you live together, you can admit it now." (I swear my sister is unyielding).

"Not now. I'm tired."

"What's the matter? Too much sex?"

Click!

"Who was that?" a groggy-eyed Richard asked.

"Just my sister."

"Oh, everything okay?"

"Yes, she's just a little nosey."

"Oh...one of those?"

"Yes, I guess you could say that."

Richard gave me a big hug and asked if I was hungry.

"Yes, but I'm also tired. I didn't sleep too well last night."

"Oh no, was I snoring?"

"No...well...yes...but that wasn't it. I guess I was just really excited about you being here...permanently."

"Permanently," he pondered. "I like the sound of that," and he got out of the bed, gave me a cute little "look at how sexy I am" pose, and went off to the bathroom.

I called out to him that I would go downstairs and see what we had for breakfast.

When he came down moments later, I asked if kid cereal was good for him.

"Sure, I love me some sugar in the morning."

"Do you?" I asked seductively.

"You naughty girl," he chastised and poured himself a big bowl of Cookie Crisp.

I was slightly disappointed he didn't take my bait, but seeing how tired I was, I decided not to push it.

"So...what do you want to do today?"

"I don't know, Lani. What are you thinking about?"

"Well, I'm not sure," I said, looking out the window. "It's a bit gloomy for paddleball. What about a movie?"

"Did anything good come out?"

I told him I didn't know, so I picked up the phone and listened to the recorded message from the theater. Although the voice was cheerful, the choices were not really good.

"Well, I guess that's out."

"I know," Richard said, "why don't I meet your sister?"

"Huh...um...no."

"Why not?"

"Well..." And the truth was, I couldn't think of a single reason besides being afraid she'd ask him questions to things I didn't want her to know. I couldn't believe I had managed to avoid the inevitable for this long; my luck it seemed had just run out.

Chapter 40

I tentatively rang the doorbell, and Richard couldn't help but notice how my hand was shaking.

"Don't worry, she'll love me," he said as he put his hand gently on mine to ebb the shaking.

My niece answered the door. "Oh, hi, Aunt Lani, is this your new man? Mom says she's surprised he's lasted this long." As I turned to leave, Richard stopped me by turning me back toward the door.

"Richard, this is my niece Molly. Molly, this is Richard."

"Oh...Richard...do come in please." My niece instantly transformed into a stern and creepy butler opening the door wide and extending her arm out for us to enter.

My sister walked out of the kitchen and greeted us. She was wearing an apron and told Richard she would hug him but didn't want to get him messy. Just as Richard told her that lunch smelled good, the smoke alarms started going off.

"Damn it," she said and ran to the oven.

"Evacuate, evacuate," my niece screamed as she ran out the door.

"I'll get her," I yelled and ran out the door in pursuit.

When we came back in the house, Richard was fanning the smoke detector, and my sister was pulling out "lunch" from the oven. Apparently, the juices from the meat loaf spilled over and started burning.

My sister was all flustered but managed a "thank you, Richard" as she pulled away the towel he was using. We all stood for a moment willing the smoke detector to stay off. Fortunately, it did.

"I'm sorry, guys. The food should be fine though."

"Yeah, Mom has been...let's call it 'flighty' with Dad out of the house so much."

"MOLLY!" my sister scolded.

Richard reassured her that it was totally okay, and he said to prove it he would eat the whole meat loaf.

"Hey...slow down there, new guy," my niece said (and I was terrified where it was going), "some of us would like a little something ourselves." (Whew!).

"Molly...Richard was totally joking, right, honey?"

"Honey? My, things are really progressing, aren't they?" Molly asked.

My sister asked me not to tell my niece that we moved in together. "I'd like to keep the façade of getting married before anything else as long as possible." If Molly thought using the word *honey* was provocative, I could only imagine what she would think of our escapades.

"This is delicious," I said. Then I turned to Richard and informed him he shouldn't expect home-cooked meals like that from me.

"It's okay. I don't mind going out to eat."

When lunch was drawing to a close, Paul came home, and Molly jumped up to give him a hug. "Daddy! I missed you! I'm so glad you're home."

My sister looked at me and said, "I do all the work. He gets all the credit."

Richard stood up and shook hands with Paul, and they went off into the living room making small chat.

When they were out of earshot, my sister started in. "He's not bad looking. I was expecting him to look a little...well...you know."

"Um...no, I don't know."

"Well, you don't exactly attract the Kevin Costner types."

"That's so rude."

"I guess. Sorry. In all seriousness, I hope he makes you happy."

"He does. He makes me very happy. How are things with you and Paul?"

"Well, he's gone...A LOT. Molly has gotten fresher since he's not around, and when he gets home, he is no help with discipline. He feels too guilty to get mad at her, and it just makes it harder on me. I mean, you hear her."

"Yes, she was overly obnoxious today. Wonder where she gets it from," I said and elbowed her in a teasing way.

At that point, the men came back into the kitchen laughing. Paul declared that "this guy is all right," and he grabbed the two of them a beer. "We'll be inside watching sports if you need us."

Chapter 41

"Well, that went much better than I expected," I confessed to Richard as we got into the car.

"Yeah, your sister is a great cook, and Paul is a cool dude. I like him."

"Sorry about my niece. I'm not quite sure what got into her."

"Ah...she didn't bother me so much, but I can see how being with her for a long period of time could drain a person."

"You're telling me." I went on to explain about the inquisition she gave me about boys not liking me.

"Well, you solved that issue, didn't you?"

I sure did!

Chapter 42

Before going home, we made a stop at the supermarket to stock up on more items now that the household doubled in size. We still picked up my old staples but added to the collection were Fruit Loops, Coco Crisps, and Hungryman meals.

I really wished I was better at cooking. I'm sure my life would be much healthier if I substituted freezer meals with chicken and fresh vegetables. I really needed to use that George Foreman. It sickened me to admit it, but it had become a dust collector. Perhaps someday I'd get the urge to open the box, but for now, Richard and I were content with kids' cereal and reservations.

When we got home, "our home" (I loved the sound of it), we put the grocery bags in the kitchen, and I started unloading them. At some point (and I'm not even sure when), Richard went missing.

After all items were properly put away, I found him sitting on the couch with his eyes closed. I thought it was odd that he left me to put everything away, but I shrugged it off as a tough day.

"Hey, sleepyhead."

Rubbing his eyes, he gave me a "hey" back.

"You all right?"

"Yeah, I'm fine. Why?"

"Nothing."

"You done in there?"

"Yes."

"Great. Why don't you grab the remote and we can see if a movie is on?"

And we sat on the couch for the rest of the night watching TV and eventually that sixth sense that was annoyed that he didn't help went away.

Chapter 43

The best part about being in a long-term relationship is that you no longer worry about shaved legs or morning breath. As a matter of fact, it is more endearing when he kisses you even though you know you're imitating Godzilla.

The problem about being in a long-term relationship is that he gets comfortable too. All of a sudden, he thinks it's cute to fart in the bed and smolder you. A "Dutch oven" he calls it. Ugh. But you think this is the price you pay for not shaving your armpits every day, so you don't complain.

After a year and a half of living together though, I uncovered so many other disgusting things. At one point I realized he thought showering wasn't a necessity and the times he did shower, I had to endure the most unattractive sounds when he loudly blew his nose. "It's the best time to do it. Your snot is all loose, so it comes right out in your hand. Then you let it go down the drain."

If the sound wasn't bad enough, there would be times I'd go in after him and let's just say it didn't always "go down the drain." On top of that, he started picking his ear and playing with the wax. I'll conveniently gloss over picking his nose (when showering wasn't happening at regular intervals). He had no idea where to draw the line of comfort.

On a day, I was feeling particularly aggravated, I decided to call my sister and get some advice.

"Well, how's your sex life?"

"What? This isn't a joke," I cried.

Lisa Brandenburg

"Um, actually, I'm not joking," she informed me. "As long as your sex life is okay, you'll be okay."

And that's when it hit me. Our sex life was not good. Richard had gained a lot of weight over our two years together that it impeded our time together.

"Oh my God, my relationship is over," I declared.

"Why?" she asked.

"Because he's overweight so our sex life isn't great," I admitted.

"Aha! I knew you were a closet slut."

"What?"

"I just fed you that bull to get you to confess. Ha, ha, it worked!"

I wanted to kill her.

"No, you don't understand, it's really terrible." I sighed.

"I'm sure it's not," she assured me. "Besides, how long are you going to wait for Mr. Right? He's the one," she continued. "He loves you, he's comfortable with you, stop being a baby."

Click!

From behind me, I was startled by a "buuuuuurrrrrp." Richard was home, and he recently had hot dogs. "Um, do you mind?" I asked. "Could you cover your mouth when you do that?"

"I always cover my mouth," he began, "when I'm in public. Here is a different story. I'm in the privacy of my own home. I can do what I want," he preached.

"Well, what about me? Why should I have to smell that?"

"Because you love me."

UGH!

"Anyway, what's for dinner?" he wanted to know.

"What do you mean 'what's for dinner?' Didn't you just eat something?" I asked.

"Yeah, a bologna sandwich."

Bologna...hotdogs, they're all the same smell, I thought.

"That didn't fill me one bit," he added.

"I bet."

He caught that one. "What did you say?"

"Uh, nothing...wait, you're right," I admitted. "I did say something."

At that moment I was fully ready to discuss my concerns with his weight when "ring, ring." Saved by the phone.

I picked it up; it was my sister. "Hey, how's Shamoo?" she asked.

"Would you stop it please?"

"Who is it?" Richard inquired.

"My sister." He was trying to figure out what she wanted. Do you know how difficult it is to think of something based on the line she just fed me?

"She wants to go to the aquarium," I blurted out.

"Now?" he questioned. "It's ten o'clock at night." Damn, I was caught.

Or was I? "Uh, well, they're doing a private event. She just got tickets." I thought he would see right through me, but he didn't. Even gave me a few bucks. Sah-wheet!

So there I was at 10:00 p.m. on my way to my sister's as it was the only place to go. "You know, you can't do that to me," I chided.

"Do what?" she said.

"You can't call me and put shit in my head," I told her. "It's not cool. I'm trying to work this all out, but you're not helping."

Having nowhere to go, I was forced to sit on the couch and watch soap operas, which are my least favorite of the TV categories. Bored out of my mind, I decided to close my eyes for a moment.

The next sound I hear is my cell phone. Fumbling to get it out of my pocket and figure out how to answer it (I only got it a couple of days earlier), I notice my sister was gone, the TV was off, and I had no idea what time it was. I answered the phone, "Hi, honey."

"Are you coming home anytime soon?" He sounded annoyed.

"Yeah, of course I am. We haven't been here too long so give me—"

He cut me off. "Are you cheating on me?"

"What?" I exclaimed.

"Well, Lani, it's 2:00 a.m., and I checked the Internet. There are no special events at any aquarium right now."

Busted!

Thinking of how to get out of this one, I slowly started with, "Well, you're right..."

He stopped me with, "Listen, we can work anything out. I'll be better, I promise. I'll clean up..." Wow, maybe letting him think I cheated wouldn't be too bad after all.

Chapter 44

I went home, and he was visibly upset. I mean, I could see remnants of tears on his cheeks. That was the greatest feeling of all. Okay, I know that sounds bad, but c'mon, how many times do you actually get a man to cry in front of you, let alone about you?

Figuring out how I would explain it all was easier than I thought thanks to the car ride home. I was listening to some radio station and it gave me the perfect idea. And so I began, "Well, Richard, the truth is..." After twenty five minutes, I had him right where I wanted him. I explained that yes, I had been out with someone who treated me with kindness and respect and was aggressively seeking to take it to the next level. I told the guy that although I felt my relationship wasn't where I wanted it to be, that before I could move forward with him, I owed it to my boyfriend to try to work it out.

Richard was floored. And crushed. I had just finished describing the perfect man, one we ladies know cannot exist, and he knew he had to kick it up at least two notches to compete.

That night in bed, he put his arm over me and gave me soft kisses on my back. It was so thrilling, but I couldn't let him get off that easily. "Uh, Richard, if you don't mind, I'd rather not be all lovey-dovey tonight. After all, I don't want you to forget there are real issues here." And so...much to my disappointment...he stopped.

Thank God the next day was a Saturday because after my late night, I didn't get out of bed until noon and only then because I smelled something burning.

Walking into the kitchen, I did not expect to see what I saw. There was Richard in his beat-up, South Park underwear trying to get bacon out of a pan and cursing every time the grease would splatter his stomach. In another pan, eggs were burning, and when I assisted by turning off the bacon flame, there was something peculiar cooking.

"Uh, Richard."

"Yeah."

"What did you put in the eggs?" I casually inquired.

"Oh, that's my favorite, corned beef hash." And seeing as things were now under control, he stuck his finger in it, got a glob, and ate it.

Trying to contain my horror, I took a deep breath and then asked, "Did you buy it?"

"No, I used what was in the cabinet."

He was clueless. "Richard! We don't have corned beef hash in the cabinet!"

"We don't? Wait a minute..." Finally, it was starting to come together for him. And as if to solidify it, the neighbor's dog we had been watching barked. His response, "Wow, it actually wasn't that bad. Why don't you try some?"

And just like that, the fact that he tried to be romantic by making me breakfast in bed was overshadowed by his total lack of couth.

We decided to go to the diner instead where he ordered, what else, corned beef hash and eggs. Having not much of an appetite, I went with a toasted bagel with butter and a glass of orange juice.

I felt like I was at a bar when the waitress brought me over a shot glass of OJ. I mean seriously, for the amount I was paying, this ounce of juice was not going to cut it.

"Richard, do you believe how small this glass is? I'm not spending $3.25 on a drink that wouldn't fill a cavity. Seriously, if I start choking on my bagel, the juice would evaporate before it reached my lips."

Richard jumped in with, "Don't worry, I can chew up your bagel for you and spit it into your mouth like mother birds do for their young."

"Just get the waitress," I implored.

When she arrived with our food, Richard didn't miss a beat and shoveled a forkful of hash in his mouth. Then, remembering my issue and wanting to "be better," he spewed out that it was an embarrassment that his woman was served such a petite amount of juice, "look at her, she's not petite."

And as if on cue, I started choking on the bagel. That's when Richard reached for the "petite" glass but knocked it over because God forbid he put his fork down. Nothing spilled on me though because there wasn't even a big enough flow to reach the end of the table.

I reached for the nearest drink, Richard's coffee, and guzzled it down. The good news was, it softened the bagel enough to dislodge it, but now, the lining of my throat was peeling away with third degree burns no doubt.

Meanwhile, while I was turning purple, the waitress chuckled at this "not petite" whale gasping for air with that sort of, "serves you right for questioning our glasses" attitude.

And Richard, he was talking to the people in the booth behind him acting all concerned and yet not once did that fork fall from his hands.

Then it happened.

This tall, handsome, God-like creature walked over to me, got down on one knee, and asked me if I was okay. He told me he was a paramedic, grabbed my hand to check my pulse, and asked if I wanted my vitals checked. I can assure you, looking at him, my vitals were in perfect check. I told him I was okay, and he asked me my name.

At the same moment, he gracefully let my hand down to the side and said, "I'm glad you're okay Lani," Shamoo...I mean

Richard...turned with a puzzled look on his face. Finally, the fork went down, he shimmied like a lame weeble-wobble out of the booth, and saddled up to my side of the table.

He extended his hand to the paramedic and introduced himself in a very "this is my turf sort of way." No, seriously, I thought he was about to whip it out and pee on the guy. The upside of that would be the guy pulling out his in retaliation. A girl can dream, can't she?

Anyway, the paramedic held out his long, masculine, hunky hand and shook Richard's. "Michael. Nice to meet you. And a word of advice if I may...pay more attention to Lani than your food."

Ahhh...Michael. And that's when I got all wet in my pants. And it felt good until I realized what actually happened. You know that petite glass of juice that started this whole thing? It finally reached the end of the table.

Eventually, the manager came over and asked what was going on. We explained the whole situation, and to his credit, as I was getting my jacket on to leave, he apologized profusely and comped our meal. Richard thanked him and grabbed the slice of toast he hadn't scarfed down yet as he walked passed the table.

"So," Richard said, "is he the one?"

"What?" I asked.

"That Mitchel guy. Is he the one you've been seeing? I saw the way he was holding your hand," he pressed on.

"Oh, Michael," I responded. "Well...let's just say he's a good friend."

"Well, if he's so good," Richard countered, "why haven't I met him yet?"

"You see the way you're acting right now," I toyed. "If I introduced him to you sooner, I'd have dealt with this reaction longer. Besides," I added, "I don't see him much anymore. He moved."

Michael really got to Richard because for the first time in a long time, Richard opened the car door for me. Mind you, this was still my car; but for masculine pride, Richard was still the primary driver.

Chapter 45

It had been a long time since Ed's funeral, and I wanted to check in with Phyllis. There were many times over the year that I wanted to call her, but the more time I let go by, the harder it was. I was at a point though where I felt I was trapped. I wasn't comfortable speaking to my sister about it, and I was positive Doris was tired of hearing about my love (or lack of love) life.

I finally picked up the phone because I had so many questions to ask Phyllis about her and Ed. Did she ever question their love? Did she ever want to leave? Did he do disgusting things?

"Hello," the woman answered.

"Hi, is this Phyllis?"

"Yes, who is calling?"

"Um...hi...um...this is Lani from the laundromat."

"'Lani from the laundromat' that has a nice ring to it," she said with a chuckle. "How are you doing, dear?"

"Well...I'm not really sure actually. I was wondering if you would like to go to lunch. It's a long time coming, and I'm sorry it took me so long to call."

"Oh nonsense. This is the perfect time to call, and I would love to have lunch. When were you thinking?"

"Um...is today too soon?"

"Well, let me check my calendar," and without missing a beat, she said, "looks free to me."

"Great. Is there anywhere in particular you'd like to go?"

"Ed and I always enjoyed that diner on Main Street."

She accepted my offer to pick her up on the way, and I jumped out of the car to get the door for her. She patted my hand that was resting on the window pane and told me how Ed always remembered his manners and opened the door for her.

It didn't take us long to get to the diner, and Phyllis was greeted by a barrage of people who obviously knew her and Ed and thought the world of them. We sat down in a booth and the waitress came right over.

"Hi, Phyllis. How are you doing? We've missed you."

"Oh Elisabeth, I'm doing well. This is my friend Lani."

"Hi, Lani."

"Hi, Elisabeth."

"Well, can I get you ladies something to drink?"

We gave Elisabeth our drink order, and Phyllis began giving me some suggestions. By the time Elisabeth came back with our drinks, we knew what we wanted so we ordered. When the menus were cleared and Elisabeth out of earshot, Phyllis leaned into me.

"So, dear...tell me what is going on. What prompted you to call?"

"Well," I began slowly, "at Ed's funeral I said we should go to lunch so I wanted to make good on that promise."

"Now, Lani, you don't have to tiptoe around it...I'm a smart woman. What's going on that prompted the call after all this time?"

"Is it that obvious?"

"Kind of," and we shared a laugh.

I then went on to explain that although Richard and I were very compatible, it just felt like things weren't progressing the way I thought they would. I confessed that I was feeling the pressure to make things more "permanent," but I thought our relationship was missing something.

I confided in her that Richard was ballooning in size, and I felt like I was playing second fiddle to food. I told her about the exchange with the paramedic and was curious if she ever hit a crossroads with Ed and how did she get through it.

She shared that things were not always easy "especially after we lost our boy," but they worked through their problems together because they took a vow. "Now...our vows didn't include having to sleep in the same bed every night, and you betcha, Ed spent a night or two on the couch, but it was never for too long."

She reminded me that I shouldn't stay with someone just because her relationship worked, but I should definitely give it all I have before bailing. She was very wise and shared a lot of information with me, but after dropping her off (promising to see her again soon), I felt like I was back at square one. She was right, I couldn't base my relationship on hers.

Chapter 46

I stopped by my sister's house on the way home from lunch. She was sitting outside watching my niece ride her bike up and down the street. I sat next to her and started idle chitchat. The conversation got serious when she brought up marriage.

"So...how long are you going to wait? People are starting to talk."

"People? What people?" I asked.

"Everyone."

When I asked her to be more specific, she said she couldn't betray their trust. "Besides," she added, "I want a niece or a nephew, and your ovaries aren't going to be able to handle babies soon."

I reminded her that I wasn't that old, and she sort of scoffed.

"Hi, Aunt Lani, look what I can do," and I turned to see my niece (at least I thought it was my niece but who could tell under the layers of padding and gigantic helmet) raise her hands in the air while peddling full speed.

"MOLLY! Don't do that," my sister insisted.

She retorted, "I'm a professional," and with that, Molly lost control of the bike and went flying into a parked car. My sister and I jumped up to check on her and halfway there, she popped up, hands raised in the air again, and exclaimed, "I'm alive, I'm alive." She picked up her bike and continued on her merry way, and I realized that those layers of padding and that gigantic helmet had their uses after all.

About twenty minutes later, Richard called and asked when I was going to be home. I assured him I was wrapping up and would see him soon.

As I pulled away from my sister's house, I rolled down the window and said, "Goodbye." My sister followed it up with "you ain't getting any younger," and I drove away knowing she was right and perhaps I was being too hard on Richard.

When I pulled into my driveway, I was determined to make things work with him.

Chapter 47

I almost knocked Richard over when I rushed into his arms and, in a very uncoordinated way, threw my legs up around him. A relief washed over me when, one, he was able to support my weight and, two, I could actually hurl my body up in the air.

"Hey, baby...what's this all about?" he asked as I kissed his neck.

"I love you. I want to make this work more than I want anything else in my life."

"Oh crap," he said as he put me down.

Completely deflated, I put my head down and whispered, "That wasn't exactly the reaction I was looking for."

He vehemently shook his head and said, "Oh...no...sorry... it's not that. I just realized I forgot to put the nachos in the oven. The game's about to start."

And with that, I realized I just committed to working harder than ever before on a relationship I was completely over.

Chapter 48

Moping around work the next day was not easy. Every time my boss walked by my desk, he gave me a puzzled look and just when I thought he would say something about my condition, he would simply turn and walk away.

Part of me wanted to leave early and go home, but the other part of me didn't want to be home where I started feeling like a stranger. By no means was I ever a neat person, but I would never step on a crumpled bag of McDonald's going to the bathroom at night. Nor would my dirty "tighty-whities" somehow end up under my bed with enough sticking out that my foot gets caught in one of the leg holes, and I have to shake it off praying I don't kick it on myself.

Speaking to Richard did nothing to help matters. He seemed to play it off as "boys will be boys." While I agree with that statement wholeheartedly, there was a major point he was missing. I didn't want a boy...I wanted a man.

Determined that I had to put my all into Richard because my ovaries were going to shrivel up soon, I put on a happy face and jumped into my next book. With newfound hope, I turned to the first page and was immediately interrupted by Doris.

"I'm worried about you."

"What do you mean?" I asked.

"You look like your dog just died. Wait a sec..." She backtracked, "You don't have a dog that just died, do you?"

"No, Doris," I said with a forced chuckle.

"Well then, I stand by my first comment about being worried about you. We are going to lunch and that's final."

I didn't even hesitate to respond affirmatively. Doris was incredibly forceful and there was no way I was going against her. So, I grabbed my bag and walked with her to the elevators.

Coincidentally, Matt was there and pressed the down button as we came through the doors.

"Ready, ladies?"

"We sure are," Doris replied.

(Coincidence...I think not.)

When the elevator arrived, Matt held his arm across the threshold for us and let "ladies first." I would be lying if I said I didn't time my deep breath at the very moment I walked passed him. I took in every scent of his being and allowed myself the guilty pleasure of imagining him in my bed. Somehow I knew he wasn't a loud snorer, and I had a feeling he would never let my side of the bed get cold as he ate popcorn and watched sports on his side. Yes, Matt was all the man I wanted, and I secretly (and guiltily) hoped I hadn't blown my chance.

"So, Doris," Matt began after we gave our order to the waitress, "Pops says the two of you are going to an art exhibit this weekend."

"Yes, it's a local fellow. He paints like the artists of my time. None of this mumbo-jumbo, splatter the canvas and roll around in it stuff," she said with a "hmpfh."

"Well, I just wanted to thank you for including him. He's looking forward to it."

"Me too," she added.

"And what about you, Lani? How are things with 'Mr. Right'?"

I was so caught up with how my name rolled off Matt's tongue that I didn't even hear his question. Doris saved me with the "Yes, Lani, how is Richard doing these days" follow-up.

"Oh...um...he's...he's okay," I finally yammered.

"Just 'okay,' Lani? I thought things were going well with the two of you?" Doris pressed. "Is that why you've been so glum?"

"I haven't been 'glum,' have I?" *What does that really mean anyway? Sounds like something I'd find at the bottom of my shoe.*

"Lani, you know full well what I'm speaking about, and don't you try to change the subject, young lady."

Young lady, I thought to myself. *I must really be dragging at work for her to use that language to get my attention.*

"I'm sorry...you're right Doris, but enough about me. Matt...how's the band?"

"We're doing great, Lani, but that's not important. Is Richard hurting you?"

Wow, Matt was truly a knight in shining armor. I wanted so badly to say "yes" just to see his reaction, but Richard wasn't hurting me; he might have been lazy, unkempt, and not as romantic as he was while courting me, but in fairness, I wasn't hurting (not in the way Matt meant).

"No," I responded while simultaneously tugging at my fingers. "He isn't hurting me. Living with him hasn't been exactly what I thought it would be." In an effort to see if Matt was still on my hook, I added, "He's not quite as thoughtful as you are, Matt."

"Wow, thanks, Lani," Matt said with a hint of redness on his cheeks (whew...he was still into me). "Actually, Michelle told me just the other day how sweet I am. I guess Pops raised me well, huh, Doris?"

Doris replied, "He certainly did, Matt," and looked in my direction. At that moment I knew that she knew I was looking for a way out with Richard, and we both just witnessed the door closing.

Chapter 49

When I pulled into the driveway I could tell that Richard was already home. I couldn't find the energy to bring myself out of the car. Secretly, I hoped that Billy would appear out of nowhere as he used to do so often. At least then I could make small talk before going inside.

I imagined that Richard was on the couch, feet up with the TV on. Dishes were probably piled high in the sink while the garbage was competing to be the tallest. It's not that Richard wouldn't take out the trash or wash dishes if I asked, but at our age, you shouldn't have to ask. I wish he would just know. Matt would just know.

Slowly I ascended the stairs leaving plenty of time for Billy to interrupt; alas, he never came. I put the key in the lock and looked back to the sidewalk one last time and pushed the door in.

"Hey, babe!" he called from the living room. I responded with a curt "hi" and put my bag down. A quick glance deemed that the garbage had in fact pulled into first place. I chastised myself for even looking, knowing it would upset me.

Richard didn't even get up to greet me. Whatever was on TV was obviously more of a draw. I thought back to all those times Billy and Matt popped up out of the blue and wished Richard would be so drawn to me that he just had to jump up to welcome me.

I sat down at the kitchen table and another man...a boy actually...popped into my head. So many years ago I made a vow that I wouldn't let anyone treat me less than Justin would. While it was true that Richard wasn't hurting me per se, he was also not treating me the way Justin (albeit it a third grade Justin) would have treated me.

I had a very tough decision to make. I could either be true to the "current me" who said I would work really hard on my relationship with Richard or I could be true to the "little girl me" who had hopes and dreams about how her Prince Charming would treat her.

Exhaling a deep breath I hadn't even realized I took, I walked into the living room and turned off the TV.

"Hey...why'd you do that?" Richard sulked.

"We need to talk."

"Oh no...did I forget to put the toilet seat down again?" he said with a laugh.

"Richard," I said while looking at the dirty dish on the floor, "I'm serious."

"Yes, I know. You told me you are serious about working on our relationship, and I'm happy to hear it! Want to go in the bedroom and start working on it?" he asked with what I'm assuming was supposed to be a seductive glance but looked more like an awkward "I just passed gas and I hope no one notices" face.

"NO! Richard, I do NOT want to go into the bedroom. You know, the bedroom that has your disgusting underwear laying anywhere you felt like undressing. The bedroom that has crumbs all over your side of the bed because you couldn't possibly eat over your plate or better yet...not eat in the bed at all. You want me to go to the bedroom where you talk a big talk but half the time I'm not sure if you're about to climax or have a heart attack on top of me never mind satisfying my needs.

"No, no, no! I do not want to go into the bedroom with you. As a matter of fact, how about you go in the kitchen, with your dirty plate, and wash a dish or two? That would probably turn me on more than you prancing around in your stained underwear acting like a Chippendale's dancer.

"I am tired of pretending I am happy because that is what people expect from me. I had expectations that are not being—"

"Marry me, Lani."

"WHAT?" Did I really just hear what I think he said?

"I want to get married. I think that I'm not taking this relation seriously enough, and if we get married, I will definitely straighten up my act."

"Wait...did you seriously just propose to me with your feet up on the couch?"

As if a lightbulb turned on, as suavely as he could, he slid off the couch and down to one knee. He took my hand and said, "I know I'm a slob, but I'm your slob, and we love each other and we have a great life, so let's do this...let's get married."

I stood there dumbfounded for a while when Richard finally broke the silence with a "So?" Followed by a car salesman grin that at one time I adored. I thought about Justin and how I shouldn't settle. I thought about Matt and how he moved on. I thought about my ovaries and didn't want to let my sister down. I thought about so many things in that moment and with my head in a tizzy I threw my hands up and said, "Fanabala."

Richard jumped up..."Is that a yes? Did you just say yes?"

"Um...I...uh...sure. Let's do this.'"

And that was my big proposal.

Chapter 50

The next day we went looking for rings. Richard was insistent we get the biggest diamond, "only the best for you." I can't say I minded too much, but on the other hand, I would have preferred to have not been there at all.

I always imagined a man on his knee presenting me with a box. He would say something so romantic that my heart would melt while slowly opening up the box. My heart would race with anticipation of what was inside. Eventually when he slipped the diamond on my hand, I would jump up and down with tears of joy shouting, "Yes, yes, yes."

Instead, I traded that all in for, "Oh...that one is nice, how much is it?" I didn't feel like I should be part of that conversation, but seeing as there were other women there who were enjoying the experience, I kept my mouth shut and acted like I was okay.

Richard had me try on ring after ring after ring, and truthfully, none of them made me happy. With tears in my eyes, I shook my head "no" to the fifteenth ring. I told him I had seen too many and that I was overly confused. When Richard said we can try another place, the salesperson looked like she was going to kill me. That one look though made me realize I did not ever want to conduct business with her again, so she screwed up her chances of getting our commission at another time.

As he started pulling me to the next store in the mall, I confessed that I was tired and just wanted to go home. The ten-minute ride felt more like two hours. As we pulled into the driveway, Billy was sweeping.

"Hey, guys! How are you?" he asked.

"We are doing awesome," Richard touted. "My fiancé and I just came back from shopping for rings."

"Oh...wow...um...congrats!"

"Thank you," Richard boasted with pride.

"Lani? Are you okay? You look like you are about to pass out."

"Oh...no, Billy, I'm fine. It's just been a long day."

"You sure, Lani?"

"Of course she is," Richard said as he wrapped his arm around me and pulled me tightly by the shoulder. "She is getting married to me!" he said matter-of-factly.

"Well...that's great, and please let me know if there is anything you need."

"We will. Thanks, Willy."

"Billy," he corrected.

"What?"

"Billy...my name is Billy."

"Oh, I'm sorry. We best be going now. We have some planning to do."

As I turned to walk away, Billy and I locked eyes, and just like Doris, I knew he knew I was in over my head.

Chapter 51

"When are you going to tell your sister?"

"Richard...I don't even have a ring yet. She will bug the crap out of me if I tell her I'm engaged, and I don't have a ring," I insisted.

"Well, I tried to get you one, but you didn't like them."

"Oh...so it's my fault?"

"I'm not saying that, but if the ring fits...?" he said with a smile realizing his pun.

"A ring is not a pair of shoes, Richard. Shoes get replaced, a ring does not. None of those rings made me feel special, and I'm pretty sure that's what's supposed to happen when it's on your finger."

"Well...maybe you are too picky. I mean, you nitpick me for every little thing?"

"WAIT a sec...You think wanting garbage to be in the garbage so we don't get roaches is nitpicking? Washing a dish for the same reason is nitpicking?" I was about to go bonkers when Richard was saved by the bell (literally).

"I'll get it," he said, relieved to escape his imminent demise.

"Oh, Will...I mean Billy. What's up?"

I heard Billy ask if I was available, and in a territorial way, Richard responded, "Yeah, sure...wait right here. I'll get her."

Not wanting to feel like an item on a shelf, I pushed passed Richard, "Hi, Billy...everything okay?"

When I saw him hesitate to speak, I realized Richard was hovering, so I stepped outside and sat on the porch inviting Billy to join me on the other chair.

"Sorry about him. I know he can come off a little pompous at times."

"A little? Ugh...wait...sorry...that was uncalled for."

I chuckled slightly. "No, it's okay. I get it."

"Do you? 'Cause when he said you were getting married, it kind of indicated otherwise."

"Is that why you are here?"

"No...well...kind of. I mean the look on your face. Full disclosure...I thought you were being held against your will."

That made me laugh even more and it felt good. I hadn't laughed in a while.

"I appreciate your concern, Billy, but I'm okay."

"Lani, I know I'm overstepping my boundaries, I really do...but..." And he hesitated.

"But?" I pried more for my benefit than his. I wanted him to tell me to run. I wanted him to be the voice that was in my head. If one person verbalized how I was feeling in my heart, I might have the courage to break it off once and for all. Just one person who didn't shove a "you're getting old," "you're being too picky," "you're ovaries are crying," and I would have all the fuel I needed.

"Well...," he started. And that's when we heard a ruckus from inside the house.

"It's okay, go on," I prodded.

"Nah...it's nothing really. Just wanted to make sure you weren't held captive." And just like that, my escape plan vanished. I thanked him for checking in on me and excused myself to figure out what on earth was happening inside.

Shockingly, Richard was in the kitchen attempting to put away dishes.

"I dropped one. Sorry."

Walking over to help him, I said, "Oh, so that's what that was about?"

"Yeah. I wanted to surprise you. Surprise!"

As I looked into his eyes, I was reminded why I fell for him in the first place. There was a boyish naivety about him that drew me in. In a sense, I felt I could groom him into the prince I was longing for. The plan obviously backfired because at his age, if he didn't know how to be a prince, he was comfortable as a peasant. I guess I was fooled by the way he spent money. To outsiders and even myself at times, I felt like a princess, but in the end, I was the servant who packed the bags, cleaned up the messes, apologized for rude behavior, and made excuses (mostly to myself) when I was ditched for poker or a cigar.

Yes, I thought I had it all. I thought we were part of a team. I thought I was "living the dream." In the end, I slept next to someone who wasn't a "stranger" per se, but he wasn't my "better half." In fact, I felt worse around him. So why on earth was I shopping for engagement rings?

Chapter 52

The weekend couldn't end fast enough for me. I spent all Sunday dodging "Why can't we go buy a ring now?" questions. At one point, I put on an award-winning performance of menstrual stomach cramps, which helped me escape his clutches in more than one way!

My head was down as I rode the elevator Monday morning. I guess you could say I was "glum." When it stopped on the second floor, my head remained down, and I backed up a bit just to avoid blocking the new comer. I only looked up when the doors opened again, and Matt said, "After you," and held his arm up for me blocking the doors from crushing me (which I wouldn't have minded one bit).

"Oh, thanks, Matt. I'm sorry. I didn't see you."

"How could you? Your head was down the whole time. Lani...I was talking to Doris this weekend..."

"You were?" For a moment I temporarily forgot my depression when trying to comprehend how they were together.

"When she came by to pick up Pops for the art show." I shook my head in acknowledgment. "Anyway..." And he paused, looked around, and must have decided that an elevator bank on a Monday morning was not a good place to have a candid conversation. "Can we have lunch today?"

"Um...I don't know."

"Why not? A girl's gotta eat right?"

He had me on that. Knowing I would be crappy company, I lied and said I brought my lunch.

"Well," he said smugly, "I don't see any bags, and if your next line is going to be that you left it here over the weekend, I'd say you are risking food poisoning if you eat it today."

A reflexive, heavy sigh betrayed me.

"Lani...it's not up for discussion. We are going to lunch. I will pick you up at noon."

I threw my hands up. "You win."

Chapter 53

At 11:50 a.m., I considered going into the ladies room and hiding out until 12:10 p.m. in the hopes Matt would think I ditched him. Unfortunately, my boss stopped by and talked my ear off until he showed up (promptly at noon).

"Well, Lani, I'll let you get to your lunch date."

"It's not a date," I said rather quickly, loudly, and more to remind myself than either of them and my boss gave me a puzzled look which was starting to become habit.

"It's okay, Lani...I think everyone knows we're just friends," Matt jumped in to break the awkwardness, and my boss took it as a sign to exit.

"Sorry...I didn't mean to..."

"It's okay, I get it."

Matt made a point to walk past Freddy's usual spot and seemed very surprised and a bit concerned that Freddy wasn't there. He explained that in the past week or two he seemed to be giving up hope and was falling ill. I can't be sure, but I thought Matt looked up to the heavens and muttered a word or two.

We slipped into a small, but very noisy pizzeria/restaurant and sat at the only open table in the center.

"So...," Matt said, trying to lift up my spirits, "what would Miss Lani like for lunch today? Anything on the menu...my treat."

"Oh, Matt, you don't ha—"

"I asked, therefore, I insist." Honestly, I wasn't even that hungry but felt I had to get something.

"Well, what are you thinking?"

"Who, me?" he said looking around thus lightening the mood further, "I'm a simpleton myself. I usually just get the ham, sausage, and meatball calzone with a side of their fantastic red sauce...or is it gravy?"

"Simpleton my butt," I said, chuckling, and I could tell he was proud to make me smile.

"You can't go wrong with anything here, Lani."

"Okay then, I'll get a house salad."

"Really? Do you eat that at home?" I shook my head no. "Then why on earth are you going to get it here? I told you...I have sisters...I know how girls really are. Live a little. Get the...," he said, scanning the menu, "chicken parm sandwich."

That did sound good. "Well...okay...since you are twisting my arm."

"Great!" And when the waiter came, he ordered for us both.

"So, Lani, what's going on? You aren't the same chipper girl you were just a short time ago."

I couldn't believe how quickly the words "I got engaged this weekend" slipped from my mouth. Although it had officially been two and a half days, I told no one. Billy knew but that was due to Richard's boasting.

"You what?" he said, and I couldn't tell above the noise if there was sadness, shock, or surprise in his voice. For all I know (and hoped) it was all three.

When he looked down at my left hand, I knew what he was looking for. "There isn't one."

"What? What type of guy proposes without a ring?" he began and then slowed down. "Sorry, I shouldn't be so judgmental. I'm sure it was a great proposal. I mean...you out of everyone I know deserves the best."

I felt myself slide down into my seat. If only he knew how badly it went down. I second-guessed myself the moment I responded with "Let's do it" and have been second-guessing myself ever since. I pictured Matt taking me to a little place like this one and having the waiter bring me a ring in a covered dish. Or perhaps he would do it while we walked on the beach. There were so many dreams I had of that moment...my living room was never one of them.

In the middle of my fantasy, Matt said, "So you said yes? Congratulations!"

I felt I had another opportunity to escape, so I took a deep breath and confessed..."I didn't want to."

"Of course you wanted to, every girl does." Over the din of the restaurant, he hadn't heard me; he thought I said, "I wanted to."

Another crossroads. I didn't know if I should correct him and claw my way out of the mess or just roll with the punches.

He continued with, "Michelle has actually been bugging me to get married. She said we aren't getting younger. But if you are going to take the plunge, maybe I should too." Rolling with the punches got me knocked out.

Over lunch, I did the best I could at deterring Matt from jumping into marriage if he wasn't ready. I felt like such a hypocrite feeding him lines I refused to accept myself. "If you aren't ready to be married, how can you be a dedicated spouse? Won't it lead to resentment?"

He did a lot of nodding and listened intently as I spoke, but the more I spoke, the more I felt I was pushing him into her arms.

"Matt, I'm going to ask you just one question. This one question will give you the answer you need with regards to marriage."

He took a deep breath, "Okay, shoot."

"Does she make you happy?"

He left me speechless with his answer..."Does Richard make you?"

The rest happened quickly. As Matt stared into my eyes, the waiter gave us the tab. Matt whipped out his credit card and put it in the waiter's hand without looking at the bill. The busboy started clearing the dishes as Matt's gaze intensified. I started squirming in my seat just as the busboy spilled the rest of my water on my lap. I jumped up breaking our eye contact, and Matt ran over to me with a napkin. The waiter apologized, and the manager grabbed Matt's credit card from the waiter and gave it back to Matt. "The meal was on the house due to the inconvenience." A lifetime of meals would not repay the inconvenience of not knowing what Matt might have said had we not been interrupted.

We walked back in silence both of us knowing we were on the cusp of something very important but not knowing how to get it back. He escorted me up to my desk, and as we walked through the doors, we heard a commotion.

A group of coworkers had gathered near my desk and formed a bit of a circle. In the middle of the circle I could see roses...lots and lots of roses. Next to the roses...Richard. Like the Red Sea, the crowd separated leaving me with a straight path to Richard.

Richard got down on one knee and, to my horror, took out a small box. One of my coworkers grabbed my arm and pulled me toward the center of the circle. Involuntarily, I turned my head back against her pull, and Matt and I locked eyes once more.

In that split second, there was no doubt in my mind that I saw a part of Matt's internal light dim. I thought about reaching my other arm to him knowing he was my last hope, but the crowd closed the path as quickly as they opened it, and I was swallowed by the sea. Just before my head turned completely back toward Richard, I saw Matt put his head down and walk away.

"Well, well, well," Sarah chimed in, "take a look at that rock."

"Oh my goodness," another girl gushed, "I guess size does matter. Way to go, Lani."

"Lani," Richard began, "you are awesome, and we are an awesome team, so will you marry me?"

Time stood still. The room spun around me. I was saved when I heard a voice exclaim, "What is all this about? How come no one is working?" It was my boss, shooing everyone back to their desks.

"We can't leave yet. She didn't answer him."

"Oh no!" I heard Doris shout. She must have been with my boss.

"Well, Lani...Don't keep the young man waiting," said my boss, "please answer him so this circus will end."

"Oh...I'm sorry...I had no idea," I said, panicking and looking for a window to jump out of.

"Well, you know now, so tell the boy." If only he knew how accurate his description of Richard as "the boy" was.

I looked at Richard. He looked anxious, but I couldn't tell if that was because he thought I would say no or if he couldn't stay on his knee for much longer. Given his ego and his blatant lack of ability to read my feelings, I went with the latter.

I played out the two outcomes. I say, "yes," everyone cheers, Richard gets off his knee and hugs me, I go back to work and act like I'm okay when everyone comes by to congratulate me.

I say, "no," and everyone looks at me like I'm a heartless bitch who refused a man so thoughtful as to show up at my job and surprise me. They would never know my side of things where the proposal was actually a spur of the moment "don't dump me, marry me," scenario because I couldn't take his slovenly nature anymore. They would only see a ring with a rock the size of a small African country and wonder how on earth I could refuse such a generous, romantic, spontaneous guy.

They wouldn't see the crumbs in the bed, the stained underwear on the floor, or the fast-food bags on the couch. They wouldn't know the fighting...ahem...excuse me "disagreements" that happen because he doesn't think he needs to shower after running around playing football "with the guys" before going out to a nice dinner. They wouldn't see how he could scarf down his bacon while I'm choking on a bagel. Nope, I would be scoffed at for years to come.

Richard broke my concentration, "So what do you say?"

Chapter 54

"Richard, I..." And I took a deep breath. It was true...I wasn't getting any younger; no one was beating down my door.

"Yes?" he prompted.

"Okay, okay, everyone," Doris jumped in. "Why don't we give these two lovebirds some privacy? This isn't a freak sideshow."

I looked over at Doris and mouthed, "Thank you," as I heard whispers of, "if she doesn't say 'yes,' I will." In that moment, I would have welcomed another woman taking my place.

Doris led us into a small conference room and told us to both sit down and offered to get us water. When she walked out of the room, Richard turned to me with a goofy grin. "I did good, didn't I?"

"What?" I asked.

"The ring, the surprise proposal, the roses...Did you see the roses?"

"Yes," I said, "I saw them. They are beautiful, thank you." I noticed I was talking with a clouded head. I felt like I was in the twilight zone. Had he really been so caught up in the pomp and circumstance that he completely missed that I didn't accept his proposal?

"Richard...I appreciate what you did, but I'm kind of a private person at work. I thought I told you that."

With an arrogance that was wearing on my last nerve, he said, "I must have forgot."

When I said, "You know...I have a real problem with that." He gave me a "what's the big deal" look.

Standing up with my hands on the table, I asked, "What's my favorite color?"

Momentarily bobbling his head from side to side and turning his palms upright he stumbled over his words. "Um...I don't know...pink?"

"Are you asking me or telling me?" I questioned while leaning in toward him and searching his eyes for the truth.

"Well, don't all girls love pink?"

"No! So are you saying you don't know my favorite color?"

"Maybe?" he said, trying to be cute but it was not working at all.

"Richard...what color is my bedroom?"

"Our bedroom," he corrected.

"My bedroom, our bedroom...you are stalling. What color is it?"

"Yeah...you got me on that."

"You are oblivious. You don't care."

"Who gives a crap about the color of a bedroom?"

"I do, Richard. Me. I care about details. It's my job to check details. When you know the details, you know not to show up at a private person's job and embarrass the hell out of them."

"How could getting married to the man of your dreams be embarrassing?"

"Because maybe you aren't the man of my dreams!" It came out louder and firmer than I ever imagined. I turned away from him realizing I just said out loud what I felt for months... maybe even years. It was then that I realized Doris was standing in the doorway with our water.

She stood there...frozen in time as she must have walked in right when I delivered the final blow. Ashamed she witnessed my lowest point, I turned back to Richard. He slowly was getting out of the chair and placed the ring on the table.

"I'm not sure what happened. You said yes this weekend. I'm sure the stress of me surprising you got you crazy. I'll leave you your ring and you can put it on when I'm gone." As he walked passed me, he took my head in his hands and kissed the top of it. He added, "I'll see you at home tonight," walked passed Doris, and left.

Doris immediately shut the door, put the cups down, and ran over to me. She took my arms in her hands and guided me to sit down.

"Oh, Lani, I'm sorry...I didn't mean to walk in on—"

I put my pointer finger to my lips and silenced her. I needed the quiet. I needed to understand what just happened, but no matter how hard I tried, I couldn't wrap my head around the fact I told Richard he wasn't the man for me, and there was still an engagement ring one foot away from me.

He was so sweet, so thoughtful to come to my job and surprise me. Just days ago I complained that he was anything but romantic. Now, I shot down the most romantic thing he'd ever done for me. Maybe he was right. Perhaps it was the surprise element that got me crazy. I took the ring box and opened it.

Doris who had been squatting in front of me jumped up. "What are you doing?"

"Richard is right. I was just overwhelmed with being at work. He's right, Doris. I have to stop running from love. I'm putting on this ring, and I'm getting married."

"Lani, NO! Don't put on that ring," and she swatted my hand.

"Why not?"

"Because diamonds have a way of clouding a girl's vision. Ironically, the less cloudy the diamond, the more blurry the vision."

I admitted that I didn't know what she was talking about, and she told me that the moment I put it on my finger, I will feel like a new person. I will float around the office on cloud nine, but it won't be about Richard; it will be about a sparkle.

Against all instincts, I closed the ring box and brought it back to my desk. Before I could finish putting it into my pocketbook, my boss beckoned me.

I swallowed whatever air I had in my mouth, sucked in a deep breath, grabbed my paper and pen (in the hopes he was giving me an assignment versus a lecture about office etiquette), and did the walk of shame into his office.

Chapter 55

"So?" he asked matter-of-factly.

"Um...uh..."

"Lani, the use of filler words is completely unflattering," he scolded.

"Sorry. That is, I'm sorry for the use of filler words and for the...um...ugh, I did it again. Sorry...for the circus today."

"Darling, I'm not asking you about that."

"You aren't?"

"No, dear. I'm asking what you said to the young man."

"Oh...I actually didn't give him an answer, but I'm leaning toward yes."

"'Leaning toward yes?'" he said with that puzzled look I became used to. "In matters of the heart, one does not 'lean toward' anything." With an elaborate use of his arm, he continued, "Love pulls you so deeply and so intently into someone that you cannot lean. It is impossible. Instead, you fall and fall hard knowing love is there to catch you. Do you understand what I'm saying?"

"I think, but truthfully? No, not really."

"Then, my dear child, you are not in love."

After a brief period of awkward silence, he looked at me with sincerity and a connection we never shared before and said, "Do I make myself clear?"

I managed a half-hearted head nod and slowly stood up. Praying I could make it to my desk without blacking out, I turned to face the door. I stopped when I heard, "One more thing dear." I didn't turn back, but he continued. "If I 'leaned toward yes' years ago, I'd be a bitter, divorced man right now. Do not let societal, familial, or biological pressures dictate your happiness."

With my head hanging down knowing the weight of the world that was now on my shoulders, I walked out of his office. An hour or so later, he appeared at my desk, asked me to take something to the post office, and to come back in the morning. God bless his heart.

Doris ran over when she saw me packing up. "He didn't fire you, did he?"

"Oh, God, Doris, no. No...on the contrary. He's giving me a pardon and letting me leave a bit early," I said, faking a chuckle.

"Oh, thank goodness because if he fired you, I was packing up and going too!"

"Thanks, Doris. I don't think that would be necessary though."

She spread her arms out and gave me a hug. "Are the girls still talking about how dumb I am?"

"Honey, I put them in their place the moment I went for water, and they haven't said a word since."

"Thank you, Doris. You really are heaven sent."

"Anytime, dear. Now...promise me that you will listen to your heart and not commit to anything that will go against it!"

"Oh, Doris! You heard him. He doesn't get it. He thinks it's just a work thing. How did he not realize I wasn't jumping up and down for joy? Isn't that what's supposed to happen?"

"It did for me," she said gently.

"Doris...I don't want to be alone my whole life. The older I get, the harder it is to find someone. Isn't it better to be with someone who isn't perfect than to be alone?"

"You are speaking to someone who has been alone for a very, very long time. I have spent more nights sleeping alone than with my husband. When you have experienced true love, you will not settle for anything less. Trust me, Lani, I had my share of losers hitting on me and not once would I let them blemish what Jack and I had. None of them were worthy.

"But now...out of the blue...a nice gentleman named Matthew happened out of nowhere." I smiled at the mention of Matt's dad. "He will never replace my Jack, but I must admit he does give me butterflies, and if I settled for someone else along the way, I might have missed out on a second chance at love."

I hugged Doris again, and this time I whispered in her ear, "Thank you."

As I let her go, I knew there was one other person I had to see before the confrontation with Richard. I ran down to the mail room.

A young girl who I looked as if she was fifteen was sitting at the window was chewing gum and filing her nails. She finally looked up when I said, "Hello."

"Yes?" she asked impatiently.

"Is Matt here?"

She replied abruptly with, "No."

"Okay," I said cautiously. "Do you know when he'll be back?"

Again, she was curt with no.

Throwing all caution to the wind and tired of her rude behavior, I put my hand on top of hers to make her stop filing and look at me. That got her attention, and I'm sure made her think I was someone really important to be that gutsy. "Listen, I need to find Matt. It's very important. Where is he?"

"Oh, hi," said an older gentleman walking to the counter from the back room. "You looking for Matt?"

"Yes," I said hopefully.

"Well, I'm sorry, miss, you missed him. He left unexpectedly about an hour or hour and a half ago. Said some emergency came up. He might have been sick. He didn't look good."

I closed my eyes and inhaled. Matt was gone, and he left right after he saw Richard on one knee.

"Miss? Miss? You okay?"

I shook myself out of my stupor and told him I was. I backed away thanking him for his time and wondering what I was going to do next. I was afraid to go home. If Richard was crying, I most certainly wouldn't kick him out, but in my heart, I knew the butterflies I carried for Richard had died a long time ago.

I stepped out of the building, looked left and right in the hopes I'd see Matt. When I didn't, I walked to the train and to the biggest decision of my lifetime.

Chapter 56

When I pulled up to my house, I was thoroughly confused. My sister's car was in the driveway. I parked the car on the street and walked up the stairs wondering what on earth was going on.

I opened the door and my sister popped out of the chair she was sitting on. "Oh my God, why didn't you tell me?"

"Tell you what?" Knowing full well what she was talking about.

"Let me see it," she said, grabbing my left hand.

"See what?"

"Lani, stop playing with me. Let me see the ring?"

"How do you even know about the ring?"

"Richard called me."

"He what?"

"He called me and told me what happened at work today. I can't believe how great he did. Do you remember how lame Paul was?" She rolled her eyes in the back of her head, and I had to admit, he didn't put much thought into her proposal. He left the box on her dresser when he went to take a shower. She opened it and asked him about it, and he proposed from behind the curtain.

I wonder if Richard told her he didn't have a ring at all when he first blurted it out.

"Okay, you know...so...why are you here?"

"Well, he said you were mad at him. I guess I'm here to get you 'un-mad.'" I had so mentally prepared myself to face him, that I was completely unprepared to face her.

She stayed with me for over an hour insisting I was completely crazy and that true love doesn't actually exist. "It's impossible for one person to be your perfect expectations." And admittedly, a lot of what she said made sense.

Molly called to find out where she was, and I was so relieved. She wanted me to show her the ring before she left and I did. True to Doris, I did not try it on, but she did. And Doris was right. Her whole personality changed. She beamed brighter than I ever saw before.

"Oh my gosh, marry him for this rock alone. You can divorce him later."

"No, thank you. If I get married, I'm not going into it with plans for divorce."

Hesitantly, she slid the ring off of her finger. I put it back in the box for safe keeping, and she headed toward the door. "Don't forget...I do want nieces and nephews." I rolled my eyes and thought to myself that there was no possible way for me to forget that.

As she opened the door, I heard her talking to someone. Richard was home and my stomach turned.

"Did you talk to her? Is she okay? We're going to get married, right?"

"Richard, I'm not going to lie. You have some issues to work out with her. Good luck."

When the door closed, I felt woozy, so I sat on the couch.

"Hi, honey," he said coyly and sat (more like plopped) next to me. He reached out to kiss me, and I pulled away.

"So I can't even get a kiss now? What has gotten into you?"

"Richard, are you that blind that you can't see I've been miserable for a long time?"

"Look, Lani," he began. "I don't know what you want from me. You tell me to clean, I clean. I know I broke a dish, but I tried. You also said I'm not romantic. Do you know how hard it was to find those roses? All you have to do is tell me what you want, and I'll do it."

As much as I wanted to tell him that having to give directions for everything I wanted was *not* what I wanted, I knew it would fall on deaf ears, so I didn't. I just asked him to give me some time. He agreed, and when he tried to get frisky, I reminded him that the "cramps" I had just the day before were still there.

Chapter 57

When Richard left for work the next morning, I called my boss and told him I needed to take a sick day. I honestly couldn't face going into work and seeing all the witnesses to my disastrous proposal. Fortunately, my boss completely understood and told me he would hold down the fort. If nothing more, I think the experience in the office brought my boss and I closer. At least I had that going for me.

I spent most of the morning vegging in my bed, and I loved it. It had been so long since I was alone in my room; I'd forgotten how much I enjoy my own space. When lunchtime rolled around, I got up and cleaned. I put every dirty piece of Richard's laundry in the hamper and washed every dish. I dusted, vacuumed, and cleaned out the moldy food in the fridge.

The more I purged, the better I felt. By 2:00 p.m., my house reminded me of how I used to live, and I felt amazing. After a shower, I went for a walk in the neighborhood. I thought about calling Phyllis but wasn't sure I wanted to rehash everything.

My cell phone startled me when it rang. "Hello?"

"Lani, it's Richard, are you okay?"

"Yes? Why? What's wrong?"

"Well, I called you at work at least five times and you never called back."

"Oh! Sorry...I took the day off."

"You did?" he asked obviously offended. "Why didn't you tell me? I would have taken the day off too."

"I didn't want to tell you. I needed some time for me."

"Oh," he said, and I could hear the wind leave his sails. "Are you wearing the ring?"

"No, Richard, I'm not."

"Oh." At that point, I knew his boat was taking on water.

"Richard...It's not that I don't love you. There are just things we have to work on before I can make a full commitment."

"Whatever you want, I will do it. You'll see."

Chapter 58

That night he came home and asked if we could go to dinner. I accepted, figuring I had to give him his chance. Like the gentleman I wanted, he held the doors open for me and even allowed me to order before jumping in with his selection.

He fed me bites of his food like he had in the beginning of the relationship and even added a new chivalrous act. When I excused myself to go to the ladies room, he half stood as a sign of respect. I didn't know where he picked that up, but I felt it was an excellent touch.

When the waiter came to see if we wanted dessert, he deferred to me. When I said I was full, that was that. I didn't have to sit through another course where Richard scarfed down a chocolate mousse cake.

He helped me with my jacket and put out his arm for me to latch onto. When we stepped outside, he took my face in his hands and kissed me under the moonlit sky. A little bubble moved in my stomach. I thought perhaps a butterfly had survived after all.

He drove us home and escorted me up the stairs. He helped me take off my coat and then asked me to sit on the couch. He slid my shoes off my feet and sat on the floor and rubbed them for ten minutes.

This was the man I always hoped for. I reached down and pulled his face to mine and kissed him with a passion that had long since left our relationship. He wrapped me in his arms, and we stayed on the couch for at least another ten minutes until I seductively led him into my...I mean our...bedroom. Given it was spotless was just icing on this cake I didn't want to stop eating.

The fact that Richard and I hadn't been intimate in a while really helped our intensity. It felt like our first time, and he was more loving and considerate than I remembered. We made love for over an hour at which point I realized I needed to get to bed or I was going to have to take another sick day.

Richard was the first to get up and shower. I enjoyed lying in the bed replaying the night before. I was giddy and the butterflies came out of hibernation. His pillow smelled of cologne; another touch that wasn't lost on me.

When Richard came out of the bathroom with the towel mostly wrapped around his waist (it was just a bit too small), he said, "All yours, princess."

I floated into the bathroom, happier than I had been in months. My euphoria was quickly slapped away though when I looked down into the sink. There was toothpaste all over. I was devastated. I would have thought after the conversation we had just the night before about how much cleaning I did, he would have made a better effort.

I told myself I was being way too picky and moved on. I scrubbed the sink clean (again) and took my shower. As I scrubbed myself with the loofah, I recalled how Richard moved his hands all over my body. The butterflies were wide awake as I recalled his touch. The Richard I fell in love with was back, and I prayed it was for good.

As I dried myself off, Richard gently knocked on the bathroom door.

"Yes?"

"Can I come in?"

"Sure," I said, and he pushed the door open. "What's up?"

"Well, I was wondering if you would wear this today," and he opened the ring box. I was drawn into it. I hadn't recognized its beauty when I first saw it. I was so overwhelmed that I must have shielded myself.

He took the ring out of the box and handed it to me. Reflexively, I took it. I was about to slide it on my finger when I recalled Doris's warning. My hair, which was still wet from the shower dripped into the sink and reminded me that moments ago it was filled with toothpaste.

I closed my eyes and handed it back to Richard. "Richard... it is the most beautiful ring I have ever seen. I want to make sure I am completely committed to this before I put it on. Can you give me a few days?"

"Yes." After a short pause, he added, "I love you, Lani."

Chapter 59

I can't say I was eager to get back to work. I knew to expect stares and whispers but what I didn't expect was the anxiousness I felt about seeing Matt. I wanted to see him so badly; to finish the conversation we started and yet I couldn't imagine how I could even start that discussion.

Taking a deep breath, I walked through the office doors and made a beeline to my desk. From his office, my boss smiled at me with a nod that said, "Welcome back, kid." I put my things down, started my computer, and sought out Doris.

She was in the copy room looking for something, and when she saw me, she stopped, grabbed me, looked at my naked finger, and hugged me. "Are you okay, Lani?"

"Yes...yes...I'm fine."

"What happened? You have to tell me. How did he take it?"

"Take what?"

"Why, breaking up with him of course," she said, confused that I didn't know what she meant.

"We didn't break up," I admitted.

She was speechless for a moment and then said, "Lani, it's none of my business, but he isn't your Mr. Right."

"How do you know that?"

"Because if he was, you'd be wearing that ring, which...I have to give Richard credit. It's a very lovely ring. But you aren't wearing it because you aren't sure."

"But I think it's just me. I'm too picky. I always have been. Richard is not as bad as my mind says he is. You should have seen how great he was last night."

We were interrupted by a male clearing his throat. "Excuse me, ladies. I'm sorry. I have to get to the mailboxes."

"Oh...Matt...um..." My knees went weak. I wanted to collapse into his arms. "Hi."

He said, "Hi," as he walked passed me quickly and not making eye contact. How much had he heard, I wondered.

"Well, I need to get back to work," Doris announced and left us in the room alone.

Matt was quickly placing the mail in the appropriate slots, and I noticed he only had a few left. My heart was beating faster than before, and I knew my window to talk to him was closing quickly. I didn't know what to say or how to say it, but I had to stall him.

"How's Freddy?" I was so relieved I thought of something to keep him in the room.

"To tell you the truth, I don't know. I go by the spot every day, and he hasn't been back. I stopped by a few hospitals to ask if he was admitted there, but without knowing his full name, it's a little hard to track."

"Oh, that's a shame. I really hope he's okay."

"Well, like I told you earlier, he gave up hope. Somehow he found out his ex-wife was going to get married to someone else. I guess it broke whatever was left of his heart." As he slid the last letter into its place, I swore I heard him say, "That happens more than you think."

Searching for something to say to keep him in the room, I asked about his band. He said they were playing their next show on Friday night. "Same place?" I asked. He told me it was and abruptly left.

As he darted passed me, I felt an electricity. There was something there, and I didn't know how to test it.

Doris woke me from my stupor when she came charging back into the copy room. "Oh...you're still here? You okay? I left in such a hurry, I forgot to get the staples I was looking for."

"So, Matt says he has a show on Friday night. Are you going?"

"Yes. Matthew and I are going to support our favorite rocker," she said with a giggle and I chuckled. It was a relief for me to know I could be so happy for someone else while I struggled with my own demons.

"I'm going to see if Richard wants to come."

Doris looked at me and visibly shook her head in disapproval then left the room.

Chapter 60

Walking through the door to the house, I wondered how I successfully made it through the day without hearing any snickers. I silently thanked Doris figuring she had to have had a hand in it. I took a deep breath and went inside.

Richard wasn't home yet, but I knew he'd be there within the hour. I also knew he'd want an answer. I went to my drawer to get the box that contained the engagement ring...my engagement ring.

Carefully and slowly (cautious of the spell it could cast), I opened the box. The ring was magnificent. I pulled it out of the box and held it up to look at it more closely. Just as Doris promised, it drew me in. I thought about what she said, and against my better judgment, I gave into the allure. I put the box down and began sliding the ring on my finger.

At the moment it touched my nail, I heard a jingle at the front door; Richard was home. Not wanting to be caught in the act, I withdrew the ring, replaced it in its box, and hid the box back in my drawer.

I ran out of the room to meet him at the front door. "Hi, honey," and even as it came off my tongue, it didn't feel right.

He greeted me with a bear hug, "I missed you. How was work?"

"Work wasn't bad. Say...Doris and Matthew are going to see Matt's show on Friday night. Same place as last time. Can we go?"

"I don't think we have anything planned. He still with that girl?"

At the mention of "that girl," my heart dropped, and I told Richard that they were still together.

"Great. Sure, let's go." It was not lost on me that he only agreed once he knew Matt was still off the market. At this point, I couldn't blame Richard for being cautious. He had every right as far as Matt was concerned.

"Listen, some of the guys asked if I wanted to grab a beer with them tonight...You know, a little congratulatory thing."

"Richard, we aren't—"

He cut me off. "I know...I know. I told them I was going to ask you soon. That was excuse enough to go to the bar. They don't know it actually happened already," and he looked away from me, and I felt terrible.

"So, are you okay if I go out for a bit?"

"Yes...sure...of course. Have fun."

"Great, I'm just gonna change. Joe is going to pick me up in half an hour or so."

I walked outside when I heard the car beep, and Richard was still in the bathroom. "Hi, Joe!" I called out.

"Hi, Lani, where's the big man?"

"Oh, he'll be out in a moment."

And in a moment he was. He kissed me on the cheek as he threw on his jacket and headed down the stairs. "Love ya, Lani."

When the car pulled away, I stood there for a moment soaking in the quiet. Reflecting back on life before Richard. I was trying to recall if I was happier then. I jumped out of my skin when Billy said hello.

He was sitting on his side of the porch, and truth be told, I was happy to see him. "Hi, Billy, how are you doing?"

"Well, I think I'm doing better than you. Want an ear?"

"Sure," and I hopped over the partition and sat next to him. As with everyone else since Monday, he looked at my finger and then back to me looking for an answer as to why it remained ringless.

"So...what do you want my ear to know?" he asked, and for the next two hours, we talked about everything from being nervous that I was settling, to the blind date he went on the week before, jobs, the neighborhood, and everything in between.

As I sat there I wondered why Billy and I didn't have these talks a long time ago. I decided it was my own fault. I kept to myself most of the time, choosing the couch and ice cream over the porch and conversation. I made a mental note that whatever happened with Richard and me, I was going to continue sitting on the porch with Billy.

At the end of the conversation, I gave Billy a final once-over and realized that I had been wrong. He was very attractive inside and out and wished I saw it sooner. Before going into the house, I gave Billy a big hug, thanked him for listening to my tale of woe, and assured him he was going to make someone very happy.

"Happy enough that they will wear my ring if I ask them to marry me?" he said, gritting his teeth, shrugging his shoulders, and raising his hands in the "c'mon, you have to see what I'm seeing here" gesture.

A few weeks ago, I might have been offended that he was so blunt. Now, I was grateful that he cared enough to tell it to me straight.

"Good night, Billy."

"Good night, Lani."

I went inside, locked the door, and lay down on the bed. My plan was to be sound asleep when Richard got home so we didn't have to have any conversation. I needed time to sort my feelings.

Chapter 61

The next day at work, my boss asked me if I could cover a book show that night. I happily (and cowardly) accepted not just for the prestige of meeting some authors, but to avoid another night with Richard.

When I called Richard to let him know, he sounded bummed, but understood. He asked if he could go to the event with me, but I told him no guests were allowed, even though I wasn't sure.

I saw Matt walk past the aisle in front of my cubicle once, but his head was down, and he was too fast for me to call out his name.

I packed up to leave for the book show around 2:00 p.m. and spent the rest of the evening "mingling" with new authors. There was not much prestige in who they were, but someday, I might be able to say I knew them when.

At 11:00 p.m., I packed up the materials I had at the show and headed home. I was surprised (and disappointed) when I saw the glow of the living room television through the window. The last thing I wanted to do was have a conversation close to midnight on a work night.

Luckily, Richard had fallen asleep on the couch and the sound of the TV masked my moves. I tiptoed to the bedroom, and before falling asleep, I spoke to God and asked him to give me a sign. I felt Richard slip into bed shortly thereafter and wondered if God would send such a subtle sign.

In the morning, Richard actually put his underwear in the hamper instead of the floor when he got up to shower. Again, I wondered if that was my sign or not.

He was out the door before me and almost left without a kiss goodbye, but thought better of it and came back. I thanked God for the subtleties but explained I'm daft and really needed something more obvious. That evening, much to my (and other people's) chagrin, I got the biggest sign God could send.

Chapter 62

"C'mon, Lani, what's taking so long?" Richard was growing impatient with how long I was taking getting out of my work clothes and into my "going out" clothes. I knew I was taking significantly longer than I should, but in my defense, I wasn't very skilled in applying makeup. A part of me knew I should stick with eye shadow and mascara, but once (a long time ago), my sister put eyeliner on my lids, and they looked amazing. Unfortunately, I was not as gifted.

I started with the left eye. Pulling the lid back toward my ear and using my right hand, made the most perfect line across the top of my eye lashes. Satisfied and proud of my work, I switched to my right eye. Being right-handed, I had to cross my left arm over my chest to pull the lid back toward my ear. In a very Twister-like way, I then put my right wrist on top of my left and began drawing the line. When I got mid-eye, my left hand twitched and my straight line inherited a speed bump. Instead of stopping, I finished the line. Realizing how bad it looked, I decided to just make the line thicker to cover up the bump.

It didn't look too bad, but the other side was way too thin. When I adjusted that line, it was totally obvious that my eyes were shaped differently (which up until that point, I hadn't noticed) and the line accentuated it too much.

As Richard paced outside the door, I knew I had to start over. I grabbed some toilet paper, wet it, and began scrubbing. It soon was apparent that water alone was not going to work so I added a little soap. This seemed to do the trick, but at the most inopportune moment, Richard called out and I opened my eye while simultaneously putting the soapy toilet paper into it.

"Ooowwww!" I cried.

"You okay? What the heck are you doing?" he asked.

"Na...na...nothing. I'm fine. Just need another minute."

Frantically, I worked through the pain, scrubbed the rest of the makeup off, and reapplied, sticking just to the eye shadow and mascara as originally intended.

As I opened the bathroom door, I heard Richard say, "It's about—" I can only assume he would finish it with the word *time*, but he stood frozen.

"What?" I asked.

"Your eye. What the heck happened?"

"Oh...that's a long story. Let's go."

As he drove to the venue, I pulled down the visor to use the mirror. He was right to be stunned. My eye was redder than I had realized in my race to apply the makeup. I was just grateful it would be dark.

We parked the car, and I noticed Richard didn't race over to get the door, so I helped myself out. The same number of young girls (if not more) were lined up against the wall. As we walked up toward the building to take our place in line, a bouncer called out to us.

"Hey...are you Lani?"

I looked around as if he had the wrong person and heard Richard tell him I was.

"Cool. Your grandma is inside. She said you had to leave the line to get her medicine so we should let you in when you got back."

I had to hand it to Doris. She definitely knew how to game the system. "Thank you."

We made our way to the booth we sat at the first time, and sure enough, there was Doris and Matthew.

"Hi, Grandma!"

"Oh, hi, dear," she said. "I'd get up to give you a hug, but I'm a bit trapped."

"Oh nonsense," said Matthew as he slid out to give Doris access. "All you have to do is ask."

Doris hugged me, nodded to Richard, and before sliding back into her seat gave Matthew a peck on the lips. I beamed from cheek to cheek, and Matthew gave me a little wink. Before sitting down, Matthew extended his hand to Richard. Richard took it and then headed to the bar asking if we needed anything. Since Doris and Matthew already had glasses in front of them, they politely declined, and I requested a Sprite.

I slid into the booth all the way around the horseshoe until I was close enough to Doris to speak to her.

"So, Grandma...I see you and Grandpa are nice and cozy."

"Oh, Lani, who'd have thought?"

"Well, I'm really happy for you."

"And what about yourself?" she inquired. "Is Lani feeling happy these days?"

Before I was able to answer her, the lights dimmed, and the girls went wild. There was no opening act; Matt walked on stage and went straight to his mic.

"Ladies and gentlemen," he began, "thank you for coming out tonight." The roar got louder than anticipated, but I could hear my heart beating above it.

"Normally, I start our shows with something upbeat. Tonight, I can't do that. I just found out a great man, a friend of mine, went to meet his maker yesterday. He was a good man who fell on hard times and lost everything. In your time of need, you certainly find out who really loves you. Freddy...this one's for you."

"Oh no!" I said as the saddest chord I ever heard played on a guitar.

"Oh no, what?" Richard asked. I hadn't even realized he returned with the drinks and took his place beside me.

"I knew Freddy. The guy he's talking about."

"You did? Who was he?"

"Well, he was this guy that stationed himself by our building."

"Wait...what?" Richard seemed confused.

"He was this guy who Matt and I used to walk by and give food to."

"Oh. So a homeless guy?"

"Yes. His wife left him."

"Well, he was probably a bum."

"No, that's not true."

"Lani, the guy is living on the street, he's a bum."

"Richard, that's not really nice."

"Sorry, you're right. I'm sorry your friend is dead. At least now he is warm," he said with a chuckle, and I couldn't believe my ears.

I had to turn away from Richard, so I looked over at Matt. He was pouring his heart out in the song, and I could see he was welling up with tears. Yes, Freddy was homeless, but he had more manners, charm, and tact than Richard ever did. I turned back to Richard and that's when I noticed he took the ring out.

"Lani, please put on this ring. Life is short. Your friend Frankie—"

"Freddy," I corrected rather agitatedly.

"Freddy, Frankie...the point is, he died an unhappy man, and I don't want to die an unhappy man. Please put on the ring and let's get married."

I turned away and looked at Matt again. As he dabbed a tear away from his eye and looked at me, I knew I wanted him and only him.

Turning back to Richard to tell him it's over, I was momentarily puzzled when I didn't see him. Leaning over the table, I saw he had taken a knee with the ring box. Panicked, I looked back at Matt who was staring at me with an even deeper sadness.

"Richard!" I exclaimed flinging my head back in his direction, "I do not want to marry you. Not today, not tomorrow, not next year. Please get up."

"Ladies and gentlemen, this next song is to my friend Lani who just got engaged. Let's hear it for her and her fiancé, Richard." The crowd cheered as I frantically shook my head no.

Matt started the song really well, but when he got to the chorus, something about, "And I won't ever let you go," his voice cracked. Richard was so excited that Matt acknowledged publically that we were engaged that he pulled me to my feet and insisted on dancing with me much to mortification.

As he pulled me up, I contemplated grabbing on to Doris but didn't want to risk hurting her. She looked like a deer in headlights having no idea what had happened as her focus was on the stage.

Richard grabbed me into his arms and started swaying me. Months ago, I longed for this sort of attention. Now, I felt like I was seized by a total stranger. One whiff of his "I don't have to shower to go out" body, and I had the strength I needed to pull away.

At the same time I was wrestling for my freedom, the song ended, and I could vaguely hear Matt saying something about how great it is to have someone and I thought I heard a boo or two when Matt said, "Michelle."

In my struggle to get out, I was able to turn my neck enough to see Michelle joining Matt on stage. Things started fogging up in my mind, and I was not sure what was happening when I saw him starting to take a knee.

Michelle obviously figured it out first because she threw her hands to her mouth as Matt began to speak. "Michelle, it's been a heck of a ride, and I know you really want this, so I have to ask you a question."

"Oh my God," I said to Richard. My fog quickly evaporated and realized Matt was about to make the biggest mistake of his life.

"Lani, come on, we're good together," Richard pleaded.

"Michelle, will you—"

"NO!" I screamed as I finally pulled free of my captor. The force with which I pulled away was so great that I wound up on the floor. I managed to see everyone (including Matt) look in my direction as I hit the floor and blacked out.

Chapter 63

"Lani? Lani?" Someone was calling my name...and...slapping my face.

"Oooww, stop, I'm okay," I said, shaking myself back into reality and waving my hands in front of my face for protection.

As my vision came back, I recognized Doris. "Oh thank God. Lani, you scared me half to death. What on earth happened?"

I struggled to remember, and when I did, I quickly tried to scramble to my feet. I was still woozy though, so I barely made it to the booth. That's where I realized there was no music and only a few gawking people. "Oh no. Did I ruin Matt's show?"

"Well," she timidly started, "I guess you can say that."

"Oh God. Where's Richard?"

"He's outside. He's waiting on the ambulance."

"An ambulance?"

"Lani, you were unconscious."

"Where's Matt?" I asked in a panic.

"Honestly, we don't know. You got hurt, and we ran to you. The next thing we heard while slapping you is Matt mumbling that he couldn't continue the show, and he and Michelle were gone.

"Did they get engaged?"

She shrugged her shoulders and rocked her head back and forth; she didn't know.

"This way, over here," I heard Richard shout as he brought the paramedics my way.

"Are you okay, miss?" they asked while unzipping their little red bags.

"Yes, yes, I'm fine," I answered as I tried pushing them away.

Richard leaned into me. "Lani, I'm...I'm...I'm sorry. I guess I got carried away."

"No, Richard, I'm sorry." And I really was. "I'm sorry I didn't tell you how I truly felt a while ago. I mean...I tried, but you would come up with an excuse and you would change, but it wasn't a real change, it was only short lived. Richard, I'm sure that someday you will find someone who will jump at your proposal but—"

"Excuse me," the paramedic said, as he held a stethoscope to my chest. "Sorry to interrupt."

"It's okay. Anyway, Richard—"

"Miss?"

"Yes?"

"I'm sorry...it's easier for me if you don't talk."

"Oh. Of course."

When he was done with the stethoscope, he shoved a thermometer in my mouth and put something on my finger. I was getting irritated by how long it was taking for me to finally be able to tell Richard how I really felt.

With the thermometer out of my mouth and the clippy thing off my finger, the paramedic asked me one last time if I was okay or if I'd like to go to the hospital. When I finally convinced him I was okay, he packed up his bag and left.

Matthew, who looked thoroughly worried and confused, had gotten me water. Poor Pops was probably torn between making sure I wasn't dead and wondering where his son was. I thanked him and nodded to signal that I was okay. That seemed to satisfy him, and he went off; no doubt in search of Matt.

I welcomed a gulp of water before I continued with the task at hand. "Richard...I'm sorry. I know you have tried your best, but there is something missing. You bought me the most beautiful ring in the world, but when you presented it to me, I didn't feel the way I always thought I would feel, the way...," and I took a big, regretful, sorrowful sigh, "the way Michelle looked when Matt got down on his knee.

"You're a good guy Richard, but it isn't enough. You can blame me. My expectations are probably way too high, but I would rather break it off now than end in divorce later. You don't deserve to live your life trying to live up to impossible expectations. You deserve to find someone who will appreciate you for what you have to offer."

Richard was uncharacteristically quiet, and I couldn't tell what he was feeling. After a few moments of awkward silence, he finally said, "Well, I can't say you led me on. I knew you weren't sure. I just thought you couldn't resist when you saw the diamond." I chuckled recalling Doris's warning.

"Well, I guess I'll pack up tonight and surprise my mom," he said with a chuckle.

"Richard, you can take some time to get your things together," and for a split second his eyes lit up with hope, so I followed it up with, "but no more than two weeks."

"Understood." He took a deep breath, and his shoulders slumped down.

Sensing the awkwardness, Doris said, "Richard, it's been a long, interesting night. Why don't you head home, and we'll make sure Lani gets there."

He looked at me for approval and I nodded.

"You sure?" he asked.

"Yes...Yes I am."

Richard walked out a defeated man, but he seemed to stand a little taller. I can't imagine I was anything more than baggage the last month or two, and breaking up had to lighten his load.

I thanked Doris, and she hugged me. It felt warm and safe in her arms, and I could have stayed there forever, but Michelle had other plans for me.

Chapter 64

"You!" she shouted while pointing in my face. "You ruined my special moment."

"I...I...uh..." I was fumbling to find the words to say. I finally managed an "I'm sorry." I thought about saying, "I didn't mean to," but I think that would have been a lie.

"How dare you take my spotlight? You know...for as much as Matt talks about how great you are, you're a total spaz. If you ruined my chance to marry a rock star, I will never let you live it down.

"I don't know why someone as cool as him would want to keep company with the likes of you anyway. He needs a trophy on his arm, not a...a...frumpy..." And she paused a moment before finding the right word: "Cow."

"Hey!" Doris shouted. "Don't you dare talk to Lani like that."

"Oh save it, Grandma. Aren't they looking for you at the home?"

As Doris and I stood there stunned, Matthew jumped in. "Don't you dare insult these women. They have more class in one finger than you do in your entire body, and let me tell you another thing, missy...I will see to it that my Matty knows exactly the type of woman you are."

"Oh please. Matt is so wrapped around my finger. You think he's really going to believe you? Look at this body. Even if he does believe you, he's not going to care. You know why?"

Matthew looked away, but she continued anyway.

"Because I give it to him good."

"Now, why don't you guys take Holly Hobbie home to her whale of a boyfriend."

"Now listen here, you vicious succubus," Matthew started, "my son will believe me, and he will toss you to the wolves."

"Really, Gramps? You're crazy. He won't give this up."

"Give what up?" Matt asked.

Michelle quickly turned the charm back on. "Oh, hey, baby," she said and attempted to hug him around his neck. He took her arms by her elbows and gently pushed them to her side. It didn't stop her though and she continued, "I'm so sorry your show was ruined. Your first two songs rocked. Was there something you wanted to ask me?"

"Yes, actually there is."

My stomach dropped again. Matthew stepped toward him in an attempt to stop him, and Matt ducked away from his outstretched hand.

"I have a very special question to ask you." He dropped down to one knee.

Doris attempted a feeble, "Matt...don't," but he moved on with the question.

"Michelle...will you..." Her face lit up like a child on Christmas, and the tears welled up in my eyes.

"Will you—," he continued.

"Yes! Yes! Matt!" she exclaimed.

"I'm glad that's your answer, but I'd like to finish the question."

"Oh, yes, of course, do finish," she said, while looking at us bystanders and smirking that she was victorious.

"Michelle, will you...get out of my life forever you selfish, inconsiderate, fame-seeker who just insulted everyone I care about?"

Her face went ashen, and Doris let out an audible laugh. Michelle flashed a furious set of eyes at Doris and Matthew started breathing again. As Matt got off his knee, she realized he was serious and leveraged the only bargaining tool she had left—her body.

She quickly adjusted her boobs in her bra to make her cleavage more appealing. I knew this "frumpy cow" was no match for the beauty queen, and I was sure those boobs would seduce him just as surely as Richard's diamond would seduce my finger.

Michelle leaned into Matt and in her most seductive voice said, "Oh, baby doll, this is all a misunderstanding. Quite frankly, I don't think their hearing is very good."

"What about mine?" he asked. "I have been standing here since you called Lani a 'cow,' which by the way"—and he looked right at me—"you are anything but. As a matter of fact, you are the most beautiful woman I have ever known. You have an innocence and kindness about you that is more appealing than any set of fake breasts.

"You have more sincerity in your stunning blue eyes than most women have in their whole bodies." On that last compliment, Michelle twisted on her stiletto heels and stormed out of the venue.

Matt turned his head to watch her leave, and I could see he let out a breath he must have been holding in all night.

I gently touched him on his shoulder, "Matt?"

He turned back toward me, and he had sadness in his eyes. "I'm sorry, Matt. I ruined your show, I ruined your engagement, I ruined my engagement. I'm a mess, and I didn't mean to drag you into this. You look so sad. I'm so sorry."

"Lani...I'm sad because that witch played me, and I almost fell for it. Pops, Doris...I'm sorry she said those horrible things to you. I had no idea she was that vicious."

"Oh, don't worry, Matty. Lani went and did you a favor by passing out. Thanks, Lani."

I held up my hands defensively. "No...I don't want to be thanked. I messed up everything. I need to go." With that, I turned to leave, but Matt grabbed my wrist and my legs went weak, and I stumbled slightly. He spun me around and grabbed my other wrist so we were standing face-to-face.

"Lani? Did you not hear a word I just said? I don't care a damn about my show, and I was only going to ask Michelle to marry me because if I couldn't be with the one I wanted, I figured I would at least be with someone who wanted me.

"But, Lani...know this...as sure as we are all standing here right now...I want you. I have wanted you for the longest time. I was devastated when Richard swooped in and took you from me before I even had a chance.

"I couldn't compete. Not a shot in hell. I don't have money, and I wouldn't know the first thing about diamond rings. I certainly am not corporate material, and truth be told, I don't know if I will ever make it with my band, and if I don't, I could never provide you with the life you deserve.

"I stepped back because I couldn't give you what he could. It broke my heart, but I did it for you."

"Did it for me?" I said with a humph and pulled away from him. I couldn't believe what he just confessed. Did I really come off as superficial? In a far more angry tone than I meant, I spewed out, "It's true, he took me on fancy trips and bought me nice things...but he was more concerned with giving me special things than making me feel special.

"I don't care about the trips and the diamonds if I don't feel special on the inside. I've never felt special. I mean, I thought I did, but they were always temporary feelings. When the nostalgia of the gift or trip wore off, I was back to feeling trapped because I didn't feel what I thought I should feel.

"I didn't say anything though because everyone expected that I should be settled down already. And I felt like a traitor," the tears started pouring down my cheeks, "I was a traitor to myself...to my heart...because I knew I wasn't happy. But I also know I'm not beautiful, even though you said so before. I know you did that to get under Michelle's skin. I never had men knocking down my door so I had to settle—"

Matt cut me off by placing both of his hands lovingly and gently on my cheeks. He looked deeply into my eyes and said, "Lani, I said you were beautiful because you are," and then quietly, in a raspy voice that was choking up, he said, "May I kiss you?"

My knees melted, and I slowly (because I was in shock and not because I didn't want to) nodded my head in approval. As he leaned in with his beautiful lips, I saw Doris nudge Matthew who was staring in awe, and the two of them turned to leave.

As if the way he caressed my cheeks wasn't romantic enough, he didn't go in for a full kiss at first. He chose to place butterfly kisses on my lips, then my cheeks, and then back to my lips.

My head was spinning, and I never wanted the moment to end.

It had to though when the bartender turned on the lights and said, "Hey, Casanova, since you scared off all the customers, I would like to call it a night."

Matt chuckled slightly and apologized. I apologized too, and the bartender informed us he was glad Matt didn't get engaged to that groupie. "She's tried to pick up every lead singer that has stepped foot in this bar. She's a fame whore. Oh...pardon my French."

Matt and I held hands as we walked outside. It suddenly dawned on me that I wasn't sure if Richard had taken my car home or not. A quick glance in the parking lot determined Richard did take the car. It's probably a good thing considering he had the keys.

"Um...I don't have a ride home," I said in a "damsel in distress" sort of way.

Matt led me to his car and walked me to the passenger side door. He was about to open it and then paused. Instead, he twisted me around and leaned me up against the car. He took my face in his hands again and told me how beautiful I was.

"Lani, you are the most fantastic girl I know, and I would love to take you out for dinner."

I frowned when he didn't kiss me as I was hoping.

"What's the matter?" he asked concerned.

"Oh...nothing," I said, shaking my head not realizing my frown showed outside of my head.

"Lani, am I being too forward? I am, aren't I?" And he stepped away. "I mean, you just broke up with your fiancé...I'm sure you need some time to process. I'm such a dope."

"No, Matt. God, no." And I grabbed his hand.

"So why are you so sad?"

I started laughing. "Well...I was actually just hoping you were going to kiss me again."

He tilted his head back and let out a cathartic sigh. When he looked back, he smiled mischievously and said, "Is that so?" and I nodded like a high school girl.

"Why didn't you just say that then?" And he leaned in and kissed me; gently at first and as time went on, our intensity turned up, and I wanted nothing more than to go home with him.

Matt had other ideas though. He dropped me off at home and offered to stay outside for a little bit in case Richard gave me a hard time. Being the gentleman I knew he was, he wanted to take things slowly; he wanted things to be "special." He also wanted to give me time to make sure I made the right decision. Little did he know I made the right decision months, maybe even a year ago. I just hadn't acted on it.

We agreed to meet for dinner the next night, and I assured him I would be fine with Richard. As I walked up the stairs, I knew I was leaving a part of my heart in Matt's car. I put the key in the lock and turned it. When I jiggled the door opened, I looked back at Matt one last time and waved as he drove away.

Chapter 65

I found Richard in the bedroom. He was almost done packing his clothes, and I couldn't help but wonder if he would ever mature enough that he would know he shouldn't pack his clean, fresh-smelling clothes with his dirty ones.

Sheepishly, I said, "Hello."

"Hey," he said as he turned and looked at me then went back to packing. "I didn't hear you come in."

"Sorry, didn't mean to startle you."

"It's okay. How are you feeling?"

"Still a little sore. I think I have a bump."

He stopped what he was doing and looked nervous. "Want me to check?"

"Nah...I'm good. I will just make sure I don't fall asleep for a bit. I hear you aren't supposed to go to bed if you have a concussion. I don't know why though."

"Me either," he added and half-heartedly folded a pair of dress pants that I knew he was going to have to iron once he took them out of the suitcase. I might not be the best as far as domestic chores goes, but I understand you can't roll up pants and expect them to be wearable. I chose not to say anything. Richard has his share of "mothering" from me, and it hadn't worked out for either of us. Instead, I asked if he wanted help.

"Sure...if it's not too much trouble."

I went into the bathroom and felt guilty with the pleasure I took clearing out his effects. Not having to deal with rust rings on the sink from his shaving cream can was exciting. I couldn't even remember how many times I asked him to put it away before it could do damage.

Looking at the toilet seat in the "up" position for the last time brought me joy. I was going to have my home back again, and I felt like a kid anticipating Christmas morning.

A tear formed when I got to his toothbrush though. I thought about the first time he stayed the night and used mine. I remembered how excited I was, and for a moment, a butterfly danced in my stomach and I wondered if I was doing right by him. After performing a mental checklist of the pros and cons, I knew setting him free was the right thing to do.

A short while later, he stuck his head in the bathroom and informed me that he was done packing his clothes. I was about to comment about how quickly he got through it and realized it goes much faster when you don't take the time to pack properly.

"Well," I said handing him his toiletries, "looks like you have most of your stuff. I can go through some stuff in the next couple of days and let you know if I find anything."

"Thanks," and we headed toward the front door.

Entering sensitive territory, I asked, "Does your mother know?"

"Yeah," he said with a chuckle (and I felt a sense of relief), "she is really mad at you, but happy to have the company again."

"I guess I can't blame her for being mad at me. I don't blame you either."

"Thanks. I'm not mad though. There are plenty of fish in the sea." He pecked me on the cheek, and before I could even ask if he needed a lift, a car horn sounded and he was out the door.

Being a curious girl, I couldn't not know who was in the car so I followed him out.

"Hi, Joe!"

He just looked at me and shook his head while Richard piled his things in the car. When the car sped off, I was caught off guard by Billy.

"Congratulations," he said as he raised up a bottle of beer and nodded at me.

Surprising myself, I turned to him and said, "Can I have a hug?"

He jumped up at the request and put his beer down. Awkwardly, he shimmied over the partition. He opened his arms to me, and I ran into them almost knocking him over. Baring my soul to him, I cried and cried and cried as he silently absorbed it all while softly rubbing the top of my head.

A few times he gently "shushed" me while saying, "It will be okay." I couldn't help but think he was going to be an amazing husband someday.

I'm guessing we had to be locked in that embrace for at least five minutes, and it was exactly what I needed. I would have stayed there a lot longer, but I had one more Band-Aid I had to rip off.

Chapter 66

"You going to be okay?" Billy asked as I headed down the stairs and to my car.

"I hope so," and I made my way into the car and drove to my sister's house.

"Aunt Lani," my niece said as she strained her neck to see behind me, "where's Mr. Lovebug?"

"That's a long story. Where's your mom? Let me guess...is she cleaning your room?"

"No. Why would you think that?" she said thoroughly confused.

"I'm up here," my sister called out.

I walked up the stairs and when we locked eyes, she knew.

"Molly...go to your room."

"Why? I smell gossip in the air."

"MOLLY!"

"Fine! But you better remember the details."

When Molly left the room, my sister turned to me, "So?"

For over an hour and for the second time that night, I let my guard down and poured my heart out. To her credit, she didn't once poke fun of me or act surprise that a rocker wanted me.

She was more upset that she had no idea about Matt.

"Well, he was kind of a dirty little secret. I figured if I didn't talk about him, I wouldn't think about him, and I would just focus on Richard."

"How'd that work out for you?"

"Not so good, Dr. Phil. Not so good."

"What's not good?" Paul asked, coming out of the bedroom. I had no idea he was even there.

"Lani dumped Richard."

My brother-in-law looked devastated. "Really? Why? He was a cool dude."

"Nah...he was a fat slob—"

I quickly interrupted with, "I didn't say that."

"No, but it was implied and anyone looking at him could tell," my sister added.

"Wait a sec...you were the one pushing me to stay with him."

"I told you I wanted nieces and nephews."

"Stop...I'm trying to understand this," Paul chimed in. "You dumped him because he was heavy?"

"NO! She's exaggerating. We broke up because he stopped caring. Not just about himself, but about me. Once he moved in, there was no effort. It was like he got what he wanted so he could stop being...well...desirable."

While I was speaking, Paul maneuvered over to my sister who was sitting. He went behind her and started massaging her neck. Her face told me this was new and she liked it. I kept talking more for her benefit than mine.

"Paul, women don't want much from their mates. I know it may seem like it, but we don't. All we really want is to feel loved, to feel special. That's it. But you see...when we stop feeling special, we start demanding other things in the hopes it will fill the void. The truth is no amount of house cleaning, lunch making, money, or jewelry can fill the void.

"Sure, it might for a week or two, but in the end, if we don't feel special, we won't be special. In fact, we'll be outright bitchy." And as the last syllable left my mouth, we heard a gasp. The three of us turned to see Molly (hand over mouth), peeking out from her room.

"I got this." And Paul shooed her back to her room and closed the door. Before he came back to the living room, my sister looked at me and said, "Wow...you just summed up in two minutes what I've been trying to explain to Paul for fifteen years."

"You sure did," he said, coming back into the living room. "And...let me tell you something, rubbing her feet is much easier than folding sheets." He leaned down and kissed her, and I took it as a cue to leave.

"You don't have to go," she said.

"Oh yes she does," Paul said. "No offense, but I need to make my woman feel special." We all giggled, and my sister looked happier than I'd seen in a while.

"Let me know how it works out with the rock star," she called out to me while Paul pulled her to the bedroom.

As I headed down the stairs, I heard Paul ask, "What rock star?" and I laughed as I walked out the door.

Chapter 67

I struggled to go to bed that night. I replayed "God's sign" over and over in my head. I laughed at how I nearly blinded myself getting ready for the night and nearly killed myself to end it. Thinking about Michelle, I wondered if I could take her on in a physical fight. I giggled realizing I beat her in a "that's my man" fight already.

I still couldn't believe the things she said to both Doris and Matthew, and I shivered at the memory of thinking Matt was going to ask her to marry him. Instead, he played Michelle much to our delight.

Richard...he caused me the most insomnia. I certainly didn't want to hurt him, but I would be lying if I said I didn't feel disappointed that he didn't put up more of a fight. Let's face facts, women have egos too.

In the end, I knew he would find someone who would be more suited for him. After all, there are plenty of women willing to sacrifice happiness for a gorgeous diamond. I say kudos to them!

At some point, I did fall asleep and was enveloped in a dream. Matt was on stage at the club singing a song and all the teenyboppers were going crazy. When the song was over, he extended his arms and parted the fans like the Red Sea. Unbeknownst to them, they just created an aisle for me to walk down. At some point, Matt's leather was replaced by a suit (and even in my dream I made a mental note to ask why he didn't choose a tux), and Pops was next to him.

I walked down the aisle, and Matt's smile changed into a look of fright and the fans started chanting, "Frumpy, cow."

I looked down, and sure enough, I was wearing a white gown with black spots, and I had hooves for feet. As the girls started pointing and their chants got louder, I saw Michelle pull Matt from the stage. I sprung up from bed and breathed a sigh of relief when I realized it was just a dream (more like a nightmare).

The clock read 6:15 a.m. It was way too early for my liking, but after the scare, there was not an ounce of sleep left in my body. I decided to get up and clean as I had on my day off.

It felt good stripping my sheets from the bed. I tugged at them with such a vengeance that I knew Richard would never lay down on them again. I scrubbed my bathroom down and sat on the toilet seat in the "down" position just because.

I found a few of his socks under the bed and put them in a bag. He really didn't have much more than clothes and toiletries at the house, so I wasn't anticipating a bunch of "left behind" items.

By 9:00 a.m., my house was back to being well...*my* house. And I flopped on my bed in victory. By 9:10 a.m., I was stir crazy and wanted to call Matt but decided to call Phyllis instead. It had been a while since we spoke, and I wanted an objective ear to hear me retell the story. Thirty minutes later I picked her up for breakfast.

We went to the diner we had frequented before, and she was greeted with the same amount of enthusiasm as last time.

Once we were seated (and her fans left her alone), I began to tell her what had happened over the past couple of weeks. As soon as I said, "There's this guy Matt at work," she raised her eyebrows and said, "I think I know how this turns out."

As I spun the tale, she hung on every word and even ignored her food when it came. When I told her to eat so it wouldn't get cold, her response was she should have ordered popcorn instead. She gasped and giggled and held her breath at the appropriate points. Had I not lived through the ordeal myself, I wouldn't have quite believed it myself.

She paused briefly when the story ended then said, "Well, I knew how it would turn out. I just never imagined the spectacle getting there." That was when she took her first bite of food.

We chatted like old friends; her asking me about Matt and what I was going to do next and me asking her how she's been doing since Ed's passing. She explained that she joined a senior center and that "Ed is having a good laugh about it." Apparently, they swore they would never be old enough for one of "those places." It was wonderful for her though. She made arts and crafts, went to Bingo, and took a computer class.

When breakfast ended, it was much closer to lunch, and as sorry as I was to drop her off at home, I was anxious about my upcoming dinner with Matt; the butterflies were in full effect.

I was happy to see Billy sweeping the leaves in front of our house when I got home. I floated out of the car and ran over to him.

"Hey, Lani!"

I grabbed his elbows in my hands and said, "Billy...I am so sorry I didn't realize how amazing you were years ago. You are a great catch, and I'm going to keep my eye out for just the right person for you!" Then in a whimsical and completely spontaneous move, I planted a kiss right on his lips.

I pulled away from him and ran up my stairs. He called out, "Thanks, Lani," and when I looked back at him, he was grinning ear to ear as he continued to sweep. My euphoria quickly evaporated when I opened the door.

"Richard...what are you doing here?"

"I think you made a mistake. I can be the man you want." He dropped to his knees and continued, "Let's go back to Disney, a cruise, whatever you want. We'll go right now."

And I had to hand it to God, he listened to me. I wanted a fight...well, here it was.

"Richard, I appreciate you coming back," I started, helping him to his feet, "but it's not about trips."

"Then what's it about?"

Angrily I said, "I told you what it's about. Why is it so hard for you to comprehend?"

"Tell me again. I'll be better."

"Fine! I'll tell you what Richard. I'm going to ask you one question...just one. If you answer it correctly, I will run into your arms, and I will never look back."

"Name it, I got this."

I took a deep breath and asked one very simple question: "What color is my bedroom?"

For a moment I panicked thinking I just sold my soul to a man I didn't love. From the look on his face I thought I might have underestimated Richard.

To break the tension or perhaps it was to distract him in case he did know the answer, I added, "I asked you this question one other time and told you it was important to me. If you can tell me the color of my bedroom, it will prove to me that you cared enough to figure out the answer on the off-chance I'd ask you again.

"So Richard...did you care enough about me to figure out the answer?"

Chapter 68

I waited for what seemed like an eternity, but he didn't answer.
He let out a deep breath and said, "You're right. I get it now.
I'm sorry. I hope your rock star treats you better."

As he headed to the front door, I called out, "Richard!"

He quickly turned around with hopeful anticipation and as
I handed him his bag of socks I realized how badly I unintentionally set him up for a movie-like ending where I jump in his
arms and declare my undying love for him.

"Oh...thanks."

A small, callous feeling of relief for not having to drop it
off at his house and face the wrath of his mom came over me.
I knew it was terrible, but I didn't care. I fought a hard battle
and I won.

When I was positive that Richard was long gone, I made a
quick phone call to my sister and jumped in the shower for my
cleansing ritual. At precisely the time I perfected my hair and
every curl was in its rightful place, my doorbell rang.

Transforming into a teenager, I ran and opened it up.
There was my sister with her caboodle full of makeup products.
"Okay, let's get to work. You're asking an awful lot of these
hands you know." I kid punched her in her arm and then pulled
her by the same one into my living room.

There, she proceeded to apply layer after layer of founda-
tion, concealer, cover-up, and a whole host of other products I
had no clue about. When she was done and held the mirror up

to my face, I almost cried; there were those two perfect lines accenting my eyes.

"Don't you dare mess up my masterpiece," she chided.

I hugged her with all my might. "I won't. I promise."

"Good," she said. "I need to get going though."

"Why so soon? Don't you want to see the finished product?"

"As much as I would love to see your wardrobe, I have a date with Paul."

"You do?"

"Yep. He totally surprised me. He asked his mom to take Molly for the night, and we are going to dinner and dancing."

"No way!"

"Yep. I have to tell you...ever since you told him about your breakup, he's been so much more attentive. I know it sucked for you, but it's been awesome for me. And it's only day two. Ha!"

"Well, I'm really happy for you." And I truly was. I was also grateful that for the first time in forever, we started a "sisterly" relationship. I was looking forward to hearing about her night with Paul, and I was sure there was much to tell her about my night with Matt.

"Have fun," I called out to her as she flew down my stairs no doubt to doll herself up.

"You too! Don't do anything I wouldn't do."

"Well, you have a kid, so I know at least one thing you do." We both laughed as she got in her car and drove away.

I walked to my bedroom and went straight to the closet. I wasn't nervous at all about what outfit I was going to wear. I went straight for an A-line party dress that fell on me in a way that hid the lumps and I only wore once on the cruise Richard and I took. I put on a pair of cute sandals, and when I looked in the full-length mirror I was completely taken aback with how beautiful I looked.

I realized that a lot of it was superficial thanks to my sister's handiwork, but I didn't care. I felt like a million dollars, and nothing was going to change that.

Billy caught a glimpse of me before I got in the car.

"Oh Lord! Look at you." He shook his head in disbelief. "What on earth?" He started fumbling over his words.

Feeling sexy and confident I gave him a seductive smile and said, "Bet you wish I waited to kiss you."

"Um...maybe, but...I still enjoyed it before." He ran (okay, limped) over to my car door and opened it for me. He followed it up with a wink and told me to have a great time as he closed it.

Chapter 69

I felt like a princess as the valet opened my door and reached out his hand to help me out of the car.

"Good evening, miss, you look lovely."

"Thank you," I said, blushing.

When I stepped up to the curb, I contemplated running away. I still felt like this was all too good to be true and was afraid Michelle would pop out from behind a tree and attack me.

Before I could make an escape though, Matt rounded the corner with his head down and nearly bumped into me.

"Oh, I'm sorry," he said and looked up. When he realized it was me, he took a step back and gave me a very long and appreciative once-over. His jaw dropped, and he was speechless.

I broke the silence by asking if he came there often.

He responded, "I will be here every single night if it means seeing you."

I put my head down embarrassed, knowing I wasn't worthy enough for such kind words.

He put a finger on my chin and raised my head. "You are..." And he paused searching for the right word and for a second I flashed back to the night before and expected to hear "cow." "You are...stunning, Lani. I didn't think you could be any more beautiful, but you...you...wow...just wow."

Only having self-deprecating humor as a defense mechanism for embarrassment, I said, "Yeah, I clean up pretty well for a 'frumpy cow.'"

He started laughing in that "Can you believe the nerve of her?" sort of way. "I don't know who she thought she was," he began. "I mean, did she really think I would be okay with her going off on you guys like that?"

"Oh, but, Matt," I teased, "she was going to hypnotize you with her fake boobs." The two of us had a good laugh and headed into the restaurant. He held the door open for me and even pulled out my chair. When he sat down, I finally took a good look at him. He was just as dreamy as I remembered, and my heart melted at the thought that this was a date, not a lunch between friends.

He ordered for the both of us, and as we waited for the meal to come, he filled me in on the night before from his vantage point.

He had been in a bad state of affairs after finding out about Freddy (from the guy who worked in the deli where Freddy used to go when he collected enough money). His head wasn't really into the show to begin with, so when he saw Richard get down on his knee with the ring, he had enough and decided to shut Michelle up and just ask her to marry him. He figured he would never have the one he wanted, so it didn't matter who he'd end up with.

At the moment he was about to pop the question, he heard me scream, "No." Thinking I was directing it to him, he stood up just in time to see me fall. Richard ran over to me and began kissing my face and calling for help. Not realizing that my "no" was directed to Richard, he thought Richard and I were still an item. Even though he was concerned about me on the floor, he knew Richard, Doris, and Pops were with me so he chose to chase after Michelle who apparently stormed off when he turned toward me.

He shouted to the guitarist to cancel the show and clear the venue, and admittedly, he felt terrible about doing it to his fans. "It wouldn't have been a good show for them anyway."

When he caught up to Michelle, she acted like she was fine; no doubt trying to keep up the facade of devoted and kind girlfriend who is close to becoming a fiancée. She told him she was fine and just needed to go to the bathroom.

Little did she know that his concern truly lay with me, and as soon as the place cleared out "and I couldn't believe how fast it did," he headed over to where we were. She beat him there, and it was a lucky thing too. By getting there second, he was able to get a candid look into the true character of his almost wife.

Being I was conscious at the point he arrived, we didn't rehash that part of the story and chose to feed each other from our forks and chat about our dreams for the next few hours. When the bill came, I didn't even have time to ask if I should contribute. Like a magician, he was ready with cash in hand, and I swore I didn't even see a wallet.

When dinner was over, we got my car from valet and left his parked on the street. He asked if I was interested in taking a walk on the beach. In all my years, I never went to the beach at night. I had no idea what I was missing.

My right hand was interlocked with his left and our "unlocked" hands carried our shoes. The sand felt amazing under my feet and the sound of the waves crashing reminded me that life will be tumultuous at times, but there is so much beauty around the chaos if you only dare to look. If I needed any other evidence of the amazing things in life, all I had to do was look up at the sky. The blue was so dark it was almost purple and the stars went on for miles. We walked in silence for a long time; no words were needed.

I loved how he tightened the grip on my hand every time a wave crashed and how he would occasionally bend down if he saw a "perfect shell" and put it in his pocket. I wanted so much for him to kiss me, but he wasn't making a move.

Recalling how long I waited for Richard to make the first move, I decided to take matters into my own hands.

"Matt?"

"Yes, Lani?"

"I think I got sand in my eye."

He put his shoes down, said, "Oh no," and took my face in his hands. "Ah, it's too dark to see. Do you have any water in your car?"

"No."

He started checking his pockets for a tissue or something and I could tell he was getting upset that he couldn't help me.

"Matt?"

"Yeah?"

"I know something that will help."

"You do?"

"Yes. I hear a kiss makes everything better."

He shook his head and chuckled knowing he had just been duped. "Is that so?"

"Um hmm," I said shaking my head. "It sure does."

I thought my plan had backfired though when he kissed me gently on my eyes. And as sweet as the gesture was, I couldn't appreciate it because all I kept thinking about was him smudging my lines.

Fortunately, he didn't linger long on my lids and made his way down to my lips. He kissed me so beautifully and softly, and I knew in that moment I would never kiss another man again. At the sound of the next wave, he bent down, grabbed his shoes, and said, "I'll race you back to the car. Be careful of the dust I kick up. You might get sand in your eye for real this time."

He beat me back to the car but not by much, and I'm fairly certain he slowed down for me. I slid my sandals back on and got into the driver's seat. In a very bold move, I drove us directly to my house.

Before we got out of the car, he looked at me. "Are you sure?" I shook my head yes, and he put a hand on my knee and gave me the "No...are you really sure?" look.

"Matt, if I didn't know any better, I'd think you weren't interested in what I have planned for you."

"Um...no. Trust me, I'm very interested."

"Then stop wasting precious time."

Chapter 70

He hesitated before getting out of the car, and I could tell something was troubling him.

"What's wrong, Matt? We...uh...we don't have to go inside."

"It's not that, Lani. I...hmmm...this is awkward."

"What is it?" I pressed.

"Can I borrow your car for a few minutes?" he asked sheepishly.

"You mean take it...like right now? Without me?" I was thoroughly confused, and I began feeling foolish. Maybe he wasn't as into me as I thought.

"Yes. I would like to borrow your car for just a quick second. I'd take mine, but...well...we left it at the restaurant."

I think he sensed my uneasiness so he said, "It's okay, Lani. I'm not going to steal it, and I'm most certainly not going to leave you for too long."

With a bit of apprehension, I slid out of the car, and he pecked me on the cheek as he took my place in the driver's seat. As he pulled out of the driveway, I began shouting, "Wait! Stop!"

Not being familiar with the car, he slammed down on the brakes much harder than he probably intended, and he jolted in the seat. He quickly rolled down the window, "What? Is everything okay?"

With foolishness in full bloom, I explained that I needed my house key, which was connected to the car keys. He walked me up the stairs "to save you a trip," and I contemplated pushing him inside because a part of me was afraid he wouldn't come back.

He maneuvered so quickly that he was already down the stairs before I stepped foot in the house. I decided to make the most of it by going to the bathroom, freshening up and giving all rooms a final inspection. I was elated when I realized just how good of a job I did cleaning.

When I was satisfied that all was picture perfect, I made the mistake of sitting down on my couch. Turns out I was exhausted. I'm not sure how long I had my eyes closed when I heard Matt whispering my name. At first I thought it was a dream, so I ignored it. I began stirring when my shoulder was gently rubbed.

As the room came into focus, I saw Matt next to me, and there was an unfamiliar glow around the room.

"I'm sorry I took as long as I did. The first place I went to didn't have candles. I made it to the second store as the guy was closing up shop. I slipped him an extra five to stay open."

"Candles?"

Matt scooched back on the couch to give me a broader view of the room. It was then that the mysterious glow made sense; Matt had set up candles for me.

"Oh my God, this is the most romantic thing anyone has ever done for me," and I hugged him around the neck.

"I only put them in here because I didn't want to intrude anywhere else," he said with a wink. "By the way, you have a very nice living room."

I laughed and he looked at me with a deep intensity and said, "I love the way you smile." He then gave me the kiss I had been longing for.

His hands caressed my cheeks as we explored each other's mouths with our tongues. Every few minutes, he would pull back to look at me as if he couldn't believe his luck. He would stroke my hair and then come back for more. Sometimes he would kiss my forehead, eyes, and cheeks before going back to my lips.

He stopped when the tears began rolling down my cheeks. "Lani? Are you okay? What's the matter?"

"I don't deserve this. You should be with someone more beautiful."

"Are you kidding me? You *are* beautiful, and if you don't mind, you're wasting precious time."

Chapter 71

I looked at him sheepishly and seductively as he stood up. He put his hand out to me and I placed mine in his. He pulled me up in a quick, "one-two" motion ("one" being the pull up and "two" being a sweep around my back with his other arm). He led me in a slow dance where the only music I heard was the beating of our hearts.

For a rock star, he was very coordinated in the ways of "cheek-to-cheek" dancing. He had my right hand lovingly in his and held it gently against his heart while his other hand slowly caressed the lower part of my back.

My other hand found its way to the nape of his neck, and I did my best to lightly stroke the hair that covered it. The flickering glow of candles completely transformed the room I had so recently come to despise. Before I allowed the image of Richard sitting in tighty-whities scarfing down fast-food to come to fruition, I squeezed my cheek against Matt's tightly to remind myself this was a new start.

That little move caused a ripple effect, and he spun me out and back into his arms.

"Oh my goodness...I had no idea you were that talented of a dancer."

"Well," he said, "Pops and my mom were always dancing around our living room. When mom was done with Pops, she'd pull me up and dance with me. Those were some fun times in our house."

"I bet they were. Now how about we make some fun times in this house?"

He smiled, slyly raised his eyebrows, and said, "I thought you'd never ask."

As I led him to the bedroom, he let go of my hand and grabbed two candles. When I gave him the "you really don't have to do that" look, he whispered, "I want this to be special" (as if dancing in my living room wasn't special enough).

He set the candles down on my dresser; a perfect place given the mirror that intensified the glow. Not knowing the proper next step, I sat on the edge of my bed wondering if I go right into getting naked or not.

Matt turned to me, got on a knee, and said, "May I?" Not knowing what the heck he wanted to do, but frankly not caring either, I shook my head yes. He gently took my right foot and began to unfasten the buckle. No man had ever done that for me before, and it was one of the sexiest things I had ever experienced.

When the sandal came off, he didn't toss it behind him (as I envisioned Richard doing), but placed it neatly at the edge of my dresser. He repeated the process with my left foot and when both shoes were safely placed, he asked if he could use some of the lotion he spied.

Figuring he wanted to get rid of the foot smell on his hands, I told him "sure," and he squeezed a bit into his hand and got back on his knees. He rubbed the lotion between his two hands and in a move I wasn't expecting, he began massaging my feet.

"As you already know, I have sisters," he began, and I shook my head in agreement. "And I have seen when they come home after a night out on the town. You know what they always complain about?"

I shook my head no.

"How much their feet hurt from the fancy shoes."

I couldn't help but giggle. And fall in love a little more.

When he was done with pampering me, he asked where the bathroom was so he could wash up. In those moments, he was gone, I imagined what it was going to feel like to have him touch my whole body. I noticed warmth between my legs and a primal shiver went through my core.

When he came back, he scooped me up again and kissed me with a passion he'd held from prior kisses. His hands explored every inch of my back, and I repaid him by sliding my hand up the nape of his neck and getting a good grip of hair. When he audibly moaned, I knew I hit a sweet spot.

He moved from my lips to my cheek, a quick nibble on the ear and finally my neck. As he tasted every inch of my neck, his hands moved down, and he grabbed a chunk of my ass at the precise moment I took another grip of his hair. He moaned again, and I felt him grow against my leg.

Boldly, I took the first step to get us to the next level. I began untucking his shirt from his pants. When he was all untucked, I began sliding the shirt up, and he raised his arms completely allowing me to take control.

There was something undeniably hot about undressing Matt. He was strong, confident, bold, but I was seeing his vulnerability and tenderness that he probably shared with very few people.

With his shirt off, I went to the button on his pants. My knuckles grazed his stomach, and while he didn't have a six pack, it felt incredible to touch a man who didn't have a belly. I felt a childish grin forming, and I did all I could to hold it back; I didn't want Matt to know just how inexperienced I was.

The ease with which I could undo his button took me off guard and sent another shiver through me. This, by far was the hottest, sexiest, most passionate man I had ever been with. As my fingers grasped the pull tab on his zipper, the phone rang. We both stopped a second.

"Do you need to get that?" he asked.

"No, it's fine," I said as I put my fingers back on the zipper. And the moment I touched his pants, the phone rang for a second time.

"You sure?"

"Yes, the answering machine will get it." It rang two more times as I lost my concentration on the task at hand and fumbled with the zipper.

It finally stopped ringing when the answering machine picked up. I was sure that was the end of it figuring the caller would try my cell phone instead which was on vibrate. But alas, from the box on the table we heard...

"Lani, are you there? Pick up. I want to know how your date was. Wakey, wakey, lazy head!" Matt and I started laughing although I was slightly mortified with the "lazy head" comment, and I was hoping she would give up soon.

She continued though, "Paul and I had an awesome time, and I really do have to thank you for it! Wow...did I just thank you?" As if she could hear me, I whispered to Matt that she never thanks me.

"God...I wish you were there, so I could tell you all about it. Anyway, let's just say, we just finished round two." There was a slight pause and then, "OH MY GOD! Are you in the middle of your own round two? Holy shit...I hope I'm not interrupting you. No...you couldn't be. You don't do that on the first date... do you? Oh crap. Call me tomorrow. Bye. Bye, rock star."

I was mortified, and Matt saw it on my face. "Wow...that's some sister you got there."

"Yes...she definitely has a way with words." I put my head down, the unzippering a distant memory.

Matt lifted my head and asked if I was okay. I told him I was, but my body language said otherwise.

"I'll tell you what," Matt said. "How about I undress you?" Apparently, I wasn't as mortified as I thought because I nodded my head quickly.

He turned me around, and when I lifted my hair off my neck so he could unbutton the top button, he kissed me and I awkwardly dropped my arm, which went weak. I tried to pull my hair up again, but he held my arm down and gently pushed my hair to the side. Using the backs of his fingers, he then teased my arms from shoulders to elbows as he kissed the nape of my neck.

My knees felt like they would buckle, and I thought he sensed it because he finally decided to unfasten the button. He raised my arms up in the air and worked the back of his fingers down my body from fingers to hips to hemline. When he reached the bottom of my dress, he gathered fabric on both sides and slid the dress up.

As his pointer fingers grazed my flesh as the dress rose, I couldn't help but wonder how many times he had done this before. He was masterful in his art of seduction, and I was happy to be his subject.

When the dress was completely off, I turned and saw him gently fold it in length-wise in half and lovingly drape it over my otherwise useless treadmill.

Seeing the treadmill reminded me how out of shape I was, and instinctively, I shielded my body with my arms. Sensing my apprehension, Matt motioned toward the bed, and I lay down. Then this...well...rock star of a man with his shirt off and his jeans fitting ever so well, crawled up next to me and kissed my stomach.

I tensed up and blocked the next kiss.

"Lani, I don't know what it is about you, but you are seriously misguided about your beauty." He moved my arm away from my stomach and shushed me as I was about to retort. I'm not sure how long it took, but Matt kissed every curve, every flaw, and every lump I had. By the end, I truly felt beautiful.

We spent the next hour or two entwined in a passion that is indescribable. My favorite moments were when he'd look at me and quietly ask if I was okay. I'd be lying if I didn't say the parts where he flipped me on top of him were a close second.

He made sure I was satisfied (several times at that), and when we finally felt like we gave it our all, we fell asleep in each other's arms.

Chapter 72

I woke up in the morning to the smell of bacon and was thoroughly confused since I hadn't had bacon in my house in years. I slipped on my robe and excitedly went into the kitchen.

Matt smiled ear to ear when he saw me. "I hope you're hungry."

"After last night...I'm ravenous."

"Great. Do you like scrambled eggs and bacon?"

"I do, but where did you—"

"I hope you don't mind, but I borrowed your car again. I swear...I won't make it a habit. I also hope you don't mind that I used this." When he stepped away, I silently reflected on the irony that was before me—the George Foreman that Richard bought was finally being used.

"No, Matt," I said with a chuckle. "I don't mind at all."

Epilogue

On the year anniversary of when Matt and I made it official, he took me strolling on the beach. We walked silently as we had a year prior, still enjoying the sound of the waves crashing.

As we held hands, I could feel Matt's palms getting sweaty. "Hey...are you okay?"

"Um...yeah...uh...why do you ask?"

"I don't know. You just seem a little pale, and your hand is slimy. I thought you might be getting sick."

"No," he said, pulling his hand away and wiping it on his pants. "I'm okay." Then he paused. "Actually, I'm not."

My heart sank at the sound of that. I knew he was bummed about not getting the music contract he was banking on, and it was causing a little bit of a strain. I feared that our relationship was getting in the way of his music although he never said so.

"Lani...I...I haven't been able to move the band forward like I wanted to this year."

I held my hand up to his mouth. "I'm sorry, Matt. You don't have to say it. I get it. I'm in your way."

He looked confused. "What?"

"I'm holding you back. If you have to break it off, I understand."

"Lani!" he interjected and grabbed my arms. "Where on earth did you get that idea from?"

"Well, I just figured since you were with me so much, you haven't done much with your music, and that in order to focus, you needed to cut out the distraction."

"My God, woman, you are unbelievable. Do you really think I would give up what I have had with you in this past year for anything?"

"Well," I said sheepishly, "I didn't think so, but...at the same time..."

"Lani, truth be told, you have given me so much inspiration. The band and I have been collaborating on awesome work. I haven't been able to move it not because of you...well actually...it is because of you, but for a good reason."

"I don't understand."

"Lani...the boys and I decided we didn't want to go out to a producer until we get some more songs in our new style...the 'Lani' style we call it." I couldn't help but laugh.

"I feel like such a fool."

"No...don't. Please, we love our new sound. I just wish I could have done it faster, you know, to get more income flowing."

"We're doing fine, Matt."

"Yes, Lani, we are, but I wanted to do better. You see, I love you, and you deserve so much more than what I can offer you right now. But I can't think of letting another day go by waiting to offer you something that might not come.

"I'm sorry that I'm not able to do more for you, but I hope that you know there is so much love inside me." Just at the point I thought I couldn't be any more confused if I tried, Matt dropped down to his knee. At the realization of what was about to happen, my jaw dropped and tears welled up in my eyes. Unconsciously, my left hand covered my mouth as I repeated, "Oh my God," over and over.

My right hand eventually went over my left hand for support. I was sure at any moment I was going to let out a scream that would knock Matt over.

He pulled out a box from his pocket, and I saw a tear slip from his eye. "Lani, when I was a little boy, my pops taught me about love by the way he treated my mother. Every morning, he made her coffee, and every night he turned down the bed. It was the only way he could thank her for taking care of all the kids while he was at work all day.

"My pops never knew this, but my mom would bring me into her room most nights and show me what he'd done for her. She used to say, 'Matty, be sure you marry yourself a girl who deserves turn down service every night.' I promised my mother I would, and I almost broke that promise to her." He wiped away the tears that were openly flowing down his cheeks.

"Lani?"

"Yes?"

As he opened the box, he asked, "Would you please accept this small gesture of a ring, and I promise that as my wife, I will spend the rest of my days treating you like the true diamond you are. I will dance with you when there's no music, I will turn down the bed, I will rub your feet, and someday...when the band gets signed, I will get you the ring you deserve."

I dropped down to my knees and finally took my hands away from my mouth. Matt, who was visibly shaking, took the ring out of the box as I moved my left hand toward him. As he slid the modest ring on my finger, I transformed into a new woman and smiled widely thinking of the warning Doris gave me so long ago. It was the most beautiful ring I ever saw.

"So?" Matt asked cautiously, "Will you marry me, Lani?"

I threw my arms around him and repeated, "Yes, yes, yes" until we both cried.

Standing in the back of the church six months later peering through the windows, I see Doris and Matthew just back from their two-week honeymoon. I am so joyful the two of them found each other.

My boss and Jasper are looking beyond dapper and completely smitten with one another. The fact that they are in a church holding hands brings me utter happiness.

I see my sister. Well...I see her back. As my matron of honor, she is the last to walk before my entrance. A sense of pride fills me when I think back to her vow renewal a month ago; she and Paul haven't been happier.

I still haven't spotted Matt no matter how far I stretch my neck and how much I get on my tippy-toes. My insecurities flare up, and I wonder if he finally realized I am not as beautiful as Michelle or Michele (I never did find out). What if he didn't show up?

When my sister reaches the altar, the music changes from "Canon in D" to the "Bridal March."

That's when I realized I'm about ten seconds from walking down the aisle, and for the first time, I'm scared. As the doors open to my anxiously awaiting guests, I finally spot Matt. I see him wipe a tear away from his eye and an overwhelming sense of clarity surfaces. Standing in the church, God has sent me a personal message and the message is *run*!

And run I did (well, more like a quick stroll) to the altar to where my soon-to-be husband, the most incredibly thoughtful man I ever knew, was waiting.

About the Author

L isa Brandenburg found her love for writing fiction in high school where she created dozens of short stories. She continued writing for fun but eventually put it on the back burner to pursue a career in theater for which she received her bachelor of arts at Brooklyn College. As an adult, Lisa went back to college and this time garnered a master's degree in publishing from Pace University.

Lisa strives to see the good in everything, and when most women dread the big 4-0, Lisa embraced it in her daily blog, Life is so Amazing, or Lisa for short.

Currently residing in Middletown, New Jersey, with her husband, Joe; daughter, Joey; and son, Robbie, Lisa is an active volunteer in her community becoming well versed in sports terms such as "baseball ready," "spread out" (for soccer), and "hands up" (for basketball). In preparing second graders for Communion, she is often heard whispering, "Prayer hands."

Although Lisa doesn't know the taste of wine, beer, or any liquor (except the obligatory sip of champagne at a few New Year's parties), she is the first to grab the karaoke mic or get the dance floor moving.

Lisa is excited and grateful that you have taken the time to support her first novel, *Run.*

Enjoy!